Cruise Mob

Robert O'Connell

Published by Green Chicken Press

ISBN: 0692295534
ISBN-13: 978-0692295533

cruisemobthenovel.com

Cover design by Robert Burger

For Lilly, Abby, and James
You're doing it *right*!

Acknowledgements

I would like to thank my family and friends for their support in this endeavor and for their inspiration.

Theresa, Lilly, Abby, and James, this is all for you.

Hilda and Oscar, this is all from you.

Rob, thank you for your eye.

Dwight, Tyrone, Ed, Hugh, Paul, Alice, Larry, Fedora, and the Parkland Writer's Café, thank you for your voices.

Cruise Mob

Tuesday, Oct 21st
~ Hoboken ~

There is the sound of waves crashing on the shoreline. Gulls are announcing their arrival and the clang of a bell is heard, possibly from a distant fishing boat. A hand is raised in the darkness. It falls on the arm of the unsuspecting man with his back turned. A rasping voice croaks out a cryptic message.

"TURN...THAT...DAMNED...THING...OFF!!"

"Ow!" shouts Scotty, jerking his shoulder to stop the pinching. "What did you do that for?"

Scotty reaches for his phone on the nightstand and manipulates the buttons sufficiently to turn off his alarm. He sits up in the darkness, rubbing his arm. Reaching for the lamp he hears yet another bloodcurdling call.

"DON'T...YOU...DARE...DO...IT!"

Scotty's girlfriend Tommy grabs Scotty's pillow and puts it over her head while wrapping herself deeper into the covers. Scotty shakes his head, slides out of the bed, and heads toward the bathroom. Along the way, he lifts the edge of the heavy blackout curtain ever so slightly to peek at the world outside.

"NGUURGH!" comes out as a guttural protest from between the pillows.

Scotty makes sure to close the bathroom door before turning on the light. He checks in the mirror to see if Tommy left a mark on his arm from her pinch.

After a shave and shower, Scotty takes a breath and exits the bathroom wrapped in a towel. Tommy has yet to move. The room has lightened due to the sun streaming against the curtains as it pops up over Manhattan. He sits on the bed next to her.

"I don't get it," he says. "You're never late, but you cannot get out of bed on time, and spend the next hour scrambling around playing catch up."

Tommy lifts a corner of the pillow on her head and peeks out.

"Did I hurt the wittle baby?" she asks.

"Wow, and nasty, too. No, you failed to draw blood this time. And why are you hating on my *Sounds of the Sea* alarm? It's supposed to help you to start the day in a mellow state. Didn't you spend your summers on the beach?"

"Yes, and my bedroom faced the east there as well. I hated it."

"I see your point. First your father buys a five bedroom summer home on Long Beach Island, and then he has the nerve to let you stay in this apartment in a high rise overlooking the New York skyline for free."

"Facing *east*...besides, the ocean sounds make me have to pee."

"I see that I'm going to have to leave this up to your therapist. Coffee?"

"Yes, and I'd like some air as well. Any other obvious questions?"

Scotty laughs and moves toward the closet to get his clothes. Tommy heads for the shower. Once she enters the bathroom, Scotty pulls open the blinds revealing a spectacular view of the city. He thinks back to last December when they first met. It was an inauspicious start which led to an incredible and unexpected adventure.

It's amazing what ten months can do. Tommy finished her doctoral coursework in Environmental Sociology at Boston University and is now working on her dissertation. She's doing research at Columbia, a short PATH ride under the Hudson followed by a subway uptown. Her brother Elmo went from being the family ne'er-do-well to a pretty successful business owner, while her father went from being an extremely successful mob lawyer and finance guru to sudden retirement.

Tommy comes out of the bathroom in her robe. Scotty walks toward her with a cup of coffee.

"God!" he says. "You look even more beautiful in the morning sun."

"As much as I despise the morning sun, it's your chipper attitude this early that really makes me want to barf," she replies. "Still, I somehow seem to be in love with you. How do you figure?"

"Beats me. You're the doctor, or at least will be soon enough. I need to go in a little early today for a faculty meeting, so you'll be happy to know that I can't stay to have you explain to me again, why we are not yet married."

"As soon as I finish my PhD and find a job, we can get married any time, place, or method that you would like. It's a deal that I made with myself and its non-negotiable...just like it was yesterday, and the day before that."

"Your parents don't love the idea of me sleeping over here, and I'm not crazy about it either, although it does slightly shorten my commute."

"Among other benefits, in case you forgot about last night. I imagine you can always go back to your apartment with Marcus and Carter. You're still paying your third anyway."

"I'll be staying there until you return from Boston on Sunday. I'll pick you up at the airport. I wish I could drop you off today."

"No worries. I'll take the PATH to the shuttle from Penn Station. You go to work and have fun with the boys this week."

Scotty picks up his computer bag and gives Tommy a big kiss.

"Say hello to your brother from me. Text me when you get there. I love you...even if you are cranky in the morning."

As he grabs his keys and heads for the door, Tommy unties her robe and lets it fall open. "I love you, too," she says.

He turns and smiles as he heads out the door.

4

Tuesday, Oct 21st
~ West Orange ~

Tommaso Pastor sits in a booth at the Wessex Diner. It is typical of Northern New Jersey with a linear design, a massive menu, and lots of chrome. He is a fit 83 years old and is nattily dressed in a suit and tie with a carnation neatly placed in his lapel. A young waitress in a black t-shirt and pants comes over. She's wearing a white apron filled with soda straws and her shirt has the restaurant logo, the name of the place over some Greek-looking columns. He holds out three fingers indicating that he is waiting for others.

He looks past the mini juke box on the end of the table in front of the window and sees a dark green SUV pull into a space. An African-American man gets out and heads for the front door. Tommaso breaks into a slight smile.

Marcus Walker shrugs off his jacket and scarf, and tosses them onto the seat across from the old man. "Sorry, I'm late," he says. "You know how it is, putting out fires at work."

"Not a problem, Marcus. I appreciate you coming on such short notice. I see you have a new car."

"Not new, but new to me. It's a Jeep. Working here in the hills, I just need the four-wheel drive in case we have another winter like the last one."

The waitress brings three menus and three glasses of water. She hesitates for a moment upon seeing Marcus, but Tommaso nods and she places the items on the table. She asks if they would like anything to drink, but they both decline.

Marcus is wearing scrubs with the logo of the West Essex Rehabilitation Center on the front. He is 27 years old and has his head shaved. He places his elbows on the table and extends out his hands to either side and asks, "Okay, Mr. Pastor, why are we here? I assume it isn't to see my new ride."

"Relax, Marcus. Let's order lunch. Carter is on his way to join us, but I know you are pressed for time, so we can start without him."

"Start what?" asks Marcus.

Tommaso picks up his menu, ignoring Marcus. Marcus knows that whatever the old man has in mind, he will get to in his own time. Marcus shakes his head, smiles, and picks up his menu.

"Ready?" asks Tommaso.

Marcus nods and Tommaso waves to the waitress. She comes over and asks, "Are you waiting for your third party?"

"No," says Tommaso, "we will order now. I will have the turkey club, with onion rings instead of potatoes and a cup of coffee, and please bring me a side of mayonnaise."

Marcus gives a short shudder and says, "Please bring me an egg white omelet with mushrooms and, um, do you have spinach?"

She nods.

"And may I have fruit instead of potatoes?" Marcus adds, staring at Tommaso.

"Anything to drink?" asks the waitress.

"Water will be fine," says Marcus, handing her the menu.

Tommaso rolls his eyes as the waitress leaves and says, "Do you have spinach? It's a Greek diner with a twelve page menu. They probably have eight varieties of spinach. Egg whites, vegetables and fruit - who wants to live so long if you can't enjoy it?"

"Onion rings, bacon, and mayonnaise, not to mention gunshots – how did you live so long, old man?"

"I guess clean living is out."

"I'm guessing spite."

"Spite, Marcus? How so?"

"I think you are too stubborn to let anyone prove you wrong."

"Not a bad theory…I'll have to let you know if it ever happens."

Marcus laughs and waits.

"I'd like to ask a favor, Marcus," Tommaso begins. "I'm taking a trip next week and I'd like to know if you might be able to stop by my place a few times and get the mail, water the plants, and check things out."

"Sure, Mr. Pastor, I practically pass your place on the way to and from work every day. But why not ask me over the phone, or better yet, when I see you for your therapy session on Thursday?"

"I'm going to miss the next two weeks. This week, I have several errands to run for the trip, and next week, I'll be away. Also, I didn't want to miss our lunch. It's one of the highlights of my week."

"For eight months, you've been coming to me for physical therapy once a week and then buying me lunch. You know, your insurance would cover these treatments elsewhere and I wouldn't have to sneak you in at work."

"And I appreciate it. You won't take money, so the least I can do is feed you. This place is nothing special, but isn't this better than that hideous cafeteria at your center?"

"I suppose so. You also should know that the physical therapy center that I recommended has pretty young girls doing the therapy."

"An incentive, to be sure, but I hobbled around on a cane for forty-plus years and you have me at nearly 100 percent. I can get laid at home. For my therapy, I'll stick with the best."

"It looks like I arrived just in time," says Carter Jackson, removing his leather jacket. "I hope that I'm still getting laid at your age…or at least talking about it."

He slides in next to Marcus and waves to the waitress. When she arrives he points to Tommaso and says, "Miss, I'll have what he's having with a strawberry shake."

"Instead of coffee?" she asks.

"That is correct," says Carter, "and thank you."

"You don't even know what he's having," says Marcus, "What if he's having tongue or tripe or some other nasty substance?"

"Mr. Pastor has never steered me wrong," says Carter with a grin. "He's one brother who knows how to live."

"So, now I'm an honorary brother?" asks Tommaso. "I got kicked out of the Sons of Italy eight months ago, and I'm still falling. I must be pretty close to the bottom by now."

"Where did you park?" asks Marcus. "I didn't see you come in."

"In the back," says Carter. "I have a limo, today, and the lot is a little tight out front. I don't need to be bringing the boss man any dings. But, enough about where I parked. When I came in someone was talking about getting laid."

"Well, now that you are here, I wanted to tell you about the cruise I am going on next week," says Tommaso.

"And you need me to score you some Viagra?" asks Carter. "I drive a guy who goes to Canada regularly and says he can get it cheap."

"What is wrong with you?" asks Marcus.

"Wait, a minute," says Tommaso. "I sure as hell don't need it, but now that I live in that god-forsaken senior complex, I might be able to find you some buyers. I have no idea what that stuff costs, but an opportunity is an opportunity."

Marcus shakes his head in disgust.

"You might be surprised," says Carter, "that those pills go for about 35 bucks apiece and they are rarely covered by insurance."

"Thirty-five dollars?" asks Tommaso. "In my day, you could get two whores for that amount, and still have enough left over to buy candy and flowers for the wife!"

The waitress arrives carrying a large tray. She hesitates a moment while Carter stares at Tommaso and Marcus has his face buried in his hands. She distributes the food, avoiding eye contact the entire time.

"Before you form your new criminal enterprise," says Marcus, "let's talk about your trip. I can't spend all afternoon here with you two clowns."

In between bites, Tommaso explains that his neighbor in the senior complex, Milton Spiezle, told him of a deal for a week-long Caribbean cruise through some Jewish senior club he belonged to. The guy he was traveling with bailed at the last minute and in a moment of weakness, Tommaso agreed to go.

"That doesn't sound like your kind of trip," says Marcus.

"Especially the part about sharing a room with another dude," adds Carter.

"We were playing pinochle," says Tommaso. "You'd be surprised how much the Italian rules differ from the Jewish rules. I was focused on the game and apparently agreed before I had a chance to think about it. Considering that my last cruise was when I was alone at twelve hiding in the hold of a merchant ship from Italy, eating garbage, I figure, how much worse can this be?"

"I actually hear that they are quite nice," says Marcus. "I mean the current ships…like a luxury resort at sea that travels from city to city. The new ones, I hear, you wouldn't even know you're on a ship unless you look outside."

"Yeah," says Carter. "I do a lot of drop-offs at the terminal. They are gigantic. Are you leaving from Manhattan, Brooklyn, or Bayonne?"

"None of them," says Tommaso. "We're flying to Ft. Lauderdale on Sunday morning. Carter, I was hoping---"

"I'll be happy to drive you, sir," says Carter.

"Are you sure you're available?" asks Tommaso.

"You can be certain of that," says Marcus, jerking his thumb toward Carter. "On Sunday morning, there are no games on, the clubs are all closed, and you sure won't catch this heathen in church."

They both make an effort to ignore Marcus.

"What time is your flight?" asks Carter.

"9:55 AM at Newark," says Tommaso.

"Then I'll pick you up at 7:45," says Carter. "The traffic will be light. I assume that your 'traveling companion' will be coming as well?"

"Perfect," says Tommaso. "I return the following Sunday at about 3:00 PM."

"That might be a problem," says Carter. "I'll be at the Jets game."

"I can get you and Milton," says Marcus, turning to look at Carter. "I'll be done with church by then. So, which cruise line are you going on?"

"I'm not sure," says Tommaso.

"Well, what ports are you visiting?" asks Marcus.

"I don't know that, either," says Tommaso. "As I said, it was somewhat last minute."

Marcus and Carter look at each other.

"Do you even know what to pack?" asks Marcus.

"I wear what I wear," says Tommaso.

Carter laughs and says, "Sir, don't take this the wrong way, but while your zoot suit and fedora might get by on formal night, it's hardly appropriate for a tropical beach."

"You expect me to wear cut-off shorts and a wife-beater like some Benny at Seaside Heights?" asks Tommaso.

"I am begging you," says Carter. "Please take plenty of pictures."

"Look," says Marcus, "As fun as this is, I've got to get back. So, no therapy for two weeks, and check out your place, and pick you up next Sunday at three. I'll get the flight information from Carter."

Carter slides out of the booth to allow Marcus to leave. Marcus grabs his jacket and reaches for his wallet. Tommaso raises an eyebrow in a gesture only they understand. Marcus shrugs and puts his wallet back in his pocket, nodding. He heads for the door.

"I'm guessing that you do that 'wallet dance' with him every week." says Carter. "It's very cute."

"Everyone is entitled to their own version of dignity, Carter."

"Well I have too much respect for you to reach for my wallet, sir."

"My point exactly. I did notice that he seemed a little tightly wound, today," says Tommaso, "even for him."

"He's got a new girlfriend," says Carter, pouring the rest of his shake into his glass.

"Is it serious?"

"I don't know about serious, but more serious than I've seen in a while. I think he sees how happy and settled Scotty seems with your granddaughter and, well---"

"Caught the commitment bug?"

"Could be. There is also some added stress since this young lady is white."

"Is that even an issue these days?"

Not for them, but she has parents, and they're from out in the sticks. They just don't know any better. You know Marcus. He'll fall on his sword to protect her from pain even if he loves her...or because he loves her. Who the hell knows?"

"Have you met her?"

"Once. She's a social worker at his rehab center working on her Masters. She seemed quite nice. He's very secretive about his love life. While we're on the subject, I'm curious about something. How would you have handled it if it were Marcus who was seeing your granddaughter rather than her being with Scotty?"

"Hmm, interesting question. I think Scotty is wonderful, and more important, my Tommasina does as well. But, while he is obviously quite funny, I don't value humor so much. I really respect Marcus on many levels."

"You know that I'm talking about him dating your *granddaughter*, and not you, right?"

"Perfect example. My guess is that you are trying to be funny, yet here I am, unamused."

"Damn. Tough room."

"Back to your question. Today, I hope that I would accept Tommasina's hypothetical choice of Marcus both because I respect her, and because I have taken the time to get to know him. Eight months ago, when I first met him, I'd have offered him money, which he clearly would not have taken. At that point, the choice would have been a severe beating or death. Any time prior to meeting him, it probably would have just been death."

Carter looks shocked.

"Damn! Well, I appreciate your honesty."

"Carter, you must understand the context. In my world, the opinions of my peers could have meant life or death to me or my family. Quite frankly, I'm glad to be out of it. There were perks to be sure, but at too high a cost. A generation earlier, I might have had Scotty killed for being a Jew. A generation before that, my own beloved granddaughter, my namesake might have been in jeopardy."

"For dating a Jew?"

"Well, more for embarrassing the family."

"Damn, in my neighborhood, most of the dads just walked out. Maybe it wasn't so bad."

"Nobility has a price. It seems that Marcus is learning that now. I hope he gets through it undamaged. Anyway, enough of that. Might you be able to drop me off at the bank on your way back to work?"

"Absolutely, sir."

Tommaso drops a twenty on the table. They put on their jackets and head toward the cashier. After Tommaso pays the bill, they get in the car and head out of the lot. After a brief ride, Carter pulls in front of the bank and thanks Tommaso for lunch. They finalize their plans for Sunday. Tommaso gets out, and closes the door. Carter opens the window and calls out to Tommaso.

"Sir," asks Carter, "just for curiosity's sake. What would have happened if I had tried dating Tommy?"

"Oh, you wouldn't have even made it to the doorbell. We'd have seen you coming up the walk and had you taken out. Speaking of which, I almost forgot something."

"Yes, sir?"

"If you ever refer to Milton as my 'traveling companion' again, you will find yourself in the foundation of a bridge abutment on the Turnpike. *Capisce*?"

Tommaso smiles and heads toward the bank. Carter raises the window. Laughing, he says, "I ka-peesh."

Tuesday, Oct 21st
~ Wayne ~

Elmo backs his pickup into a space in the parking lot of the Willowbrook Grove condo complex. After locking his door, he reaches into the truck bed and takes out two magnetic signs. The signs are blank and he uses them to cover the company logo on the sides of his truck. The logo shows a picture of some tastefully artistic leaves around a silhouette of a house surrounded by the words 'Pastorini Landscape Design'. He grabs his computer bag off of the hood and heads toward his condo. He lets out a growl when he passes the sign displaying 'No Commercial Vehicles Allowed', attached to a fence. Elmo fishes out his keys in the dark as yet again, the front porch light is not on.

"Where the hell have you been?" he hears, before getting across the threshold.

It's Linda, of course. He slumps his shoulders and blows out a breath to compose himself as he closes the door.

"I had to stop by a client on the way home," he says. "One of the subcontractors moved some slate tiles and they were having a meltdown. I talked them off the ledge and headed straight here."

"I didn't move in here just to sit around all night waiting for you. I wanted to meet some people at Star Tavern."

Elmo puts his case on the table and absently reaches for the candy dish. It is empty. He attempts to slump his shoulders before realizing that he had already used that affectation. He wonders what he would look like at this point were his arms not attached at the shoulder.

"First," he says, "it's only 7:45. It's not that late. Second, it's Monday. Isn't it a little early in the week to be going out?"

"Well, if you didn't work all day, seven days a week, we'd be able to go out on the weekends. I gotta sit around here all day. I get bored."

"Besides the obvious option of getting a job to occupy your time, you might have also considered taking a few minutes to, I don't know, maybe prepare some food."

He walks to the kitchen and opens the refrigerator. Of course, it is nearly empty.

"Or possibly buy some food," he adds.

"Hey, I made pizza yesterday!"

"And while I do appreciate your efforts in putting two frozen pizzas in the oven, I'm not sure that going out for pizza makes a whole lot of sense a day later."

"I LIKE pizza, and Angie and Sal are gonna be there. She was gonna talk to me about a salon job."

"A salon job? You quit the last two after a week. Let's see...the first was because they wanted you to work on weekends, when people like to get their hair done, and the other...what was the problem there?"

"You know what the problem was. They wanted me to sweep hair off of the floor."

"Oh, that's right. You're too much of an 'artist' for that."

Elmo's use of air quotes around artist is more than she can handle.

"Fuck you, Elmo Pastor!" she shrieks.

"You recall that I asked you to work with me at the shop, right?"

"So I can come home smelling like dirt every night? Ooh! Why did I move in with you? What the hell happened to you? You had plenty of money, and we went out all the time. Ever since you started that damned nursery, you've gotten...um...um."

"Pride?" asks Elmo. "My father is retired now. It is time for me to pull my own weight. I also need to pay rent."

"What rent? Your father owns this place!"

"We've been over this. I agreed to pay rent, especially since he's doing all of my accounting for nothing. Look, Linda, obviously you want the old Elmo back – the big shot with plenty of time, money, and no direction. You are looking at the new Elmo, now – hard-working, responsible, and exhausted. I personally like this Elmo better. I guess you need to decide. I'm sorry that we didn't discuss this in more detail before you moved in."

"Isn't there something in between?"

Elmo looks at the candy dish. He pulls out his phone and pushes a few buttons.

"Sal," he says, "...yeah, Elmo. I assume you're at the Star...yeah. You got the truck?...Can you and Angie come over in about a half-hour? Linda needs a ride. Yeah... Thanks, dude."

Linda looks stunned and begins to cry. Elmo puts his phone in his pocket and sits at the table.

"Linda, please sit down," he says with surprising calm. "I'm terribly sorry. I want you to be happy. I really do, but this is not working and is not going to work. I think that you know this already. We've just been playing house here and you deserve more than that. I know I have changed and while that may be unfair to you, I need to keep going. You'll see that this will be for the best, hopefully sooner than later."

Linda has her head down and is whimpering softly. Elmo gets up and kisses her on the head. He takes his keys out of his pocket.

"I'm sorry, Linda," he says. "Sal and Angie are coming with the truck. I think it's better if you cleared out before I get back. Please leave the key in the mailbox and leave everything the way you found it. Sal will call me if there is a problem."

Elmo turns and heads out of the door.

Tuesday, Oct 21st
~ Glen Ridge ~

Ramona is sitting on the kitchen counter wearing a plush robe. She has one foot on a barstool and the other on the counter.

"Stop moving!" says Robert.

He is sitting at the counter, also in a robe, on another stool. Ramona cannot stop giggling.

Elmo walks in through the back door and they both jump with a start. Ramona yelps and closes her robe tightly around her. Robert deftly grabs the open bottle of nail polish before Ramona can kick it over.

"Jesus Christ!" shouts Elmo. "What the hell are you doing? Wait, I don't want to know. Jeez, don't you have like, five bedrooms in this house?"

Robert's face is bright red. He realizes that he closed his hand on the wet nail brush. He reaches for a paper towel. When he opens his hand, Elmo sees the nail polish. He shakes his head like a cartoon character doing a double take.

"Pop? Are you...oh, God, Pop...You're painting her toenails?"

"Just never you mind that," says Ramona. "What are you doing sneaking in on us like that? Suppose we were doing...something else?"

Elmo immediately covers his ears.

"Oh, Mom! Gross! I was gonna eat off of that counter!"

"Okay," says Robert, "everybody calm down. Everybody's been frightened and embarrassed enough. Is everything alright, Elmo? To what do we owe this surprise?"

"Yeah, sorry about that," says Elmo. "I just asked Linda to leave. She's packing up. Sal and Angie are picking her up in his truck."

Ramona carefully hops off the counter holding her robe closed. Standing behind her son, she silently gives a Robert a big smile and pumps her fist like Tiger Woods. Robert shows no reaction until she whips open her robe and flashes him. Robert's eyes nearly pop out of his head causing Elmo to turn around. Ramona has already assumed her motherly pout and reaches out to Elmo.

"Oh, I'm so sorry, baby," she says.

He accepts the hug, but does not appear upset at all.

"It's actually okay, Mom," says Elmo. "Surprisingly, I don't feel bad about it at all. I'm not even angry."

"Well, I'll bet that she is," says Robert. "I hope she's not in there tearing up the condo, or even worse, setting it on fire."

"Don't worry, Pop," says Elmo. "Sal won't let her get out of hand. I actually think that Linda is relieved as well. To be honest, I actually came over to get something to eat. Any leftovers?"

"Sit down and I'll get you something, baby," says Ramona.

Before she can move, Elmo holds up his hands.

"If you don't mind, Mom, I'll get the food. Maybe you could---"

Elmo makes a wiping motion with his hand in the general direction of the counter.

"Oh, of course, sorry," says Ramona as she goes under the counter for a bottle of Fantastik. She sprays some on the counter and takes a paper towel from Robert to wipe it off.

Elmo returns to the counter with an armload of Tupperware containers, a bottle of beer and a plate. Ramona brings him three forks, a knife, and a napkin.

"Three forks?" asks Elmo.

"Yes, dear. One for serving, one for eating, and one for your father," says Ramona, as she gets another plate.

Elmo puts an assortment of leftovers on his plate.

"This looks great, Mom. While I miss Merola's, you've done a pretty good job at making your own."

She pours a cup of decaf for Robert.

"Thanks, but your father is the real expert. I just help him assemble and clean up, mostly."

"Gee, Dad, master chef *and* manicurist? Where do you find the time?"

"Being retired has some advantages, Son. I still find time to do your books, you know. Besides, your mother just chipped one nail. I came down here because the light was better. She still goes to the salon for that. We haven't been completely wiped out, yet."

"Does that mean that you are going to hire a contractor for the chip in the bedpost?" Ramona asks, giggling.

Elmo nearly spits out a mouthful of lasagna.

"Oh, gross!" he shouts. "I'm trying to eat, here."

"I'd prefer if you kept the nail polish thing to yourself," says Robert, "if you don't mind."

"Your secret is safe with me...and possibly a future therapist," says Elmo.

Ramona sits down with a cup of tea.

"So do you want to talk about it?" she asks.

"There's really nothing to tell," says Elmo. "I never should have asked her to move in. She wanted the old Elmo, who was immature and had no trouble showing her the good life with Dad's money. I've got to tell you, the business is hard work, but I really like it, and honestly, I feel so much better about myself."

Robert and Ramona look toward one another and Ramona dabs her eye with her napkin.

"It's called pride, Son," says Robert, "and no one deserves it more than you."

"Well, I have the two of you to thank, Pop."

"Nonsense, pride comes from within. We may have helped you find it, but it comes back to us double. You'll find out when you have kids. Oh, will you look at this one."

Robert points to Ramona crying and hands her his napkin. She blows her nose so daintily that it appears almost regal. She reaches across the counter and takes Robert's hand. She takes Elmo's hand as well.

"Elmo," she says. "You look exhausted. Please sleep here, tonight."

"I think I had better, Mom. I am wiped. I'll just crash on the couch."

Robert winces. "So much for harmony," he mutters to himself.

"Nonsense!" says Ramona. "Your room is all set up. I insist that you go upstairs."

"I thought you were gonna make an office out of it," says Elmo.

Robert shakes his head.

"It's more of a shrine. I think you'll find that very little has changed. The same is true for your sister's room and your brother's."

Ramona slaps Robert on the arm as she bounds up the stairs.

"I'll take out some fresh towels!" she sings.

Wednesday, Oct 22nd
~ Glen Ridge ~

Ramona opens one eye, looks at her alarm clock and smiles. She reaches to turn it off. In the split second before she hits the off button, there is a soft popping sound. Before the music can come on, she has, like she seems to do every morning, literally beat the clock. She leans over and gives Robert a tender kiss on the cheek. He responds by grabbing her pillow and sliding it over his head.

Ramona slides out of the covers and heads toward the bathroom. Along the way, she takes a quick peek through the drapes to check the weather. "ARRRRGH!" comes out from between the pillows.

About a half hour later Ramona emerges from the bathroom in her robe, her hair and make-up already in place. "Are you coming in with me?" she asks.

Robert sits up in bed and shakes out the cobwebs.

"My God," he says. "I dreamt that Elmo moved back home."

"Don't be silly. He spent the night, but left an hour ago. My guess is that he wanted to check the condo before heading into work. I hope that every trace of that skank Linda is gone."

"Skank? Isn't that a bit harsh? I could see lazy or entitled, maybe even crude, but a skank?"

"It's a mother thing. Can you get up so I can make the bed?"

Robert knows that this is no time to protest. Delaying will only result in being required to help with the process. If he can somehow manage the intricate origami folding pattern of the sheets, he will still need to pick up and deliver the twenty or more pillows arranged in a mosaic that would stump Rubik himself. Robert manages a quick "Yes, ma'am", and darts into the bathroom.

Fifteen minutes later, Robert emerges and finds his beloved bed replaced by a king-sized piece of artwork. Another 'mother thing', he muses.

"Ro, what were you asking earlier? I was a little out of it."

"I asked if you were coming to the shop with me this morning."

"I think I'm going to go in later. I want to read the paper and catch up on some paperwork, if that's okay."

"It's fine with me. Things have calmed down considerably since the summer. Elmo looked awful last night. He was going to take some time off next week and go to the shore house with Linda. As happy as I am to see her out of the picture, I still want him to take a break. Maybe you could offer to go with him."

"I thought you wanted me to help you. I'm not sure you and Donny can handle it."

Robert suddenly realizes that he made a poor choice of words. Ramona immediately stops adjusting her earrings and gives him the death stare. Robert rushes in to hug her before she can speak.

"Sorry, baby," he says quickly, "poor choice of words. I just want to be available to help you only if you need it."

She smiles and kisses him tenderly. "That's better. While we're on the subject of helping, did you get the package to Tommy that I put together for Pep? There was some important mail for him. She's leaving for Boston in a few hours and is staying with him."

"I took care of it."

"What do you mean, you 'took care of it'?"

"Now who's the untrusting one? I took care of it."

"You brought it to her?"

"I took care of it!"

"Please explain."

Robert rolls his eyes, but knows he has no choice.

"I saw Papa on Sunday. He said he was having lunch with Marcus, who was to give it to Carter, who was to pass it on to Scotty who is the guy who happens to be boinking your daughter."

"So now, instead of nagging one forgetful husband, I have to count on the responsibility of five of you."

"Five of who?"

"Men, that's who. And why when she's getting boinked, as you so classily put it, is she *my* daughter? I'll bet when she gets her doctorate, she'll be *your* daughter."

Robert looks at her sheepishly for a moment, then comes in for another hug, but Ramona fends him off.

"Don't even try it, Buster. I'll see you later at the shop."

Wednesday, Oct 22nd
~ Cedar Grove ~

Elmo backs his truck into the side lot of Pastorini's Nursery. He is glad to see Donny's Chevy Nova already parked next to the building. There was some concern about bringing Donny into the business. Elmo and Donny have been best friends since middle school, but it wasn't always the most fruitful relationship. Between Donny's penchant for dangerous ideas, and Elmo's follower personality, they spent most of their time together getting yelled at, lectured, and performing community service.

Elmo heads toward the shop stopping for a moment to look at the sign above the door. While it was his father's idea to incorporate the nursery and the landscape service separately, it was Elmo's idea to use the name Pastorini.

They had found out only last New Year's Day about the heroic sacrifice by a young woman named Pastorini who saved the life of his grandfather and started their lineage in America as the Pastors. That name now required a lower profile due to some rather serious changes in the leadership and management of the New Jersey organized crime landscape.

Elmo's father bought the fading Bellino's Nursery from a former business associate after noticing his son's affinity for plants and landscaping. The hope was that Elmo would find some direction and things could not have gone better. With Robert doing the accounting and Ramona helping out running the store, Elmo has been able to spend more time on the landscaping work. He has developed quite a following. When spring rolled around, it was evident that more help would be needed.

When Elmo had suggested bringing in Donny, it spurred a rather lengthy family discussion. Robert was vehemently against it for no other reason than Donny's toxic influence over Elmo. Ramona countered with the fact that Donny had left the auto shop where he had been working and was now on the staff at her gym. She reported that he had seemed to clean up his act both physically and temperamentally, and was at work every morning. Due to their conflicting schedules, Elmo and Donny spent what little social time they had on the phone.

They agreed to a trial with the restriction that Elmo and Donny could not be roommates for at least six months. It was also expected that Elmo and Donny would both begin taking college courses in September, paid for by the Pastors. It was as though the two young men had grown up overnight. Donny was a model employee who arrived promptly and worked efficiently with little direction. He often made suggestions that were implemented and successful. He had a talent for working with his hands that saved hundreds if not thousands of dollars in maintenance on the trucks, sprinklers, plumbing, and electrical systems.

Elmo and Donny surprised the Pastors by signing up for on-line summer coursework at their own expense. While Robert remains skeptical, Ramona has taken Donny under her wing. She began mentoring him in presenting himself to customers and in the social graces in general.

Elmo raps on the locked front door. Donny looks up from the work he is doing behind the counter. He glances at the clock and heads toward the door. Donny stops to flip over the Open/Closed sign to Open and unlocks the door.

"Good morning, boss," says Donny, with a grin. "Looks like I beat you here again. It's a good thing somebody's looking out for this place."

"Yeah, yeah. It's been slowing down, but thanks anyway. I slept at my parents place, then got up early to shower at the condo."

"Trouble?"

"Yeah, I suppose so. I asked Linda to move out last night. I left so she could go quietly."

"I'll bet she wrecked your place."

"Nah, I had Sal come get her. He kept her in check. I was there this morning. The only thing missing was the beer."

"Small price to pay, Bro. Looks like I win the pool. I had two weeks. Your pop had four."

"Damn, such confidence. What did my mother have? I'm sure she had my back."

"Are you kidding? She was out after three days. She was never a big fan of Linda."

"Jeez, what did you all see that I didn't?"

"E, look, for many years you listened to my screwy ideas. At least you get it now. Is this gonna affect your vacation next week?"

"Probably. My parents think I need the break, but there's no point in going to the shore myself and if I go, you gotta stay."

"That's not a problem. I agree that you could use a few days off. I'm just not looking forward to being here alone with your parents. Your pop still pretty much hates my guts."

"Well, you did almost get him, his father, and his son killed. Besides, you've really turned it around with my mother. You're like her special project."

"I know. I'm worried she's hot for me!"

Elmo is looking for something heavy to throw at Donny when the door jingles. Elmo quickly turns to greet a customer. Ramona comes in and he hears Donny laughing from the back room.

"Are you boys doing some stapling?" she asks.

Elmo realizes he is still wielding the stapler and quickly puts it down behind the counter.

"Uh, no, Mom. I thought I saw a cockroach around here somewhere."

"You leave Donny alone. You should always treat your employees and co-workers with respect."

"Good morning, Mrs. P," says Donny, as he enters from the back room. "I guess you heard Elmo's news."

"Oh, yes. I owe you something."

Ramona reaches into her purse. She takes out a ten dollar bill and hands it to Donny.

"Seriously, Mom," says Elmo. "You bet on the length of my relationship?"

"Don't look at me. Your best friend here had two weeks."

"Nice try, Mom. Donny told me that you had three days."

Ramona wags her finger at Donny who looks at the floor.

"Why thank you, Donald," she says. "I guess it was just wishful thinking on my part. I knew you would come to your senses, Elmo. By the way, Donald, are you expecting a delivery today?"

Donny immediately turns red and slips into the back room. Ramona smiles and moves behind the counter. Elmo looks confused. He is about to speak but thinks better of it and pulls the schedule up on his computer.

Wednesday, Oct 22nd
~ West Orange ~

Tommaso Pastor walks up to the door of his condo in the Azalea Gardens section of Essex Village. He stops for a second in thought, and puts his keys back into his jacket pocket. He hangs his dry cleaning on his doorknob and heads further down the walk toward #116. Tommaso firmly knocks on the door. After a few moments, a short, bald, and round man opens the door.

"Bernie," he says, "thanks for coming…Oy! Tommaso, my apologies. I was expecting Bernie Solomon, you know, the director of Essex Village. Come in, come in."

Aside from being a neighbor, Milton Spiezle was one of the few people Tommaso could call a friend. He was also one of the few people that knew of Tommaso's past in organized crime. Milton was the top money launderer east of Chicago for several decades. His vast knowledge of the world organized crime landscape afforded him a quiet retirement.

"I can come back if you are in the middle of something," says Tommaso.

"No, no, that won't be necessary. I just need to confirm with the little *pisher* that I'll be out of town for a week. I usually don't like anybody knowing my business, which is tough enough already with all the *yentas* here. You know what I mean by *yenta*?"

"I get the idea. Kind of a cross between *chiacchierone* and *ficcanaso* in my world. So no one knows where we're going?"

"Not from me, and I'm quite confident that you didn't tell anyone."

Tommaso nods and Milton continues.

"Since I have no family or loved ones, if you will, I keep all of my affairs neatly in order. When something happens to me, I just need someone to contact my attorney and my mortician. Everything is neatly planned."

"How so?"

"I get cremated, there is a little service here, my stuff gets liquidated, and the Jewish War Veterans gets whatever is left minus the twenty-five grand cash in an envelope for Bernie."

"Neat."

"Well, I never married, but had a full life. After the hitch in the Army, I realized I had two skills – taking care of dirty money, and keeping my mouth shut. I lived first class, all the way and schtupped more woman than you can imagine. I usually travel alone, but since you moved in, I figured it might be time for a change of pace. We have a similar background, so why not?"

"Sharing a cabin, I assume will be an adjustment. The last ship I was on was no luxury ship. I stowed away in the cargo hold."

"Trust me, this will be better. The Fiesta Line is not the top, but is in the upper half. You get a more mature clientele, you know, less families with kids, and plenty of lonely women."

"Will I be cramping your style?"

"The truth is, Tommaso that I don't have the stamina I once had. When I was in the ZBT house at Princeton, we would put a necktie on the doorknob to the room if we were entertaining a girl. God forbid either of us gets lucky, we'll just use that. The good news is that the ship has something happening at all hours. I'm sure we'll have a blast."

"Well, Milton, I'm actually looking forward to trying something new."

There is a knock on the door.

"That must be Bernie," says Milton. "Can you come over in the morning to finalize our plans?"

"Sure, 9:00 okay?"

"Perfect. I might be in the garden. If I don't answer the door, come around the back."

Bernie opens the door. Tommaso nods to Bernie on the way out and heads toward his unit.

Wednesday, Oct 22nd
~ Cambridge ~

"Pep," says Tommy, "I'm happy to crash on the couch."

"Nonsense," says Pep. "It's my place, and I will decide who sleeps where. Besides, I took the time to wash the sheets, and I don't want to waste it. I made you some room in the closet in case you want to hang anything up and there is some room on the bathroom sink for your things."

"I can't believe it."

"What?"

"You've turned into Mom."

Pep smiles as though this is a compliment. He places his sister's carry-on bag on the freshly made bed as she puts her backpack on the desk chair. He gives her a big hug. Pep is a slim college senior who is five years younger than his sister. Tommy begins to unbutton her coat but Pep stops her.

"Wait," he says, "let me take you to dinner. I'm starving, and I'm sure your lunch was limited to peanuts on the plane."

"Well, actually it was pretzels, and now that you mention it, I am kind of hungry."

"Great! We have sushi, pub grub, and a very nice Mediterranean place in the neighborhood. I recommend the latter even though it's lamely called Casablanca, but the food is great."

"That sounds nice, and since you've apparently turned into Mom, I won't even try to wrestle you for the check."

Pep laughs and wags his finger at Tommy as he picks up his wallet and keys. They head toward the door.

It's a perfect autumn evening in Cambridge. Pep's apartment is right off campus at MIT on Green Street. Tommy and Pep cut through to Massachusetts Avenue and turn left. In the middle of the block, they find Casablanca, a small restaurant between a florist and a bike shop. They enter and are met by a hostess in a nondescript Mediterranean outfit. The restaurant has a dozen tables, two of which are occupied by five students from the looks of it. They are shown a table across from the empty bar.

A blonde waitress in a colorful embroidered jacket with sheer sleeves comes by. She's also wearing jeans and sneakers. Pep gets up and gives her a big hug.

"Kim, I'd like you to meet my big sister, Tommy."

Kim smiles and waves, and then steps back to give an ostentatious *salaam*.

"Welcome to Casablanca," she adds.

"Wow," says Tommy, "the royal treatment."

"Actually," says Kim, "everyone gets the same greeting. The owner has deluded himself to think that people come here for the ambiance, but it's almost all students and hipsters."

"Hence, the costume?" asks Tommy.

"Oh, this is nothing. Wait until you see Brad at the bar. He's in the back getting some stock. I've actually heard quite a bit about you, Tommy, particularly about your adventure meeting your boyfriend last Christmas."

"Oh, really?" asks Tommy, shifting her gaze toward Pep.

Pep tries to quickly change the subject.

"Um, Kim, here is a Math major. We've been in a few classes together and she is a star in her department."

"That's great, Kim," says Tommy. "I hope that you can inspire more females to pursue math and the sciences."

"Why thank you. I typically get smirks and eye rolling from the guys, at least those who are honest enough not to be patronizing."

"Let me guess. The women are worse."

"I'll say. They're either derisive or, well, you're the sociologist. Pep, tell her about my Urban Spoon review."

"Are you sure?" asks Pep with a smile. "Okay, one night, some of us are looking for a new place to eat, so we go on line. Manny is looking at reviews and sees one flaming Casablanca with half a star. The thing is, that the jerk writing the review, keeps mentioning the 'ditzy blonde waitress' over and over. Well, we all know that they're talking about Kim, who is probably one of the one hundred or so top mathematical minds in the country."

Kim strikes her ditsiest pose and they all laugh.

"Well," says Tommy, "I will have Pep send me the link and I will immortalize you by adding your story to my collection of gender stereotypes."

There is an older gentleman behind the register demonstratively clearing his throat. Kim looks at the owner and then scans the room filled with empty tables. She shakes her head and says, "I'll be back."

They scan their menus and make their choices. Kim returns with two glasses of water and a carafe of the red house wine. As she is taking their order, Brad comes out of the back room and takes his position behind the bar. Kim wasn't kidding about the costume. He is wearing a fez and a short embroidered jacket not unlike Aladdin.

Tommy notices Pep's extended stare. Brad places a box below the bar and looks their way. He immediately brightens and waves to Pep. Pep returns the greeting, possibly a bit too enthusiastically. After Kim leaves with their order, Tommy grins at him.

"You must be quite the regular here to warrant such a greeting," she says.

Pep's face reddens.

"A bunch of us come here pretty often. Brad goes to Harvard."

"Oh? I don't recall asking about Brad."

Now, Pep is completely embarrassed.

"It's okay," says Tommy. "Apparently my relationship story is so epic that you shared it with all of your friends."

"First of all, Brad and I do not have a relationship. Second, your story *was* epic. Quite frankly, I don't even know if Brad is gay."

"I am now using all of my sociology training to avoid making a cheap joke about his outfit. You don't suppose he's wearing those curled up slippers, do you?"

"You're not helping."

You know, with all of my gender research, I never really thought about that. For a straight person to assume that someone else is straight, they have an eighty-plus percent chance of being right. Your odds go way down."

"Plus," says Pep, "there is a significant portion of the population that might take offense at the inference, let alone the question."

"This reminds me of a conference I attended once. There was a guy who was the life of the party and was pretty much flirting with everyone. Several people, both gay and straight, were speculating on his orientation. One of the suggestions was from a guy who said, 'Ask him if he plays golf'. This spurred further discussion on what question you could ask that would get you an answer in the least embarrassing or awkward way."

"What happened?"

"Well, several of us met for breakfast. We're all siting down at the table when this woman walks by wearing the same outfit she had on the night before. She simply announces, 'He plays golf.', and just keeps on walking."

"Jeez, Sis, what happened to you? I vaguely remember you being a hero to me at one point."

"You could use *my* methodology and go over and barf into the samovar by the bar. That should get his attention."

"The fact that Scotty was charmed by that debacle never ceases to astound me."

Kim brings the food and refills their drinks. The place begins to fill up, mostly with college students. Pep and Tommy discuss his schooling, his plans for the summer, and for after graduation. Tommy fills him in on her relationship with Scotty."

"I can see it in your face when you talk about him," says Pep. "I've never seen you look so happy."

"I *am* happy. I'm glad it shows."

"Tell me what you have found that you like least about him."

"That's an odd question. Let me think about it. I guess maybe it's that he's not an animal guy. I know that we never had pets because of Mom's issues, but I rode horses and always kind of liked the idea of a house full of pets."

"Interesting. And what do you like best?"

"Wow. That's tougher. He's smart and very funny. Never underestimate the value of someone who can make you laugh. I know. It would be his fierce loyalty. He has this weird heroic streak that I wish I had. It's like he wants his tombstone to read, 'He Had Principles'."

"Neat," says Pep.

"Why did you ask?"

"I'm not sure. I've found that the best way to learn about someone or something quickly is to ask about the superlatives. You know, the best, worst, most and least."

"Why don't you try that on Brad?"

"When I'm ready. How's the family?"

"Mom and Dad are acting like teenagers, speaking of barfing."

"Good for them. And Elmo?"

"Elmo really has changed. I might actually like this version of him, except for that girlfriend of his. She can really bring him down."

"You need a new source for information. He already threw her out. Didn't Mom text you? She blew up my inbox. I had my phone on vibrate and I think it actually danced in my pocket."

"I guess I have been dumped by Momnet. I hadn't heard. Did you know that Grandpa is going on a cruise?"

"Yeah, with some guy from his complex. I just can't picture Grandpa playing the tourist in an Hawaiian shirt."

"Speaking of travel, can we expect you at Thanksgiving this year? Mom keeps bringing it up. I wish you'd commit. Why don't you bring Brad?"

Pep wads up his napkin and throws it at her.

"I'll call her tonight, all right? Hey, I'd like to introduce you to some of my friends. Are you available if I invite some people over on Saturday night?"

"Sure, I'd like that. I'm meeting Libby for lunch at the wharf, but I'll be back in the afternoon. Just not too late, I can't party like I used to."

"Puh-lease, Sis. You've always kept farmer's hours. You can take a nap in the late afternoon. We don't get warmed up until midnight. You can sleep on the plane on Sunday."

Wednesday, Oct 22nd
~ Montclair ~

Marcus sits at the kitchen table staring at a large pile of paperwork. He sighs and grabs a report off of the tallest stack and begins to read it. He hears the rattle of keys and some laughter outside the apartment door. It opens and Marcus' roommate Carter staggers in laughing with a girl in tow.

Ever the gentleman, Marcus stands in the presence of a lady. He quickly sees that the term 'lady' is generous. Carter shrugs off his jacket and tosses it onto the couch. Marcus clears his throat and Carter instinctively reaches for his jacket, to hang it up. Marcus smiles inwardly realizing that his training of his roommate seems to be working. Carter finally gets that Marcus is waiting for an introduction.

"Oh, yeah," stammers Carter. "Marcus, this is Gwen. Gwen, this is my roommate Marcus."

"Hello, Marvin," she says, a little too loudly. She clearly has had more than a few drinks. She's a full-figured woman who is having trouble removing her jacket while holding her purse. Carter eventually helps her out of her entanglement.

Marcus pulls Carter aside and lowers his voice.

"Dude, Scotty's here, so you'd better take her into your own room."

"What? I didn't know he was coming here."

"Well he *is* here and came home fried from a series of meetings, so you might want to keep it down a little."

"Damn, my room is a mess."

"First of all, I told you to clean it up, but we can argue about that later. I doubt she'll notice and it looks like you're gonna need to work fast."

Gwen is sprawled on the couch and is fading fast.

"Damn," says Carter, "I'll catch you in the morning."

Carter pulls Gwen toward his room. Marcus laughs to himself, shaking his head.

Thursday, Oct 23rd
~ Montclair ~

Scotty awakens to *The Sounds of the Sea* alarm and turns on the lamp next to his bed. He sees something glinting in the light and finds a long blonde hair on the pillow next to his. He opens both eyes widely and sits bolt upright in bed. He grabs the pillow and gives it a deep sniff, immediately breaking into a coughing spell.

"Carter!" he spits through gritted teeth.

Scotty gets out of bed and slips on a t-shirt. He carefully grabs the offending hair between his thumb and forefinger and heads out of his room.

He bursts out of the door and nearly plows into Marcus coming out of the bathroom. Scotty maintains his hold on the evidence.

"Where is that son of a bitch?" asks Scotty.

Marcus steps aside allowing Scotty access to Carter's door. He bangs on it with his free fist.

"Get out here, you pig!"

When there is no response, Scotty adds, "What blonde slut were you screwing in my bed?"

This gets Carter's attention and he immediately slides out of the door while slipping on a robe.

"Shhh!" hisses Carter. "Bro, I got a girl in there."

Scotty holds up the hair between his fingers.

"Can I assume that this belongs to her?"

Upon seeing Carter's look of panic, Scotty finally realizes that the hair clearly does not belong to his current visitor. He tries to switch to 'Bro mode', but it is too late. Gwen pushes her way out of Carter's room. She is barely dressed, but that doesn't stop her from slapping at him quite hard and pushing past him.

"Sharonda was right about you," she shouts. "I cannot believe that I let you bring me here!"

She moves past Scotty and picks up her bag and jacket from the couch. Gwen pulls open the door, but before leaving turns back toward Carter. She looks like she is about to speak, but just quakes in anger and lets out a guttural growl. She turns, heads out, and slams the door.

Scotty and Carter are too stunned to move for a moment. Marcus comes out of his room, adjusting his tie.

"You guys want some breakfast?" he asks.

"What the fuck is wrong with you?" says Carter, to a stunned Scotty.

"Me? You're the one screwing your nasty women in my bed. How was I supposed to know you had one in there, especially a different one?"

Scotty holds up the blonde hair. Marcus steps between the two of them and holds up his hands.

"Why don't you two shower, get dressed, and most of all, calm down. I'll make breakfast and we can all discuss this like civilized human beings. I'm trying to get rid of a headache but I also don't want to miss any of this."

Scotty and Carter gruffly return to their rooms and Marcus heads into the kitchen and takes out the eggs, butter, two tubes of biscuits, and a block of cheddar cheese from the refrigerator. He turns on the oven, and puts up a teapot of water to boil. He is about to put the biscuits in the oven when he stops to look at the clock. Marcus reaches for the tap and turns on the hot water, full blast. He hears Carter scream from the shower and smiles. He puts the biscuits on the counter for a few extra minutes.

Scotty comes out first, dressed for class in khakis, a long sleeve, blue cotton dress shirt, and a tie with a big smiley face on it.

"Did I hear a bloodcurdling scream a minute ago?" asks Scotty.

"Yeah, I was checking to see how long Carter was gonna be."

"Oh, the old cold water trick."

"Works every time."

Carter comes out dressed for work in black slacks, a crisp white shirt and a thin black tie. He tosses his jacket over the back of the couch before making himself a cup of instant coffee. He turns toward Marcus while stirring his mug.

"Did it ever occur to you to just knock on the bathroom door and ask how long I'll be?"

Marcus puts the tray of perfectly golden brown biscuits on the table.

"Perfect timing is an art form, Brother. I don't mess with success," he says.

They each sit down and dole out the eggs and biscuits. Scotty pours a glass of orange juice and holds the pitcher up toward Marcus. Marcus waves him off while pointing to his water glass, but Carter holds out his juice glass and Scotty fills it.

"First," says Scotty, "I want to apologize for mentioning another woman in front of whoever that was this morning. I should have determined if you were alone, or at least boffing the same woman twice in a row."

"Apology accepted," says Carter, "although I believe you meant to say *whomever*. I have been on an unusual hot streak as of late, and you certainly could not have expected that. I, in turn, apologize for using your bed without explicit permission and for failing to wash and change your sheets. I was planning on doing laundry this evening and did not expect you to return last night."

"See," says Marcus, "how much better things are when we are civil? Anyhow, who is this blonde you are talking about? Apparently I missed her completely, and why was, um, Gwen was it, so agitated?"

"If you must know, Gwen and Marcie, the blonde, are partners in a flower shop in Clifton."

"Wait," asks Scotty, "you brought home business partners to sleep with on consecutive nights? And who the hell is Sharonda? Dude, you're going to get yourself stabbed one of these days."

"And," adds Marcus, "he was going to do them both in your bed if I hadn't stopped him last night."

"Jesus Christ, Carter! Marcie's perfume is still on my pillow!"

Carter shrugs and takes another forkful of eggs, cleaning his plate.

"Ask him who he was buying flowers for when he went into the shop in the first place," say Marcus.

Carter gets up to put his dishes in the sink.

"I wish I had time to explain all of this, but I have a pickup. Ever since you guys entered committed relationships, you've become a little judgmental. Maybe I just want what you both have."

"You may have to give them a little more than twelve hours, before trying the next one," says Scotty. "Are you both gonna be home tonight? I'd like to make dinner."

"Not me," says Carter. "I'll be at the Laundromat."

"Can you go tomorrow?" asks Scotty.

"No can do, Bro. There's a lady who goes every Thursday that I want to meet. I haven't seen her yet, but she has great taste in lingerie."

"Jesus, you're a pig" says Scotty. "Just make sure you wash my sheets."

"No biggie," says Marcus. "I can't make it either. I gotta date with my girl. We moved up to tonight because she has a girl's weekend with some of her college friends."

"Sweet. Grading projects and Thursday Night Football. I can't wait. Please remind me why we were in such a hurry to be adults."

Thursday, Oct 23rd
~ West Orange ~

Tommaso walks over to Milton's condo. He rings the bell, but there is no answer. Tommaso slides through the foliage partially blocking the narrow pathway between the buildings and heads toward the patio area. He walks into an impressive garden of flowers, plants, and herbs. Milton is nowhere to be found, but Tommaso sees that the screen is closed and the sliding glass door is open.

"Milton?" calls Tommaso, to no reply.

Tommaso slides open the screen and notices that the television is on with some sort of business program. Milton appears to be asleep in the leather chair facing the two men arguing about the next hot stock, but Tommaso already knows. He touches Milton's neck to verify that Milton is indeed dead.

Tommaso lets out a slight sigh and reaches for the remote. Before touching it, he stops and remembers the caution that kept him alive for this long. Tommaso walks toward the phone to call Bernie. On his way, he passes Milton's desk and sees the cruise documents neatly laid out along with the airline tickets. Tommaso stops and stares at the items while thinking. He takes out his handkerchief and opens the top desk drawer. Right on top, he sees Milton's passport. After a short pause, Tommaso picks up all of the travel documents and Milton's passport. He looks around to make sure that he did not touch anything else.

Tommaso heads toward the back door. He stops beside the chessboard, where Milton has a game in progress. Using his handkerchief, he carefully tips over the black King. Tommaso whispers, "Goodbye, my friend," before wiping off and closing the screen door.

Thursday, Oct 23rd
~ Cedar Grove ~

"Robert, can you help this customer place these items in her car?" asks Ramona, from behind the register in the front of Pastorini's Nursery.

Robert is in the office working on reconciling the receivables.

"Where's Donny? I'm in the middle of something," he says.

"He's on a delivery, Robert. We mustn't keep the customer waiting."

Ramona's explanation was delivered with the perfect mix of directness, customer service, and ice. Robert knows from her tone that any further delay on his part will result in more trouble than either of them would like. He quickly gets up from the desk and heads out to the shop.

Robert is relieved to see a wagon containing two azalea plants and a small bag of topsoil. As he begins to wheel the items outside, Ramona adds, "There is also a small dogwood outside and Mrs. Gennaro needs three of the forty pound bags of peat moss as well."

Robert shivers in exasperation, not sure if he is angrier with Ramona, Donny, or himself, for buying this shop for Elmo in the first place. His frustration is compounded in finding out that Mrs. Gennaro has a new Lexus and is quite particular about the slightest amount of dirt in it or on it.

Twenty minutes later, Robert returns to the shop and gives his wife the evil eye. His shirt is filthy and he has a few leaves in his hair. Ramona takes one look at him and begins to laugh. Robert smells his hands and makes a face.

"Where the hell is Donny?" he asks. "What are we paying him for if not to do this sort of work? And could you please tell me what is so God damned funny?"

"I'm sorry, honey, but I was watching you from in here. What were you trying to accomplish out there?"

"First of all, for someone who doesn't want any dirt in her car, the lady bought an awful lot of dirt. Didn't you tell her that we would deliver it for free?"

"Of course, but she didn't want to wait."

"How will she get the stuff out of her car when she gets home?"

"I assume that will be Mr. Gennaro's headache. I would expect that he is used to it."

"I empathize with him. You seem to have little difficulty in getting *your* way."

"Are you complaining? At the end of the day, Mr. Gennaro gets to take Mrs. Gennaro into their boudoir. You get *Moi*."

"That's assuming my back is not broken."

"Hey, Buster, she could have ordered gravel, or some of those fifty pound bags of decorative stone. If you are too infirm to handle me, I suppose you could trade places with Mr. Gennaro for a few days."

"No thanks! I've taken enough orders from her. I appreciate the fact that you rarely criticize me in the bedroom."

She walks around the counter to give him a kiss, but as she gets near, she recoils and scrunches up her nose.

"Ugh!" she says. "But no treats for you until you clean up."

"But, I'm wearing nature's cologne."

"If you try to touch me with that peat moss on your hands, you'll be sleeping out in nature."

Robert holds out his hands and begins to chase her when his phone rings. He carefully fishes it out of his pocket and looks at the screen.

"It's Papa," he says. "He never calls my cell. I wonder if he's all right."

"Why not answer it and ask him?"

Robert looks at her for a moment and slides his finger across the device to accept the call.

"Papa? Is everything okay?...Dinner?...Uh, yeah, sure..."

At this moment, Elmo walks in. He smiles and kisses his mother.

"I got the contract for The Willows!" he says. "It's our first commercial gig."

She holds up a finger nodding her head toward Robert on the phone.

"He just walked in, I'll ask him…"

Robert moves the phone from his ear.

"Elmo, what are you doing for dinner?"

"No plans, I was just gonna pick something up."

"Great, you can pick up your grandfather and bring him to the house."

Robert goes back to his call.

"Okay, Papa, Elmo will pick you up at 6:15."

Robert ends the call.

"What was that all about?" asks Ramona.

"Beats me. Papa wanted to come over for dinner. I can't remember him ever asking before."

"Better get busy with those take-out menus, Mom," says Elmo. "Pop, we got the contract, at our price!"

"Great, Son," says Robert. "Come back to the office and tell me about it."

Robert reaches to put his arm around his son. Elmo gingerly sidesteps the gesture.

"Jesus, Pop, you really stink!"

Thursday, Oct 23rd
~ Glen Ridge ~

Ramona sighs as she sets the dining room table. Since Elmo moved out, they have rarely used this room. The subject of downsizing has not come up, but she is sure that it has crossed Robert's mind. While he has assured her that they are financially secure, she knows that they are carrying a lot of obligations and properties. With the kids using three of them she also knows that things cannot stay this way forever.

Robert comes in through the kitchen carrying several bags of food from Martucci's. Ramona sends him right back into the kitchen where she has laid out the serving platters. She follows him in.

"What do you suppose your father wants to discuss?" she asks.

"I wouldn't worry, babe. It could be anything. Papa has never been much trouble and I'm sure, whatever it is, we can deal with it."

Robert has been emptying the bags and opening the containers while Ramona has been transferring the food to the platters. He tries to hand her a tray of meatballs, but she is staring at him agape with her hands on her hips.

"Never been much trouble?" she asks. "Aren't you forgetting something? Remember last Christmas?"

"Well, I suppose if you want to be a Debbie Downer---"

Ramona gasps and throws a pot holder at Robert.

"Debbie Downer? Let's see...you lost your job, your father and children were facing jail or murder, you had your daughter's boyfriend arrested---"

"Hey, it all worked out, and look how happy Tommasina is. You were worried that she'd never find anyone."

"God, you're impossible!"

"I guess my glass is half full these days."

"Yes, full of your marbles. It's a good thing I love you, Buster. Help me get this stuff on the table."

The front door opens and Elmo comes in with Grandpa. Ramona gives them both a kiss and takes their coats.

"Smells great!" says Elmo. "I need to wash up."

Robert kisses his father on the cheek and asks, "Is there anything we need to discuss while Elmo is out of the room?"

"No, Son. We spoke at length in the car about the business. He is an impressive young man and you should be very proud of him."

"Of course we are," says Ramona.

"Wait, that's not how I meant it," says Tommaso. "You should be proud of yourselves. I see so much of both of you in him. I know you had your worries, but all of your efforts can clearly be seen in him, now."

Ramona mists up and gives Grandpa a hug as Elmo walks in.

"Did you make Mom cry again, Grandpa? You're not dying are you? Can I have your Rolex? C'mon, let's eat!"

After some laughter and head shaking, they sit down for a nice dinner. Ramona is anxious, but Robert knows that his father will say what he wants to say in his own good time. Robert is pouring a dessert wine when Grandpa clears his throat.

"I have two plane tickets and two tickets for a cruise for a week, leaving this Sunday. My traveling companion is no longer able to travel and I would like to know if you and Ramona would like to go. I know that it is short notice, but I also know that you have fewer commitments than in the past, so I thought you might like to get away."

Ramona looks shocked and turns to Robert who is his usual implacable self. Elmo seems only interested in the tiramisu that he is enthusiastically shoveling into his face.

"Papa, what a wonderful gesture! While I would love to take my bride on such an adventure, I have been with her long enough to know that a month is probably the minimum amount of time for Ramona to prepare for such a trip. Don't you have another friend, perhaps a lady that would like to go with you?"

"Normally, I would, but a cruise is new to me. I would prefer to travel with someone I was more comfortable with."

"Elmo!" shouts Ramona.

"Hmmnn?" says Elmo, with a fork in his mouth.

"What do you mean, hon?" asks Robert.

"Why doesn't he take Elmo? This way Papa doesn't miss his trip, Elmo still takes a little time off, and they get to know each other better."

"Mom, I can't be gone from the business for a whole week."

"First, swallow your food. Second, you and what's-her-name were going to the shore house for a vacation anyway."

"Her name is Linda, and I was just going to miss Monday and Tuesday, our lightest days. I don't want you and Pop to have the place for a whole week. Besides, I have no idea what to pack for a cruise."

"Honey, you're exhausted. You've done amazing things with the shop. It's the down season and your father and I can handle it with Donny's help. Just pack a t-shirt and a bathing suit and sit by the pool all day. Look, we'll go out tomorrow and I will help you pack."

"Son," says Robert, "she's got the shopping fever, now. I think you'd better consider it. Papa, what do you think?"

"You know, Son, I like it. This trip was supposed to be something new for me, and this would certainly be that. What do you say Elmo? How about going on an adventure with your old Grandpa?"

Elmo removes the fork from his mouth and holds out his hands as he chews his last bite of tiramisu. He swallows and says, "Do I have a choice?"

They laugh and finish their shopping plans. Elmo and Grandpa get their coats and head to the door. After the goodbye kisses and hugs they head down the walk. Ramona shouts after them.

"Papa, what happened to your original traveling companion?"

"Oh, he died," says Grandpa, as he waves and gets into Elmo's car.

Friday, Oct 24th
~ West Orange ~

"His cleaning lady came in and found him dead," says Mrs. Diamond.

Tommaso nods in condolence as he squeezes between her and Mrs. Silverman into the Activity Room of the Clubhouse at Essex Village. Although he is of average height, he has a clear line of sight to the front table. He wonders to himself if Jewish women stop growing at five feet tall, or if they just shrink faster than other people. He also wonders how he will navigate the sea of outsized rear ends and massive bosoms all covered in black that are roiling between himself and his destination.

The table contains a photograph of a young Milton Spiezle in his military uniform and a few pieces of memorabilia from his time in the Army, including a Purple Heart. It is surrounded by some nice flower arrangements and two gentlemen wearing military caps identifying them as representatives of the Jewish War Veterans group.

Tommaso eventually makes his way to a front corner of the room to face Bernie Solomon, the apartment complex director and the person who organized the memorial service.

"I'm sorry for your loss, Mr. Pastor," says Bernie. "I know that you two were close."

"We don't live forever, and this seems sedate and tasteful. It suits Milton. It would seem that he was particularly popular with the ladies."

"Oh, these women come just to gossip and get some free sponge cake."

"Well, in any case," says Tommaso, "thank you for taking the time to set this up."

Bernie holds out his hand for a handshake. Tommaso's begins to reach out to reciprocate, but pauses. Instead he holds out his left hand. Bernie looks momentarily confused, but after a barely perceptible shrug, switches to his left hand as well.

Tommaso's grip is like a vise, which takes Bernie by surprise. He pulls Bernie's left arm slightly closer to himself causing Bernie's jacket sleeve to ride up. Bernie's wrist is revealed to show a Patek Phillipe watch. Tommaso leans in slightly toward Bernie's left ear.

"I will assume that you found this watch under Bernie's sofa after you donated his belongings. Since we both know that you have already received a substantial bonus, I'm sure we can agree that the Jewish War Veterans will get everything that Mr. Spiezle has directed. Do we understand one another?"

Tommaso leans back, still squeezing Bernie's hand. Bernie's face is now a bright pink and is beaded with sweat. He quickly nods and mouth's the words, "Yes, sir."

Tommaso finally releases his grip, pats Bernie on the shoulder, and heads for the front table. He nods at the two veterans and looks at Milton's picture. He crosses himself and gives a salute.

"Once again, goodbye, old friend."

As Tommaso heads for the exit, he overhears Mrs. Silverman speaking to Mrs. Diamond.

"Look how upset Bernie is. I never knew he and Milton were so close."

Friday, Oct 24th
~ Cedar Grove ~

"Donny, Elmo is going out of town next week, so it will just be the two of us," says Ramona.

She continues into the shop and places her bag safely behind the counter while Donny flips the OPEN sign.

"Um…what about Mr. Pastor?" asks Donny.

"Don't you worry about him, Donald. His bark is worse than his bite."

Her use of the full 'Donald' increases, rather than decreases his level of worry.

"The thing is," she says, "is that I need to take Elmo shopping tomorrow, so it will be just you and Robert."

Donny slumps back onto a stool and places his head in his hands.

"Oh, man," he says.

"Oh, don't be such a baby. It will be fine. He will be here to help you and I will make sure that he knows who is in charge. You just do what you normally do and he'll be here for support."

"I just want the place to still be here when Elmo gets back. Where is he going, anyway?"

"It seems that his grandfather is taking him on a cruise tomorrow."

"Wow, I wouldn't have guessed that, but he sure could use a break. He put an awful lot of hours into this place this summer."

"I agree. So when the opportunity came up---"

"You made him an offer he couldn't refuse?"

"Yes, Donald, and while we're on the subject, I need you to get along with Robert tomorrow, so I believe the expression is 'Grow a pair'."

"Yes, Mrs. Pastor. To that end, I have a quick repair to the irrigation system that I'd like to make before the customers arrive. Can you handle the store here, while I take care of that out back?"

"Yes, sir, boss!"

She gives him a salute as he smiles and heads out. Ramona does a little straightening up when Robert walks in causing the bell over the door to jingle. Ramona smiles and runs around the counter to give him a kiss and a hug.

"You're here early," she says. "What's the occasion?"

"Actually, I'm not here. I was asked to join a foursome by some of the people at the Chamber of Commerce. I wanted to let you know, since I was passing by. We're playing in Wayne."

"Does Elmo know?"

"Yes, he does, and to be honest, he was actually the one who was invited. He had to see some clients today, so he suggested that I go. And, before you ask, I am all caught up on my paperwork."

"Oh, Robert, I imagine this is a little different from the way it used to be."

"You know, honey, it's not so bad. Oh, I miss the 'star treatment' I got at the fancy private courses, but that was all business, and I never knew how stressful that business was until I got out of it. I have fewer opportunities to play, but the guys playing at these municipal courses have a much greater appreciation for the chance to get out and have some fun."

"Well, I will let you play hooky under one condition."

Ramona hugs him and grinds up against him.

"Oh, yeah? What condition is that, baby?"

"I need to take Elmo shopping tomorrow, so you need to come in first thing in the morning and help Donny run the shop."

"What? Can't you go shopping in the afternoon?"

"Absolutely not! He's going on a week-long cruise with two days' notice. We'll be lucky to get him ready as it is. And, I need you to *help* Donny. This is a big opportunity for him. I can support him while Elmo is away, but I need you to be on your best behavior tomorrow to build his confidence."

"Just make sure he shows me some respect."

"Robert, he's afraid of you."

"Better, yet."

"No, it's not better. Respect through fear doesn't work. Look at your organization. Please try this my way."

"All right, honey, you've got a deal. When did you get to be so smart?"

"I thought that's why you married me."

Robert slides his hands down her back and firmly grips her rear end.

"There were a few other reasons. The brains were more of a bonus."

"Men are such pigs."

They share a deep kiss.

Saturday, Oct 25th
~ Cedar Grove ~

Ramona and Robert arrive early at the shop and are about to enter.

"Be good," she says.

Robert grumbles as he holds the door for her. Elmo is already behind the counter, however, he is not in his uniform shirt. Donny is there as well, looking a little pale, even for him.

"Okay, here is the plan," says Ramona. "First we go to Elmo's to see what he has and to lay it out, and then we shop for the rest. After that, we pack. Meanwhile, you two play nice and we all get to pick up the shattered pieces of our lives on Monday."

For a moment, no one moves. Ramona shakes her head in exasperation.

"Donny, what do you normally do on a Saturday morning?"

"Well, since you and Elmo are typically at the shop, I use the early hour or two to clean the trucks. I guess I can still do that if Mr. Pastor covers the store, or I can come in and do it on Sunday."

"Wait a minute, Donny," she says. "Can Robert operate the register? Can Robert answer questions? Can Robert handle the customers? Maybe, but in any case, you will be needed in here. Can the cleaning wait? Maybe, but we have a schedule for a reason. I see no reason why Robert cannot clean the trucks."

Robert is flabbergasted, but Ramona shoots him down with a look before he can protest.

"Donny, tell him how you do it," she says.

"Well, there is a broom and a shopvac just inside the bay door for the inside and a mop and a hose for the outside. It usually takes me about twenty minutes per vehicle times four. If the shop is quiet, I also hit the cab windows with Windex."

Donny avoids eye contact with Robert and Ramona gestures with her head from Elmo toward his Father. Elmo gets the message.

"Pop, would you mind?" he asks. "It sounds simple enough."

Robert glares at his wife and takes a deep breath. He then looks at his Italian leather shoes.

"I don't want to cause any trouble," says Donny.

"Nonsense," says Ramona. "You're the boss today. Donny, what size shoes do you wear?"

"Uh, ten-and-a-half."

"Perfect," she says. "Take off your boots. You can switch with Robert. That way they won't get wet."

Robert appears to be ready to explode, but Ramona takes him to one side.

"Robert, please take a moment to remember why you married me, and to consider if you would like to ever see any of it again."

"I thought that I married you for your brains."

"You made your position on that clear, yesterday. Bonus, remember? Elmo, dear, we have a lot to do today!"

She grabs Robert's rear as she and Elmo head out of the door.

Saturday, Oct 25th
~ Wayne ~

Elmo is driving Ramona's car up Route 23 toward the mall.

"You actually don't need as much as I thought," she says. "It's mostly some dress clothes and maybe a little cruise wear."

"What exactly is cruise wear, Mom?"

"Well, one of the things that make a cruise special is the fact that you are not limited in the amount of luggage you can bring. Also, the ship has a lot of activities requiring different attire. Finally, at dinner, you are expected to dress up, sometimes a little, and sometimes a lot."

"It sounds like kind of a hassle."

"Well, it is and it isn't. Part of the charm of a cruise is to spend a week living at a level of luxury that most people rarely, if ever experience. While you can take it as a lounging vacation, most people actually are more active on a cruise, taking advantage of these luxuries."

"You mean like at a casino?"

"Not exactly. Casinos are so glitzy as to be fake. A good cruise ship and crew actually make you feel like an aristocrat from the 1920's."

"You mean like the high-class douchebags on the Titanic?"

"Close, but they actually *were* wealthy and that was in 1912. Also, it was a movie, so I can't be sure that they were all douchebags. The biggest problem today, is that there will be many passengers aboard who have so little exposure to culture that all they bring are shorts and t-shirts."

"While that sounds fine by me, Grandpa said we would be dining with others, so I certainly want to meet his expectations."

"Actually, this will be an adjustment for him as well. I typically wear three to four outfits per day on a cruise as does your father, believe it or not. Of course, I have to lay out his clothes. Grandpa won't do that. Maybe we can find him some casual cruise wear as well. I'm a little concerned about finding summer-season clothes at the mall. Plus there will be two formal nights on a week-long cruise."

"Formal nights? How formal are we talking?"

"At minimum, a suit, and many men still wear tuxedos. Unfortunately, your father's would be two short for you and your brother's won't fit your broad shoulders."

"Pep has a tuxedo?"

"Are you kidding? With all of his band functions, he wore a tux more often than James Bond."

"Well, I have a black suit."

"Quite frankly, a year ago, I would have just taken you to a men's store and plunked down the $500 or so we needed to get you one. These days, we have to be a little more careful. Hey, do a U-turn here!"

"But Mom, the mall's still a mile ahead."

Ramona raises an eyebrow.

"You think that *I* don't know where the mall is? Just turn around."

Elmo slides over and waits for an opening in the oncoming traffic. He turns and Ramona waves him over to the right lane.

"Go in here, where the blue car just came out," she says.

They pull into the parking lot for a row of stores. At the end of the row is a Goodwill Thrift Store. Ramona points toward it.

"Mom, are you okay?"

"Elmo, I have been fortunate enough in my life to have never had to shop in a thrift store. Some of the women at the gym were talking about it, and this might be a place to find a tuxedo at a low price, particularly if you are only going to wear it once."

They park and head for the door. Elmo opens it for his mother. Ramona takes a deep breath and heads inside.

"Just so you know," says Elmo, "it appears from the sign that the orange tags are half price."

Both Ramona and Elmo are surprised by the cleanliness and organization of the store. They find a Brooks Brothers tuxedo that fits Elmo perfectly for $24.99. They also find several dress shirts including some requiring cufflinks. Elmo has a few sets that he received from his grandfather and is looking forward to showing them off.

They are doing so well that they continue to shop in the hope of finding some cruise wear for Grandpa. They find some interesting things including some colorful button-down shirts and casual slacks. They even find a nice linen blazer.

"These aren't too much of a departure for him, so I hope he'll try them," says Ramona. "I will put them in a separate bag and you can hang them in the closet when you get on board. That way, neither of us has to argue with him."

"Gee, thanks," says Elmo. "Hey, check this out. We're gonna be traveling on Halloween, right?"

"Yes, next Friday, I believe. There will probably be a costume event of some sort."

Elmo puts on a black fedora from a rack.

"What do you think of this with my black pinstripe suit?" he asks.

"Just as long as it's for costume purposes only. I worked too hard to get us out of that life. We'd better get going. I should be able to get this to the dry cleaner for a one-hour job."

"Don't they close early on Saturday?"

"I may have to loosen a few buttons for Armando, but I'm sure I can convince him."

"Jesus, Mom, I'll drive as fast as I can, so you don't have to slut yourself up too much."

"Actually, if we weren't in a hurry, I would have liked to look at the ladies clothes. There appeared to be some very nice things."

"Aren't you concerned that…um…someone might see you there?"

"Poise, Sonny Boy."

"Poise?"

"Yes, it is the carrying oneself with grace or refined movement. Focus on who you are rather than where or what you are."

"Hmm, you never cease to amaze me, Mom."

Saturday, Oct 25th
~ Cedar Grove ~

Ramona pulls into the parking lot of Pastorini's Nursery and heads for the door. She enters to see Donny behind the counter straightening up the space. He looks up at her, but cannot manage his usual smile.

"That bad?" she asks.

Donny rolls his eyes and jerks his thumb behind him indicating that Robert is in the office.

"We did alright," he says, "considering that this is the off season. It seems that the constant chill in the air isn't so good for business."

Ramona gets the reference and smiles.

"Perhaps I can help with that next week. The forecast indicates a warming trend. Robert? Are you ready to go? I need to stop at Armando's for some dry cleaning. He is doing a special job for me and I don't want to keep him waiting."

Robert comes out almost immediately and says, "I didn't want to disturb your discussion about the weather."

He walks straight out of the door toward the car. Ramona turns back toward Donny and gives him a sympathetic look.

"He'll come around Donny. He knows how much you've changed, but he has his own changes to deal with. He spent the last thirty years as a big shot and now, he's a, well---"

"A big pussy?"

Ramona slaps a laughing Donny on the arm.

"Ooh, Donald! I'll be here next week so you shouldn't have to deal with him one on one. In any case, he's going through a lot of the same things that you're experiencing. Please try to be patient with him."

"I will, Mrs. Pastor. I'll see you on Monday."

He holds the door for her, flips the closed sign and locks the front door behind her. Robert is standing impatiently next to the locked car.

"You don't expect to get into my car wearing those filthy boots, do you?" she asks. "Where are your shoes?"

"I told Donny he could keep them."

"Well, if you want to give away a pair of $250 shoes in a snit, that is your decision. You still are going to have to remove the boots. Also, I don't expect that Donny agreed to a trade. He may actually need his boots."

Robert opens the door and sits on the passenger seat. He removes the boots and hands them to Ramona. She walks over to Donny's car and places them next to the driver's side door. Ramona gets into the driver's seat and starts the car.

"Robert," she says, "I noticed something very interesting back there when I brought back the boots, something I think is very important that I tell you."

"Oh, yeah? What's that?"

"I must say, those trucks looked very clean."

Robert glares at her and Ramona bursts out laughing. Robert looks down at his bare socks and starts laughing as well. They pick up the dry cleaning and head to Elmo's condo. Elmo answers the door and immediately notices that his father is in his stocking feet. He shrugs rather than to ask.

Ramona moves to the bedroom to check on Elmo's packing job. She shudders at the sight of it and puts the dry cleaning on a chair. She immediately empties everything out and starts over. Robert and Elmo give her some space and sit in the living room.

"I assume you left our place in one piece, today," says Elmo.

"Everything was fine, son. I assume you have your passport?"

"Yeah, I have everything only I don't see how the tickets can be in my name. We only heard about this a couple of days ago. Are we assuming that Grandpa took care of this?"

"You know, now that you mention it, that never occurred to me. Your grandfather has amazing attention to detail for a man his age, but on the other hand, he has done very little traveling. Other than the trip to Italy several years ago, he hasn't really gone anywhere."

"And didn't you and Mom make all of those arrangements? I mean, he just told me to pack and be outside at 7:45 tomorrow morning."

"Well, I guess you'll find out soon enough. I do not recommend mentioning this to your mother. She has enough to worry about."

Ramona calls them into the bedroom. Her packing job is nothing short of miraculous. She tells Elmo what needs to be hung up immediately and how to repack the items well enough to get it all home.

"Thanks, Mom. You guys want to go grab some dinner?"

Ramona points to Robert's feet.

"Jesus, Dad. How about if I just run out to get some Chinese?"

"I'll set the table, sweetie."

Robert shrugs and reaches for the remote.

Saturday, Oct 25th
~ West Orange ~

Marcus is sorting several vials on a counter in a lab room at the West Essex Rehabilitation Center. He feels a slight vibration on his hip and reaches into his pocket for his phone. He is momentarily disappointed to find that it is not the expected call from his girlfriend, but he accepts the call anyway.

"Hello?...Oh, good evening Mr. Pastor...wait a second, I'm doing something that requires the use of my hands...I'm going to put you on speaker...Can you hear me, sir?"

"Loud and clear, Marcus. Am I interrupting you?"

"No sir, not at all. I came in to the office tonight to clean up some things."

"Marcus, it's Saturday night. Carter told me you had a girlfriend."

"Well, Carter has a big mouth, but it's true. She's just out of town this weekend meeting up with some girlfriends from college. She'll be back tomorrow, so I'm trying to get ahead."

"*Good, I was worried that you spend so much time there, that you started dating some old bag with a hip replacement. I'll bet even now, you are doing somebody else's job.*"

"Okay, you got me. So what can I do for you?"

"*It's actually good that you are there. I need a few things.*"

"Things? Go on."

Marcus listens to Tommaso, frequently shaking his head. He considers asking why he needs them but decides he has enough chaos in his life.

"When do you need the stuff?"

"*I need it by the time Carter picks me up tomorrow morning. I also need to contact him, since I need to get picked up a little earlier.*"

"I doubt you'll get him tonight. I spoke to him earlier and he has a problem with one of his girlfriends being late."

"*Is he at the airport?*"

"No, CVS. He's buying a home pregnancy test. It's a different kind of late. I will see that he gets this package and I will see that he gets you earlier. What time would you like?"

"*Since you have been so kind as to deliver my goods, I only need him fifteen minutes earlier at 7:30. I need to stop on the way to pick up Elmo.*"

"I'll make sure he's there, sir. Is there anything else? I'm expecting another call any minute."

"No, Marcus, and thank you for your assistance. Tell your lady that Grandpa says 'Hello'."

Marcus smiles and disconnects the call. His smile grows broader when his phone vibrates again.

Saturday, Oct 25th
~ Cambridge ~

Tommy is in the kitchen of Pep's apartment slicing tomatoes to be placed in a taco dip. Pep is spreading a layer of sour cream on the bottom of an aluminum lasagna pan. He looks over at his sister and grits his teeth.

"What?" she asks. "Am I doing this wrong, too?"

"Well, based on the size of the chips in proportion to your chunks of tomato, I'm a little concerned about the structural integrity of---"

"Fine, I get it," she says, as she drops the knife onto the counter. "Just tell me what I *can* do."

Pep surveys the kitchen and frowns.

"Can you put the chips into the bowls I took out?"

"God, Pep, you ask as though this is my first day of kindergarten. I'm not completely incompetent."

Tommy opens the first bag with sufficient force to scatter several chips across the counter.

"You were saying?" asks Pep. "I'd hate to see you up this late without a nap."

"Who the hell has a party starting at midnight, anyway?"

"This isn't the party school that you went to. Those of us talented enough to get into MIT and Harvard spend a lot of time in the library."

"Stuff it, twerp. You just want to let your boyfriend get off of work."

"I don't know if he's even coming, and he's not my boyfriend."

"Pep and Bra-ad sitting in a tree, K-I S-S-I-N-G!"

"Jeez, Sis, you *are* in kindergarten! Can you take people's coats and put them on the bed? Freddie will be here any minute."

"It's only 11:30."

"I know. He's from India. He hasn't gotten the whole 'making an entrance' thing. You'll see. Anyhow, all stereotypes aside, shouldn't you develop some domestic skills before you get married?"

"Scotty is quite skilled in the kitchen and besides, he patronizes me as badly as you do."

"Oh, so there *is* talk of marriage, then?"

There is a buzz and Tommy heads to the intercom and presses the talk button.

"Saved by the bell," she says, and presses the intercom button. "Pep's party palace"

"Um...it's Freddie."

"C'mon up," she says as she presses the door release.

In a minute, there is a knock on the door. Tommy opens it and somewhat shocked as to what she sees. Freddie breezes in wearing bellbottoms, a skin-tight Lycra shirt, a long white silk scarf, and some sort of jacket from the British invasion, not the 1960s but rather the 1770s.

"I'm, um, Tommy. Can I take your coat?"

"Heavens no, dahling," says Freddie. "It's part of the ensemble."

Freddie demonstrably breezes in.

"You're the first one here," says Tommy.

He slumps his shoulders as Pep comes over and gives him a hug.

"I keep telling you Freddie, that if you want to make an entrance, you need to arrive an hour after the start time at the earliest."

"But then I miss so much."

"Freddie, this is my big sister, Tommy."

"Ooh, the dancer!" says Freddie.

Tommy gives Pep a questioning look.

"Oh you simply *must* tell me the story of your adventure with your boyfriend! Oh, I hope I'm not speaking out of turn. You *are* still together, I hope. Otherwise I might snap him up myself!" says Freddie, as he leads her toward the living room.

Over the next half hour, a dozen or so additional guests arrive, most of who are from Pep's study groups or the campus LGBT organization. Pep is busily passing out food and drinks while Tommy alternately takes coats and relates her tale of her flash mob adventure of the previous winter. She wonders how an event that left her shattered in a puddle of tears could be so fascinating to everyone.

Pep continues eyeing the intercom as though he can somehow see the guests walking up to the stoop. Tommy hears a buzz and answers.

"It's Kim."

Tommy buzzes her in and turns to Pep to give him a thumbs up. He sneaks away from the party as Freddie is entertaining with his lip sync routine to "Killer Queen". When he opens the door, he is clearly deflated.

Kim puts her hands on her hips and says, "Hey, Kim. Welcome to my party. Oh, why thank you for inviting me. I wouldn't miss it."

Tommy comes over, gives her a hug, and takes her coat.

After an appropriate amount of torture, Kim tells Pep, "Oh, Brad is right downstairs. Some guy out front was having trouble with his car and Brad stopped to help. It was too cold for me. He'll be up in a few minutes."

Pep leans up against the door jamb, swooning.

"He can fix a car," he says.

Kim and Tommy look at each other and burst out laughing.

In a few moments, Brad is at the door and is rubbing his hands together for warmth. Over the course of the next three hours, Tommy tells her tale a few more times, some games are played, and Freddie has at least three dramatic meltdowns. During the lively conversation, they learn that Brad is in pre-law with a minor in art history.

"The law is for my mom," he says.

He has had a few incredible internships, mostly in Latin America. He is a former military brat that moved frequently and never was able to establish roots.

"By the end of this semester, I will have lived in Cambridge longer than anywhere else in my life," he says.

Soon, the apartment empties and Tommy is cleaning the living room, while Pep, Kim, and Brad are working in the kitchen.

"Kim, can you give me a hand out here?" asks Tommy. "Freddie made quite a mess."

Kim pop's her head out with a curious look and Tommy waves her over.

"Sorry," says Tommy, in a hushed tone, "I just wanted Pep to get some face time with Brad."

"Oh, me too. He was kind of dumbstruck, so I thought I might help him along."

"That's so sweet. You are a good friend. As you can tell, I'm from a different school of nurturing. I'm trying to kick him out of the nest."

They sit and begin to swap Pep stories.

"Sometimes, I wish he were straight," says Kim.

Eventually, Brad and Pep come in.

"Hey, you guys are doing a great job cleaning out here," says Pep.

"Sorry kiddo," says Tommy, "but I shut down after three AM. It will be here in the morning."

"Well, Brad and I are meeting for coffee at ten," says Pep. "Would either of you care to join us?"

Pep's face clearly is stating that he is asking to be polite in front of Brad, but that he also expects both of them to politely decline.

"Not, me," says Tommy. "I'm sleeping in and then it's off to Logan for my flight home."

Kim cannot resist the opportunity for some fun and pulls out her phone.

"That sounds like fun. Let me check my schedule," she says.

Pep looks like he is going to cry.

"Damn," says Kim, "I'd love to, but it seems that I'm meeting Tom Brady to give him a blowjob before the game. He says it relaxes him."

Everyone laughs except Pep.

"What an amazing coincidence," says Brad. "The Pats are playing the Bears. I'm blowing Jay Cutler!"

After they leave, Tommy closes the door.

"I *like* her!" she says.

Pep leans against the door and swoons, "He knows who the Bears quarterback is."

Sunday, Oct 26th
~ West Orange ~

Carter pushes the doorbell of Tommaso's condo. The door opens almost immediately and Tommaso greets Carter wearing a grey suit and a fedora. His luggage is right next to the door. Carter picks it up and moves toward the shiny black Lincoln sedan. Tommaso locks his door and carries a shoulder bag to the car. He opens the front passenger door and sits while Carter loads the trunk before getting behind the wheel.

"Are you sure you don't want to sit in the back, Mr. Pastor?"

"Wait, this isn't the back? Is it possible that I've gotten so old that I don't know where I want to sit?"

Carter laughs and shakes his head.

"Sir, you are one piece of work. You know that?"

Tommaso hands Carter a slip of paper.

"We need to pick up my grandson. Here's the address."

"Yes, sir. I know where it is."

"Do you have a package for me from Marcus?"

"It's in the trunk, right next to your carry on bag."

Carter pulls out of the complex and heads toward Wayne.

"So what happened to…what was his name…Milton?" asks Carter.

"He died."

"Excuse me?"

"He died. He was an old man. It happens."

"Well, it is not uncommon for there also to be a hail of bullets involved with you and your friends."

"Not this time. Just a bad ticker. Speaking of dodging bullets, how did your test go last night?"

Carter swerves slightly, weaving partially onto the shoulder before recovering.

"God dammit! How the hell could you possibly…oh, wait a second. Fucking Marcus! The good news is that the test was negative. The bad news is that I'm gonna strangle that son of a bitch so you might want to start looking for a new physical therapist."

"I think this was retaliation for you blabbing about his new girlfriend. In any case, I'm glad it worked out. I do recall reading something about medical science developing some rather cutting edge technology to avoid unwanted pregnancy. You may want to look into it."

"Have you considered taking that *schtick* on the comedy circuit? I'd like to think that I have learned my lesson. Here we are."

Carter pulls into the complex and heads toward Elmo's unit. He sees Elmo waiting outside with his luggage. He is wearing jeans, a polo shirt, and a fedora.

"What is it with you people and the hats?" asks Carter.

"Elmo, do you still have that ridiculous suit of mine you showed me last year?" asks Tommaso.

"As a matter of fact, I have it packed right here in the hang-up bag. I thought I might wear it on Halloween with my new hat."

"Take it out and put it on, please."

Elmo is about to question his grandfather, but upon meeting Carter's shrug, decides that it is easier to comply. Carter loads the suitcase and in a few minutes, Elmo comes out wearing a pinstripe gangster suit along with his fedora. He hands the remaining bag to Carter and they head toward the airport. Now, they are both in the back seat.

"Hey, Carter," says Elmo. "How's it going and thanks for the ride."

"No problem, Bro. Since you two appear to be headed on some kind of a gangster cruise, it won't surprise you that your grandfather made me an offer I couldn't refuse."

"Speaking of the cruise, Grandpa, I have my passport, but I can't see how the tickets can be in my name."

Tommaso reaches into his jacket and hands Elmo Milton's passport and ticket. Elmo looks at them for a moment.

"Grandpa, have you figured how I'm supposed to get through security with this?"

"How carefully do they check?" asks Tommaso. "Carter, you go to the airport frequently. What are we looking at?"

"Probably five years in a Supermax prison. TSA is part of Homeland Security. That's federal. These are the people that brought us The Patriot Act and other little loopholes in the Constitution. They don't even have to give you a reason why they're arresting you."

"Really? I guess we'll have to try Plan B."

"Plan B?" asks Elmo. "What the hell is plan B?"

"Carter, walk me through the process."

"Wait, this is Plan B?" asks Elmo. "There actually is no Plan B?"

"Relax, Elmo," says Tommaso. "Let's work the problem. Besides, this is supposed to be a vacation."

"Okay," says Carter. "We have three areas of contact to worry about. First, you need to check the bags. Second, you need to check in, since I assume you failed to get a boarding pass. Finally, and this is the big one, you need to get through security."

"Can't we do the first two together at the check-in counter?" asks Elmo.

"Sure," says Carter, "if you have the proper credentials. They don't check as carefully as TSA, but it's too risky. I do have a suggestion, however. Since I drive rich white folks around, I can check your bags outside at the curb. They are supposed to check, but can easily be distracted if you know what I mean."

"A gratuity," says Tommaso.

"It makes the world go 'round, sir. I'm sure that I can get you that far. Now, we need the boarding passes. If you have the ticket code, you should be able to use the kiosk. I assume Elmo can handle that since it requires a rudimentary understanding of technology. Even if you have to go up the clerk, you should be able to have Tommaso get both of them. If that doesn't work, he should be able to go up twice since he can probably pass for Milton if they don't check carefully."

"Can you get us a wheelchair?"

"Are you feeling alright?"

"Of course I'm all right," says Tommaso. "We might need it as a distraction."

"I might actually need it for my stroke," says Elmo.

"Wheelchair is a piece of cake, but I have no suggestions for the TSA at security. There have been so many screw-ups at Newark that they have become pretty careful. And don't try bribing anyone if you ever want to see daylight again. The good news is that the cruise people will probably not be as careful as they are in the airport."

"Assuming we make it that far," says Elmo.

They pull up to the terminal and Carter gets out. He pops the trunk and moves over to the men at the baggage drop-off.

"May I help you, my brother?" asks the taller and heavier of the two men.

"I have a 'special' passenger," says Carter, "who would like to have you check his bags. He says there is a Mr.

Jackson from him and his colleague should they be permitted to wait in the car."

"That sounds like it might be a job for The Jackson *Five*, if you get my drift."

"I'll tell you what, my brother. I hope you like Christian music. I can get you an Amy *Grant* assuming you can also get me a wheelchair. Otherwise, I may have to seek out another listener, if you get *my* drift."

"Deal, brother."

The man takes a cart over to the car and gets the luggage. Carter hands him the tickets so he can route the bags to Ft. Lauderdale. He hands Carter the tickets and the claim vouchers and goes inside. He returns a few minutes later with a wheelchair. Carter deftly slips the man a crisp fifty and waves him off.

Tommaso gets out of the car and sits in the chair. Elmo takes the documents from Carter and they shake hands. Tommaso calls Carter over. He tries to hand him a wad of cash.

"Save it for bail money, sir. Step two should be easy. I wish I could help you with TSA. Have a safe trip and call me if you decide to turn back."

Carter drives off as Elmo and his grandfather enter the terminal. They move into position to observe the check-in process.

"Carter said the kiosk uses a ticket number," says Elmo. "This must be it. It's a six character set of numbers and letters. We should be able to go up to the kiosk and get the boarding passes."

"Not we, just you. There is a woman assisting the people. If you are alone, you can always claim ignorance. Wheel me over there next to that sign."

Elmo wheels Grandpa next to a sign advertising an airline depicting a young woman and child enthusiastically waving to some unseen loved one. Elmo heads to the kiosk and follows the instructions by entering the code on the ticket invoice. Suddenly, a woman in a colorful polyester shirt and red, white, and blue scarf comes over.

"Can I help you?" she asks.

Elmo hesitates awkwardly, but finally stammers out, "I'm trying to print my grandfather's boarding pass. He's over there."

Elmo points toward Grandpa, who is waving to the people on the sign. The woman gives Elmo an understanding nod and turns to the screen.

"Well it seems that you already have your seats assigned. We just have to hit print. Oh, wait a minute. Are you Mr. Spiezle or Mr. Pastor?"

Elmo closes his eyes tightly as though this will help him think faster.

"Uh, neither. I'm just helping them get to security. Mr. Spiezle is in the bathroom. He has to go like every fifteen minutes. I was just trying to save him a few steps with his walker."

"Oh, that is so sweet of you. Well I hope they get to Ft. Lauderdale safely. Here are your boarding passes."

Elmo lets out a deep breath and walks over to Grandpa.

"You can stop waving, now. We've somehow made it to step three. I'm gonna need a vacation from this fucking vacation, Grandpa. Any bright ideas about security?"

"I'm working on it, and watch your mouth. Go over to where the people come out. We can observe the procedure from there."

Elmo wheels Grandpa to the best spot to view security without being noticed.

"Are you okay here, Grandpa? I gotta use the bathroom."

"Sure, Elmo. I'll be right here."

Grandpa watches and sees that the first person only checks to see if you have a boarding pass. He also sees that the wheelchair people get routed into a much shorter line. The next stop is to one of two TSA agents who look at both the boarding pass and the passports. They also check each face against the photo. It appears that once through this checkpoint, everything else is routine. Grandpa notices that Elmo has returned.

"Take me to the bathroom," says Grandpa.

When they get to the bathroom, Grandpa gets out of the chair.

"Sit down, Elmo."

"You mean in the wheelchair?"

"No, on the floor. Of course, in the wheelchair."

Elmo sits down.

"Take off your hat."

Elmo takes off the hat. Grandpa reaches into the bag he received from Marcus. He pulls out a clear plastic bag and opens it. He hands Elmo a plastic oxygen mask. He then removes a bundle of plastic tubing.

"Put on the mask."

Elmo shakes his head and puts on the mask. Grandpa takes the tubing and runs it from under the mask to Elmo's waistband. He tucks the tubes in and lays the side of Elmo's jacket over them. Grandpa takes an electric razor out of his bag and hands it to Elmo.

"Place this in your pocket on the same side as the tubes."

Elmo complies and Grandpa gives him a pair of white gloves.

"Here, put these on and give me your hat. Okay, here is the drill. We turn on the razor so it sounds like you're on some kind of breathing machine. I wheel you up to the first checkpoint and give them the boarding passes. We take the fast lane because of the wheelchair. We go slow enough to ensure we get the fat, older agent. I will give him all the documents and you just have to look old. Once we are through, you turn off the razor and we go through security normally. Remember to look old."

Grandpa takes Elmo's hat and goes into the bathroom. A few minutes later he returns and places the hat on Elmo's head. Grandpa pushes Elmo about three feet before Elmo jams down his feet and stops the wheelchair.

"Grandpa, this hat smells like piss!"

"Quiet down. It's supposed to. I pissed on it. We can deal with this later. The sooner we get through security, the sooner you can take it off. Now turn on the razor."

They reach the first checkpoint and Grandpa hands the boarding passes to the woman there. She is about to ask for ID but gets a whiff of Elmo and points them in the direction of the speed line. Since the agent they want is working at half the speed of the younger one, it requires a little maneuvering to get to him. Grandpa hands the boarding passes and passports to the agent.

"You'll need to take off the mask, sir," says the agent.

"Oh, I'm sorry, but he cannot hear. I'm taking the poor fellow home for the last time. A man should die in his own bed. It's going to take me a minute to unhook him from his breathing apparatus. Oh, my, did you have an accident, Milton?"

Upon smelling the urine, and seeing the line back up, the agent quickly makes the appropriate marks on the documents and hands them to Grandpa.

"Go," he says.

Grandpa wheels Elmo to the table to prep for the x-ray machine. Once out of sight of the Agent, Elmo gets out of the chair and Grandpa gets in. There is a trash can for plastic bottles and banned substances. Elmo throws out the gloves, mask and tubing as well as his new fedora. They go through and the only incident is when one of the agents picks up Grandpa's razor from the bin.

"Sorry," says Elmo, "my grandfather thinks it's his transistor radio."

He makes a swirl with his finger around his ear in the international symbol for crazy. Grandpa just smiles. The agent gives Elmo a knowing wink and hands him the razor. They ditch the wheelchair and walk toward their gate.

Sunday, Oct 26th
~ Montclair ~

Carter parks his car next to the apartment and heads inside. As he walks up onto the porch, he hears a beep and checks a text on his phone. Marcus, who is returning from church, pulls into the driveway. Carter waits for him and they go in together. Scotty is in the kitchen setting the table.

"Perfect timing," he says. "I've got bagels, juice and coffee. I also have some muffins about to come out. How did it go, Carter?"

"Elmo just texted me. They made it through security, but don't ask me how. That old man is crazy."

"And how was church?" asks Scotty.

"It was good," says Marcus. "As usual, I learned something and I owe you an apology, Carter. I let a confidence slip to Mr. Pastor on the phone last night."

"Don't worry, Brother," says Carter. "The old man already lectured me and he reminded me that I told him about Sandy. Go figure. I duck the Reverend and get the same lesson."

"From a Pastor," adds Scotty.

"Har-de-fucking-har-har," says Carter. "I miss this."

"How did your thing go last night?" asks Marcus.

"False alarm," says Carter. "I'll be going with you to church next week, for sure, and it won't be to pray for a point spread. I need to light some candles."

"Did I miss something?" asks Scotty.

"Yeah," says Carter. "Remember Monique, the girl from the old neighborhood?"

"Your 'friend with benefits'?"

"Yeah. She had a pregnancy scare last night, but it turned out she was just late."

"Yours?" asks Marcus.

"Maybe, probably. I'm just glad it's over."

"Except the lesson," says Marcus.

"Damn, I hope so," says Carter. "I certainly hope so."

"I've got a question," says Scotty. "How is it that Mr. Pastor heard about this before I did?"

"That's on me," says Marcus. "I'm not sure how it happened. He's an oddly powerful dude."

"When you go to pick up Tommy later," says Carter, "don't take 78. There's some sort of construction going on. You going back to Hoboken tonight?"

"Thanks and yes. I'll probably be there all week. Feel free to use my room so long as you clean up after yourself.

I'd prefer if you kept your women in your own room, however."

"I probably will be taking a break from indiscriminate sex for a while after last night."

"I'll believe it when I see it," says Marcus. "Just take proper precautions. Also, it wouldn't hurt to think of the woman's position once in a while."

"That's what got him in this trouble," says Scotty.

"Can you please be serious once in a while," says Marcus. "Yo, pass me the muffins. Lemon poppy? Yeah!"

"When does Sandy get back and how is all of that going?" asks Carter.

"About four," says Marcus. "I'm taking her to dinner. We're fine, but she was visiting her college friends. She's worried about a few of them not taking it so well."

"She shouldn't be hanging out with racists," says Carter.

"It's nothing that overt. You know, the 'friend' subtly suggesting that it's not fair to the families or potential children. Most of them are privileged from the sticks. Hell, so was Sandy."

"Wait," says Scotty, "Sandy's white? Why am I always the last to know these things?"

Laughing, Marcus throws his last chunk of muffin at him.

"Why don't you shut the fuck up?"

Sunday, Oct 26th
~ Newark ~

Elmo and Grandpa walk through the gangway and onto the plane. They are pleased to find that Milton had paid in advance for an exit row. Elmo puts the bags in the overhead and sits closest to the door while Grandpa takes the aisle.

"So how's the vacation, so far?" asks Grandpa. "Nice seats. Only two across here and we have extra legroom, it would appear."

"Let's see. I lost my new pissed-up hat, I sweat through a wool suit, I had to wash my hair in an airport bathroom, and I have eight inches of extra legroom. I'd say it's about even so far. Oh yeah, and we're still in New Jersey."

"Really? I feel invigorated. Youth really is wasted on the young."

"Well this youth needs some rest before the next leg of chaos. As soon as we take off, I'm going to recline and sleep."

"Did you do any research about the ship? Milton was quite the veteran at this sort of travel. We are going to have to figure it out on our own."

"All I know is that we will be on the Fiesta Cruise Line. Their ships have a Latin theme and are all named for dances. We will be on the Mambo, which is an older ship. It had a sister ship called the Macarena that was destroyed in a storm in the Bermuda Triangle in 2005. Most got off safely, but it was a big story."

"I remember it."

"They have the Rumba, the Merengue, the Salsa, the Lambada, and several others in the Caribbean and Europe, plus one in Alaska. Even though ours is like a fifteen story luxury hotel at sea, they are currently building a new one called the Tango, that will be nearly twice the size."

"Maybe we can board it in Florida, walk to the other end, and get off in the Bahamas without ever lifting anchor."

The plane takes off and levels out in a few minutes. Elmo leans back his seat and pulls out a pair of ear buds. Grandpa reaches into his pocket and pulls out his razor and holds it out to Elmo.

"Are you sure you wouldn't like a shave?" he asks.

"You are out of your fucking mind, Grandpa. Just wake me when we land, alright?"

Grandpa is laughing hysterically.

Sunday, Dec 26th
~ Newark ~

"I'm walking out now," says Tommy.

"Perfect," says Scotty. "I just pulled into the airport. JetBlue, Terminal A. I'll be there in a minute. Can't wait to see you."

Scotty disconnects the call and follows the signs for arrivals. He squeezes to the right and is looking for Tommy. It is crowded, but not so much that he shouldn't be able to find her. He stops his car, but immediately gets whooped at with a siren by an officer on a motorcycle. Scotty puts his car in gear and heads back into the loop. He picks up his phone and calls Tommy.

"Hey, lover," she says. "Where are you?"

"Just a minute. I'm putting you on speaker. There are too many cops around. Can you hear me?"

"Yup, loud and clear."

"I must have just missed you. I'm going around again. An officer chased me. What are you wearing?"

"An orange peacoat. There's hardly anyone here. Have you forgotten what I look like already?"

"Hardly. The image is burned into my head. Maybe the clothing is throwing me off."

"Well, that's not an option. It's a little too chilly for that."

"Okay, I'm coming around again. I still don't see you. You're sure you're at Terminal A?"

"How should I know? I got off the plane and came out. I flew JetBlue if that helps, but you already knew that."

"What do you see near you?"

"I see buses and a lot of taxis. The sign here says JetBlue. There are some other numbers and letters."

"I don't understand. I'm in the same place. Can you wave your arms? Shit, I'm getting chased again. I have to go back around."

"Wave my arms? Are you blind? I'm the only one here. If you came inside to meet me like a real boyfriend, this wouldn't be happening."

"You know what they charge for parking here? Besides, since you did carry-on, this was supposed to be faster."

"Well, how much are you spending on gas right now?"

"Wait, carry-on, can you see the sky from where you're standing?"

"What? Yes, I can see the sky. Why?"

"You must be on the departure level. I've been looking for you on the arrival level."

"By baggage claim? Why would I have gone down there?"

"Oh, I don't know, maybe to meet your ride. You are arriving and not departing, you know."

"Well, I hope you're not blaming me for this. Inside, it just says 'Exit to street' or something."

Scotty pulls up to the curb where Tommy is standing nearly alone. He hops out of the car and gives her a big hug and kiss. He takes her bag and puts it in the back seat while she gets into the passenger seat.

"I assume that you are hungry for lunch," he says.

"Particularly with all that extra waiting," she says.

"What kind of lunatic arrives on the departure level?"

"Apparently the kind who will remain blameless if you expect to see her naked later."

"Hmm, fair enough. How was your trip?"

"I got done what I needed to. I'm on track to finish and defend. There was a time when the advisors wouldn't want to let you go. Now, they can't afford to keep you. I had a great visit with Libby. She sends her regards. She says the ad game is more cutthroat than ever. I wish she would settle down."

"And Pep?"

"He's so sweet. He has a great group of friends. He seems to have an interest in this guy Brad, from Harvard. He says he expected us to be engaged by now, especially since I will be finished in May."

"Well, I've been meaning to talk to you about just that."

Sunday, Oct 26th
~ Ft. Lauderdale ~

Elmo wipes some drool from his mouth as the flight attendant asks him to put his seat back up. He elbows Grandpa gently and rouses him as well.

"We'll be landing soon," says Elmo.

Elmo lifts the shade and peers out of the window and is surprised to see a lot of nothing. Soon the plane crosses out of the Everglades and the landscape immediately changes. There is a series of tight clusters of homes, nearly all with swimming pools. The developments are interspersed with canals, ball fields, golf courses, and rows of retail stores. Some of the canals are large and stretch toward the ocean.

After an uneventful landing, they leave the plane and head to the baggage level. There are several people holding signs from various cruise lines gathering people together. They find the person holding the sign for the Fiesta Line. It is held by a middle-aged woman wearing a brightly colored skirt, white blouse, and a multi-colored scarf.

"Please retrieve your bags and place them on one of these carts. When we have enough for a group, your bags will be placed on a bus and you will be driven to the ship.

Please make sure that you have the cruise line tags on all of your bags so they can be routed to your stateroom."

In less than fifteen minutes, Grandpa and Elmo are on the bus and headed through the checkpoint at Port Everglades. The bus goes past a series of incredibly large ships before pulling in front of the Mambo.

"Damn," says Elmo, in awe.

The baggage tenders take their bags to the ship while Elmo leads Grandpa into the terminal. This is a much less chaotic venue than the airport. They go through the x-ray stage without incident, but are amazed at the variety of items that are being confiscated. Aside from some rather frightening looking knives, there are several steam irons and coffee makers on a row of tables.

"Who the hell would bring that on a cruise ship?" asks Elmo.

Grandpa shrugs.

They enter a large room with signs directing passengers to one of several lines based on the color of their tickets. There are several sofas and plenty of open space, so they can observe the process without holding up anyone else. Unlike the airport, everyone here is smiling.

"Apparently, they're serious about customer service in the cruise industry," says Grandpa. "Maybe it's something to consider for your business, Elmo."

"Why do you think Pop isn't allowed near the customers?"

Grandpa chuckles.

"I think that we should go through separately," says Elmo. "This way, since you have proper credentials, you can see what they need and we can work out the next scam."

"Agreed, but maybe I should go through as Milton. If there's a problem, I can just claim senility."

"Not much of a stretch there. Just pay close attention to what information they need."

Grandpa heads for the blue line and quickly gets to an agent. He uses Milton's passport and information, but the agent never looks to compare the photos. Everything goes quite smoothly including the part where she asks Grandpa to stand on a pair of footprints glued to the carpet. She snaps his photo and in a few minutes, the agent hands Grandpa a card.

"Sir, this is your 'Dance Card'. It is your room key, as well as your charge card anyplace on the ship. You also need it for debarking and embarking at ports. Just head up those stairs to the ship and you're all set."

Grandpa heads toward the ship, but slips under a rope to loop back toward Elmo.

"Okay, Elmo, I went through with Milton's credentials. Now I can go through again with my own with no problems. Here is your room card. Follow me over here."

They walk to the rope near the stairs where Grandpa had exited.

"Just wait here," says Grandpa.

Grandpa goes around and gets back on line. He makes sure he gets a different agent and goes through the process smoothly. He walks toward the ship and lifts the rope for

Elmo to join him. They go over a series of ramps and eventually arrive at a wider area where a couple of crewmen are standing near an electronic device. They are taking the Dance Cards and sliding them into the machine. The passenger's pictures come up and the crewmen are verifying to match the pictures with the passengers.

"Grandpa," says Elmo.

"Relax," says Grandpa.

He hands the crewman his card and smiles. The man checks it and returns it.

"Welcome aboard, sir," he says.

Elmo hands over his card and Grandpa's picture comes up. The crewman looks at Elmo, and then to Grandpa.

"Oh, I thought this might happen," says Grandpa. "There was some confusion when we checked in. I hate to say it, but I believe that we had a trainee. They were having some trouble with the camera, but I didn't want to get anyone in trouble. We'll go back downstairs."

"No, sir. It's no trouble at all. We can fix it here."

"Are you sure?" asks Grandpa. "We don't want to hold up the line."

"It's nothing, sir, really. Mr. Spiezle, just stand on that line."

Elmo moves to the line and the crewman takes another picture. In a moment, his face replaces Grandpa's on the screen. Elmo is grinning in the picture and retains his smile as the crewman hands him his Dance Card.

"Welcome aboard and have a great cruise!" says the crewman.

After a few steps, someone takes their picture in front of a decorative lifesaving ring printed with the words, 'Welcome Aboard'. They walk onto the ship and are in awe of their surroundings. A young woman in a naval looking dress with epaulets steps toward them.

"Can I help you with anything," she says.

"Food," says Elmo. "We'd like some food, please."

She smiles and directs them to the Embarcadero, which is the buffet area available for all meals. She informs them of when they can go to their cabins and what to expect for the Muster Drill and for the Sailaway Celebration. Elmo and Grandpa head for the elevator.

Elmo puts his arm around his grandfather and says, "Bon fucking voyage."

Sunday, Oct 26th
~ Fiesta Mambo, Port Everglades ~

"That was a pretty impressive buffet," says Elmo. "Let's see. We're on Deck 9. Room 9368 is even, so it should be on the port side."

"Which is the port side?" asks Grandpa.

"Well, it's on the left, but that's assuming we're facing the front of the ship. I'm a little turned around here. Wait, here are some signs. It should be down this corridor. We're pretty much in the center of the ship."

They walk past several cabins and the hallway is bustling with stewards delivering luggage. They squeeze by a heavyset woman complaining that she has yet to receive her bags, even though they are clearly in the middle of the process.

"Here it is, Grandpa. It looks like all of our stuff is here."

Elmo takes his Dance Card and slides it into the slot on the door. A green light pops on and they enter the room.

"Wow," says Elmo, "It's pretty tight, but it looks comfortable."

"According to Milton," says Grandpa, "these ships are an engineering marvel. He said that there's enough room to unpack your clothes and put the suitcases under the bed."

"Speaking of which, there is only one bed here. I assume that you and Milton weren't planning to share."

They are interrupted by a knock at the door. Elmo opens it to find a black man in his mid-thirties wearing a white steward's outfit and brandishing a huge toothy grin. He is speaking in a heavy island accent.

"Welcome aboard, Mr. Pastor and Mr. Spi-zel. I am Jameson, your room steward for your stay with us. My I bring in your bags?"

"It's Speizle, but you can call me Elmo," he says, extending his hand.

Jameson vigorously shakes Elmo's hand and says, "Elmo, you mean like the---"

"Yeah, the Muppet," says Elmo. "Jameson, we seem to have only one bed here."

Jameson is already bringing in the bags.

"No problem Mr. Elmo. There was a time that we could guess the sleeping arrangement based on the names on our manifest. These days, you never know. I will rearrange everything while you are at dinner. I see that you have the early seating."

"What does that mean?"

"May I see your Dance Card?"

Elmo hands it to him.

"Do you see here? It says that you are in the main dining room at 6:00PM. It is called The Ballroom and is on Deck 3 toward the rear of the ship. You are at table number 347. Oh, this is very good news. Your assistant waiter will be my very good friend Fabrice. I will make sure that he takes extra good care of you."

"So we don't go back to the buffet?"

"I can see that you are new to cruising. The Embarcadero is quite nice and is available for all of your meals. The dining room is also available, but is extra special for dinner. Most passengers eat breakfast and lunch upstairs at any of our specialty restaurants or the Embarcadero. Dinner in the dining room however, is first class, and not to be missed."

Elmo turns around to find Grandpa already asleep on the bed.

"Oh, I guess my grandfather is worn out from the trip. I have a couple more questions for you. I am going to shower and go to the Muster Drill. Can he stay here?"

"I am required to inform you that Admiralty law requires participation in the drill."

"What I'm asking, is do they do a head count or a room check?"

"Elderly passengers, and those with special needs, may watch the safety video on the TV in the cabin. I'll make a note for our records."

Jameson winks, and then opens the closet and gets a life jacket out for Elmo.

Elmo pulls out his wallet.

"Oh, no, Mr. Elmo. We are not permitted to accept gratuities outside of the regular process. That takes place at the end of the cruise."

"Okay, then thank you, Jameson. One last question, can you show me how to operate this shower?"

"Yes, Mr. Elmo. You need to rotate the right handle from blue to red to control the temperature, and the left handle for the water flow. Have a very special cruise, sir."

Elmo opens his suitcases and quietly places his clothes into the closet and drawers. He hesitates for a minute, and then does the same for his grandfather. Elmo takes out a nice button-down shirt and khaki slacks for dinner. After sliding the empty bags under the bed, he goes into the bathroom for a quick shower.

The announcement for the Muster Drill comes over the PA system while Elmo is drying off. Grandpa does not move a muscle. Elmo quickly dresses, puts his Dance Card in his pocket, grabs his life jacket, and heads for Deck 4.

Sunday, Oct 26th
~ Fiesta Mambo, Deck 4 ~

Elmo exits the staircase onto Deck 4 and looks for his Muster Station. There are crewmembers directing the passengers out on the deck where the lifeboats are suspended. He sees a cute redheaded crewwoman and recognizes her as the person who originally had directed them to the Embarcadero upon boarding. Even though he knows he's in the right place, Elmo asks her anyway.

"Can you please assist me?" he asks. "I want to make sure I'm in the right place."

"Oh, hello again. I remember you from when you got on the ship. Fellow redheads are always remembered."

She points to her head. Elmo is not sure whether this is a reference to her memory or hair color, but he is primarily focused on keeping his knees from buckling. Her accent is quite simply the most beautiful thing he has ever heard. A quick look at her nametag identifies her as Olivia from New Zealand.

"Wow, how many jobs do you have?" asks Elmo. "You're not the Captain, are you?"

"Hardly, but we tend to help out in many ways. Will you be going to the Welcome Aboard show, this evening?"

"I hadn't thought about it. Should I?"

"It's really is worth seeing and there might be a surprise in it for you. It was nice meeting you again. I'm sure it won't be the last time."

She points to her hair as she moves on to help more passengers.

"Oh, and my name is Elmo!" he shouts, as she turns and waves.

After the Muster Drill, Elmo heads back to the room to check in on his grandfather. He opens the door to see Grandpa standing on the balcony looking out at the port.

"Hey, Grandpa, how was your rest?"

"Perfect. I really needed it. That was quite a morning, wasn't it?"

"I've already tried to block it out. This ship is pretty amazing. There's a Sailaway celebration in a few minutes. I figured we could then explore the ship before heading to dinner. There's a show tonight that comes highly recommended."

"I'll tell you what, Elmo. You seem to be dressed for dinner. Go to this Sailaway and then come back for me. I'd like to shower and get dressed. Thanks for unpacking, by the way. Also, take this. It is apparently a map and schedule of all the ship has to offer. I think that we get a new one each day."

"Okay, Grandpa, just let me show you how to use the shower."

"You think I can't operate a shower?"

"Not this one, unless you've been on a space ship or a submarine. And don't drop the soap. Bending down in there is tricky, if not impossible. The toilet is pretty crazy as well."

After giving Grandpa a quick tour of the bathroom, Elmo says, "I'll be back at quarter to six."

He heads up to the Lido Deck to check out the pool area. Grandpa looks up at the ceiling, shakes his head, and then looks down at the floor and says, "What have you gotten me into, Milton."

Sunday, Oct 26th
~ Fiesta Mambo, Deck 12 ~

Elmo is leaning on the rail on the starboard side of the ship overlooking the water side of the port. From this height he can see all of the port, the barrier islands, the ocean, and quite a bit of the coast of South Florida.

There is another cruise ship pulling out which really does look like an enormous hotel floating by. Hundreds, if not thousands of people are laughing, pointing, and taking pictures. He is on the Sun Deck, which rings the pool deck in the middle of the ship. Below, there is a salsa band at poolside playing party music and some people are already dancing.

Elmo pulls out the document given to him by Grandpa. It is a colorful tri-fold schedule called The Treasure Map. It describes all of the restaurants and has a schedule for all manner of events for all ages. There are discos, a theater, and bands. There are contests and sporting events. There are bars and a casino. There are also detailed descriptions of the ports, excursions, and onboard shopping. Elmo is overwhelmed by the number and variety of the options.

He jumps with a start at the blast of an air horn and even though he cannot feel any change, he can see that the ship is now moving. Several people begin to cheer and Elmo wonders how many of them are already drunk. He looks down toward the pool and sees a crowd of at least twenty-five people of a wide range of ages all wearing the same bright yellow T-shirt. He shades his eyes from the setting sun enough to see that they are all part of the Gilliam-Willis Family Reunion.

Elmo is in awe of something so large floating so smoothly, even in the calm of the inlet. On the way out, they pass The Allure of the Seas, which dwarfs The Fiesta Mambo by comparison. Eventually, the ship clears the breakwater and heads out to open sea. Elmo considers heading to the back of the ship to see the sunset, but checks his watch and heads to meet Grandpa instead.

Elmo picks up Grandpa and is not surprised to see him nattily dressed in a navy sport jacket and light blue slacks. His shirt is open at the collar and he is not wearing his trademark fedora.

"Sorry, sir, but I was expecting my grandfather. He's kind of your size, but is a lot more sinister."

"Very funny. Is it a crime to fit in a little?"

"Now that you are talking about crime, I can see that it's you. Shall we go?"

"Oh, what a couple of fine looking gentlemen," says Jameson, who catches them in the hall.

"Jameson, can you take our picture?" asks Elmo. "No one will believe me otherwise."

"Of course, Mr. Elmo, and Mr. Pastor."

Elmo is impressed that Jameson remembers their names. Jameson takes Elmo's phone and frames them in the picture.

"Say cheese," he says and there is a flash. "Mr. Elmo, I notice that your phone is on. You can pick up extensive charges once we get more than a few miles off shore. Unless you have an international plan, I suggest that you consider turning it off for the duration of the cruise. If you need it as a camera, Airplane Mode will protect you as well."

"Gee, I never thought of that," says Elmo. "Thanks, Jameson. Grandpa, you'd better give me your phone."

"I didn't bring my phone. Who would I call? The only other person I know here is sleeping three feet away."

Elmo rolls his eyes.

"I will have your room made up when you return," says Jameson. "Enjoy your dinner."

Sunday, Oct 26th
~ Fiesta Mambo, Deck 3, The Ballroom ~

Grandpa and Elmo follow a line of people into the dining room at 6:10. An assistant Maître d' points them in the direction of their table. The room is incredibly ornate with chandeliers and draperies. The room is packed, but is so efficiently laid out that you would think you were in a small, quiet bistro. Elmo spots the table and is surprised to see that it is set for eight and that some of the seats are already occupied...by old people.

"Welcome," says one of the men. "My name is Paul. To my right is Larry, and to my left is Alice. The seat next to Alice is taken, but the other four are unaccounted for."

Tommaso nods and takes the seat one away from Alice and Elmo sits next to him leaving two empty seats to his left. Almost immediately, a young dark-skinned man in a fancy vest turns over their water glasses and fills them. Elmo notices from his nametag that it is Fabrice from Cameroon. Elmo has no idea where Cameroon is.

A moment later, two women, one older and one younger, come by pointing at the table number. They smile as the younger one sits next to Elmo and the older one, next to Larry. The older men all rise and after a moment, Elmo does as well.

All of the women are in colorful dresses and all of the men besides Elmo are wearing jackets. Tommaso notices several different levels of dress throughout the dining room. Before anyone can speak, a waiter comes by and hands out menus to everyone.

"Good evening. My name is Handy, and I will be your waiter for the duration of the cruise. My assistant is Fabrice and we are here to provide anything that you need. The wine steward will also be by to take care of your bar needs. Tonight, I recommend the seasonal butternut squash bisque, the pecan encrusted snapper, and the *rayuela*, a *yuzu* infused cake for dessert."

"Wow," says Elmo, looking at the menu, "how does this work?"

"Is this your first cruise?" asks Alice.

Both Tommaso and Elmo nod.

"You're in for quite a treat," says Paul. "The food on the Fiesta line is excellent. It is not uncommon to gain seven to ten pounds on a week-long cruise. Basically, when Handy returns, you tell him what you want from this list. Most choose a soup or salad, and appetizer, and an entrée, but if you want to try two things, just ask, and they'll bring them."

"The portions are small by American standards," says Alice, "but the food is rich. Dessert comes later. We tend to get one of everything and share. The pacing of the meal is perfect as well."

Handy returns and goes around the table taking orders from the ladies first. Elmo notices from the nametag that he is from Indonesia. He also has a more ornate vest than Fabrice. Tommaso orders exactly what was recommended. Elmo orders the onion soup, the Caesar salad, a shrimp cocktail, the prime rib, and for good measure, an additional entrée, the scallops risotto.

"What do you have to drink?" asks Elmo.

"Water, iced tea, coffee and hot tea are complimentary. Soft drinks and alcoholic beverages are available through the bar service, sir."

"Iced tea will be fine."

"Since this is your first cruise," says Paul, "you will probably be very impressed."

This turns out to be true as Fabrice deftly serves the bread and Handy delivers the first course. This is interspersed with introductions and lively conversation.

"I'm Paul Kreppel. I live I a retirement community in Boca Raton. Cruising is quite a bargain for Florida residents. I went on several with my wife who passed four years ago. My friend Larry, to my right, and his wife helped me to get through it. His wife just passed in March, so I am hoping to return the favor. We went to grade school together in Brooklyn if you can believe it."

"My Sylvia and I were together for seventy-one years," says Larry. "Paul also has an ulterior motive. He and Alice have been keeping company."

"It's true," says Alice. "We live in the same community. I lost my husband Stanley eight, no nine years ago. As you can see, my traveling companion is absent. My cousin from

Iowa has had a little trouble getting her sea legs and is lying down in our cabin. She should be fine by morning. She lost her companion last year. Her husband was a miserable wretch. He was an abusive alcoholic and womanizer, and Sarah is the sweetest person I know."

The conversation rolls around to Tommaso.

"My name is Tommaso. I live in New Jersey and this is indeed my first cruise. I lost my lovely wife over thirty years ago and I am traveling with my grandson, Elmo."

"Um, my name is Elmo and I, um, I've never been married but I did break up with my girlfriend last week."

Paul roars with laughter.

"I'm sorry, son," he says. "I guess at our age it's something we all have in common. We didn't mean to be grim."

The young woman next to Elmo realizes that it is her turn for an introduction.

"Hello, my name is Shana. I am twenty-six and make my living as an artist. I grew up with my mother, here on some sort of a hippie commune in New Mexico. She takes me on these trips when she is between step-fathers."

After a stunned silence, the last person speaks.

"Why thank you, my dear. My name is Melody. I left my wealthy parents in Connecticut when I turned eighteen and did indeed join the 'hippie culture', living in co-ops and communes for several years. I too was an artist and was in my late thirties when I became pregnant with…Shana. I had avoided pregnancy so long, that I figured I was barren and I just got careless. Her father was a rover who quickly moved on. I can't even remember what he looked like. I named her Shoshone after a tribe I had lived with in Nevada. Obviously, she has chosen to go by a less ethnic name."

Everyone has stopped eating as to not miss one sordid detail except for Elmo, who is managing to do both.

"When Shana was nine, an older gentleman came by our stand looking for antiques. There was something special about him, but I had no idea what. We quickly fell in love and married. He treated my daughter like his own. He was quite wealthy and he taught me everything about class and culture, how to dress, how to act, not much differently from how my parents lived. Quite frankly, I liked it. He died suddenly, five years later. I have been married twice since to wealthy men and am currently looking for number four."

"Well," says Alice, "who's going to the show, tonight."

"Not me," says Shana. "If the trip here didn't wear me out, this dessert certainly did. I'm turning in early."

"Tommaso," says Melody, "since my daughter lacks the stamina, would you please escort me?"

"It would be my pleasure," says Tommaso.

"I am going to take a walk in the fresh air with Alice," says Paul. "We'll meet you there, maybe."

"Elmo," says Larry, "I guess that leaves you and me."

"Sure, why not," says Elmo. "It came highly recommended to me."

Sunday, Oct 26th
~ Hoboken ~

Scotty is lying in bed with Tommy snuggled up against him in the afterglow of lovemaking. Unfortunately, this afterglow is raising Scotty's body temperature beyond comfortable limits.

"This is so nice," says Tommy. "I really missed you."

Scotty is trying to carefully slip at least one foot out from under the covers to let in a little air flow before he bursts into flames. He is trying not to squirm which might disturb Tommy's reverie, but a sweat ball rolls into his eye.

"You seem quiet," she says. "What's on your mind, Babe?"

Scotty has his eye shut tightly to try to stop the burning sensation. He is also now breathing through gritted teeth in order to get more oxygen into his searing lungs. Tommy finally feels him quaking and looks at his face. It is bathed in sweat and he is turning a bright pink.

"Jesus!" she shouts. "Are you having a heart attack?"

When she lifts her head off of his shoulder, he seizes the opportunity to quickly roll out from under the covers.

"I'm sorry," he says. "I was a little warm, but I didn't want to disturb you."

"A *little* warm? You're soaked with sweat. This is disturbing. Go towel off and I'll put on some pajamas. I'm actually quite chilly."

After he towels off and puts on shorts, Tommy returns wearing flannel, long-sleeved pajamas with pants. She also is wearing slippers.

"Are you going mountain climbing?" asks Scotty.

"So we're on different climate zones. I'm more worried about my sleep schedule. I don't know how those kids do it. I have jet lag and never left the time zone. I probably shouldn't have taken that nap. I'll be up half the night."

"You'll catch up in a day or two."

"Speaking of catching up, what was that cryptic line on the trip home from the airport?"

"Oh, that. I just thought we should talk more about an engagement."

Tommy starts to speak and Scotty holds out his hands.

"Not, marriage," he says. "I said engagement. A marriage needs planning, and I don't want to wait a year or more *after* you graduate."

"Okay, I'm listening. Aren't you supposed to make some grand gesture on your knees?"

"Remember when that guy proposed at the Jets game and the girl ran off instead of saying 'yes'?"

"Yes, I said 'Good for you, girl', I believe."

"Exactly. You also said that the jerk had it coming. I don't want it to be a surprise. I want us to decide together."

"Okay, sounds fair, so far. What do we need to discuss?"

"Well, I assume we need to agree on some level of commitment to each other, possibly in some romantic way."

"You're doing great so far, although in my fantasy, I would expect you to be wearing a shirt."

"See, now you're making fun. Let's move on to the ring. I know that you wouldn't want me to bankrupt myself surprising you with a piece of jewelry that you will wear every day of your life and, that you didn't pick out. Besides, there's also the issue of blood diamonds."

"I'm sorry. You really have thought about this. Okay, I can see picking out a ring together. And you're right. I do have a big problem with how diamonds are obtained. What are the alternatives?"

"Well, there are fakes, many of which are pretty good now, and there is another type of stone, although many of them are mined like diamonds."

"Neither of those addresses your budget, which might get us something in the Crackerjack line."

"Come on, I'm trying to be serious. Any thoughts other than comedy?"

"What about an antique?"

"What do you mean?"

"An antique diamond might predate the blood diamond trade. I, and by I, I mean you, will have to do some research on that. It might also be cheaper and fit my style."

"There, that wasn't so bad. I assume I'm going to have to ask your father for permission."

"Ooh, let's not get into that just now. Start on the ring research first."

"Whatever you say, baby."

Sunday, Oct 26th
~ Fiesta Mambo, Deck 4, Olvera Street ~

Elmo and Larry are walking through Olvera Street, the promenade of shops and restaurants running through the middle of Deck 4. Elmo looks down to see the Art Gallery and the Photo Area. There are a few bars with live music and several upscale retail stores.

"It really is amazing all the stuff they get in here," says Elmo.

"These ships are amazingly well-engineered," says Larry. "Compact, no wasted space. This is why the Japanese are beating our brains in. Do you know that the main pool is directly over our heads?"

They walk past a staircase leading down to the casino.

"There are a lot of people down there already," says Elmo.

"They say the slots are loosest on the first day of a cruise," says Larry.

They walk a flight up to the main entrance of the Teatro Real, which is a surprisingly large theater in the front of the ship. It is thirty minutes before Showtime but the place is already filling up, mostly with older passengers. Several appear to be saving seats. They move to a place in the center section, about ten rows back.

"Do you think we should save some seats for the others?" asks Elmo.

Larry looks at Elmo and smiles.

"I don't think that will be necessary," he replies.

They continue with light conversation interspersed with declining drinks from the enthusiastic bar staff. They talk about the band setting up in the corner next to the stage and the optical illusion caused by the lights on the gold shimmery curtain. All the time, Elmo scans the room for Olivia, to no avail. He is beginning to think that she was playing him for a fool.

The lights dim and some announcements come on about flash photography. The band starts an entrance vamp and a man bounds out in front of the curtain.

"Welcome aboard the Fiesta Mambo! I'm your Cruise Director Mark Daddier, but you can call me Mack Daddy! I hope you are ready for a great show, and here it is! The Fiesta Mambo orchestra, singers, and dancers are here to perform for you...Latin Rhythms!!!"

The curtain rises and an amazingly elaborate and colorful set is the backdrop for 40 minutes of Latin dancing and singing. Elmo is quite impressed with the quality. About halfway through the show, there is a number featuring each dancer individually. Elmo is watching a raven-haired woman doing an athletic routine when he finds something familiar about her.

"Shit!" he says, a little too loudly when he realizes that it is Olivia wearing a wig. She's one of the dancers! From this point on, Elmo focuses on her rather than the show in general.

As they mill out of the theater, Larry says, "Thanks, Elmo, for accompanying an old man. I guess it's time for me to turn in."

"Do you need help getting to your room?"

"Son, I survived fourteen months in the infantry fighting the Nazis. I think I can find my stateroom."

"I didn't mean---"

"No, it's fine son. You're polite. It shows you were raised well."

"Thanks. Hey, Larry, how did you know we wouldn't have to save any seats?"

"Well, I know Paul and I know Alice, and I saw the way that the other woman---"

"Melody?"

"Yes, I saw the way that Melody was eyeballing your grandfather, like you were ogling your crème brulee."

"Maybe they went to the casino. You said the slots were loosest on the first day of a cruise."

"Son, who said I was talking about the casino?"

Sunday, Oct 26th
~ Fiesta Mambo, Deck 9 ~

Elmo heads down the corridor toward his room. Too exhausted for exploration, he decides to check in on his grandfather. He knows that Grandpa has to be on the ship, but has been known to get into trouble in a much smaller space than this. He pulls out his Dance Card to unlock the cabin and suddenly stops.

"Shit!" he says, as he looks at the door handle.

There is a necktie draped around the handle in the international symbol of 'If this room's a'rockin', then don't come a'knockin'.' At that moment, Jameson comes by carrying an armload of towels.

"Is your card not working, Mr. Elmo?"

Elmo points to show Jameson the tie. He checks Jameson's nametag and asks, "Does this mean the same thing in Jamaica as it does in the U.S.?"

"I see. We rarely wear ties, but a shirt or beads will do. Your grandfather is a lucky man."

"More than you can imagine. I guess I will do some more exploring."

"There are worse ways to spend an evening, Mr. Elmo."

"I suppose," says Elmo, with a chuckle. "You know what the funniest part is?"

"Tell me, Mr. Elmo."

"The son-of-a-bitch used my tie."

Jameson gives Elmo a big smile and a wink and heads down the hall. Elmo heads toward the stairs to go out on deck.

Elmo starts out on Deck 12 walking around the rail by the running track. He can see another cruise ship off the starboard side. There are some stars and barely a sliver of a new moon. He considers lying down on a deck chair, but the salt air gives him a second, or maybe a third wind.

Elmo checks out the disco and some of the bars. Most things are wrapping up now that it is after midnight. He catches the last few acts of karaoke, mostly drunken caterwauling, but there is an older gentleman doing a credible Frank Sinatra imitation. He must be a regular, because there is a sizable group of old ladies applauding and even swooning. Elmo wonders if he'll have groupies in his seventies and beyond.

Eventually, he ends up on a very quiet Olvera Street, at La Bamba, the twenty-four hour quesadilla and dessert place. Elmo is nursing a decaf and a churro when he hears a voice.

"Elmo?"

Elmo looks up and is shocked to see Olivia in a leotard and long sweatshirt, carrying a gym bag.

"Do you mind if I join you?" she asks.

"Sure, if you don't mind me hallucinating. I didn't expect to run into you at three in the morning."

"Actually, it's pretty common for me with my schedule. What's rare is to see passengers up this late, or early, I suppose."

"Oh, it's late, all right. I was up at six for my flight."

"I trust you have a cabin. You know that they can be used for sleeping."

"Long story. The short version is that my roommate is entertaining."

"That seems pretty simple."

"He's my grandfather, and he's eighty-three."

"Impressive. I look forward to meeting him."

Elmo gives her a strange look.

"I'm only kidding, silly. Sorry, we typically rehearse after a show since we are already backstage and the theater is not being used. You'd think I'd be exhausted, but I'm so wired afterward, that I cannot go right to sleep. It's not a good way to be on a ship."

She goes on to explain the life of a dancer, and the additional responsibilities that she has, including greeting guests and the Muster Drill. She also gives a few dance lessons and hosts the Art Show at the end of the cruise. Elmo admits that he almost missed her in the show due to the wig and was quite impressed with her dancing.

"The dancers share a room, but the singers get their own. Luckily, my roommate is shacking up with the lead singer, so I get to sleep in peace."

She tells Elmo that she is terribly homesick and is looking forward to the end of her seven-month contract in two weeks. She received an offer from a theater company in New Zealand, based in Auckland. There will be some travel to Australia as well. Elmo could listen to her all night. Actually, he is.

"Would you like to see where the crew lives?" she asks.

Elmo nearly falls off of his chair.

"Uh, sure."

She leads him down to the lowest level of the ship.

"I shouldn't be doing this, but we probably won't run into anyone who would care at this hour. Just look like you belong."

"I don't want to get you in any trouble."

"Oh, it's not that. Quite frankly, there are security cameras nearly everywhere, but no one could watch it all. They only monitor critical areas and record the rest in case they need to look back. There are just a couple of security guys who patrol who can be difficult. We're unlikely to run into them. If we do, you can be my cousin. At least you have the hair for it."

Elmo shrugs as they make a turn. Other than some personal touches on the doors and a lack of carpeting, it doesn't look all that different than the passenger corridors. They arrive at her room and go inside.

"Elmo, I have to ask you a personal question and it's going to sound odd."

"I'm way past odd. Fire away."

"Are you circumcised?"

"Never mind. You win. That was pretty odd. Why do you ask?"

"There is a lot of sexual activity on a cruise ship. Quite frankly, there's not much else to do. Only, I have an aversion to uncircumcised genitalia. I don't know why, but it just makes my skin crawl."

"While I can see why some might find your aversion unusual, I can safely say that I agree with your position one hundred percent. I, myself happen to be circumcised and am quite proud of it. I actually wish that I had more opportunities to show it off."

Olivia peels off her sweatshirt and begins removing her leotard and says, "Great, I'm really looking forward to being in the audience for a change!"

Monday, Oct 27th
~ Fiesta Mambo, Deck 9 ~

Melody is zipping up her dress as Tommaso puts on his robe.

"Thank you for a lovely evening, Melody. Are you sure that I cannot get you some coffee or breakfast."

"No thank you, Tommaso. I really need to get back to Shana. She's quite judgmental for someone who grew up in a 'free love' environment. I did have a wonderful time and I appreciate your chivalry. We both know that you are not up for the level of commitment that I am seeking. I did however, have a lovely evening."

She gives him a peck on the cheek and heads out of the door. As Tommaso is watching her leave, Elmo is walking up from the other direction. Tommaso turns and is surprised for a moment.

"Elmo, you look like hell."

"Really? I was just getting started. I only came to pick up a tie."

Grandpa laughs.

"Sorry about that," he says. "Come in and talk with me."

They fill each other in on their adventures, each making no specific mention of sexual activity. They decide that Grandpa is going to head to the Embarcadero for some coffee and possibly breakfast. Elmo is going to sleep for a while and they agree to meet at 1:00 for lunch.

Tommaso enters the Embarcadero and is surprised to find it so crowded. He overhears people on line explain that since this is a cruise day at sea, there are more people having breakfast on board. Tommaso collects a variety of food items and looks for a seat. There are none to be found other than a few jammed in corners near large families with loud children. He decides to keep looking.

A group of four is getting up near the rear window and Tommaso moves in to claim the table. At the same time, a woman is moving in from the other side.

"Oh, my apologies," says Tommaso. "I didn't know that you were going to sit here."

The woman smiles and says, "Would you like to share? I am here alone."

Tommaso starts to answer, but is still thinking about her smile. It is somehow disarming and familiar.

"Uh, yes," he says. "I too am alone."

They put their trays down while Tommaso tries to figure out why his last statement sounded so awkward to him. A young man in a vest immediately comes over to bus the table from the last group.

"Can I get you some coffee or another beverage?" he asks.

"Yes, thank you. That would be nice. I would love a cup of tea, chamomile if you have it."

She turns toward Tommaso.

"Um, coffee for me, please."

"That worked out nicely," she says. "That young man was from Nepal. Can you imagine how different this must be for him? Even living at sea level must be odd. Actually, I suppose on the ship, he really sleeps below sea level."

Tommaso is desperately trying to clear the fog in his head. The server returns with the beverages. This exchange and the act of putting cream in his coffee helps him return to reality, except he quickly realizes that he never uses cream. There doesn't appear to be anything noteworthy about the woman. She is of average size and weight, with short salt and pepper hair. She's wearing a subdued long sleeveless shift dress.

"I'm sorry to seem so fascinated by the people on the ship," she says. "This is my first cruise. Oh, pardon me. Allow me to introduce myself. My name is Sarah."

"Good morning, Sarah," says Tommaso, who is finally recovering. "My name is Tommaso, and this is my first cruise as well. There is no need to apologize, although I believe that I must. You seemed so familiar to me at first that I was quite tongue-tied."

"Really? This is actually my first foray out onto the ship. I was struck with a slight case of the *mal de mer* yesterday after boarding."

"Mal de mer?" asks Tommaso.

"Oh, I'm sorry. Seasickness. It's the French term."

"Again, there is no need to apologize for my ignorance. It actually sounds almost pleasant in French."

"I wish it were, but I'm fine this morning. As for the apologizing, it's a bad habit I picked up from my late husband. I'm working on it."

"Wait, Sarah, are you Alice's cousin?"

"Why yes, but how---"

"I am at your table in the dining room. I am traveling with my grandson, and we met everyone except you."

"I can see that Alice told you a few things about me. Maybe that's why I seem familiar to you."

Tommaso is convinced that there is something else behind his impressions, but doesn't pursue it.

"She only mentioned that you were from Iowa, recently lost your partner, my condolences, by the way, and that you were slightly under the weather."

He decided to leave out the part about her husband being abusive. He's also unsure why anyone would refer to an abusive spouse as a partner.

"Oh," says Sarah, looking at her watch. "I am supposed to meet Alice and Paul for some sort of a tour of the ship. I expect that I will see you at dinner. It is a formal night, I believe."

"What a coincidence," says Tommaso. "My grandson is sleeping in after a late night and I was going to take the ship tour myself. Would you mind if I walked with you?"

"I don't see why not," she says.

Monday, Oct 27th
~ Cedar Grove ~

"Yes, ma'am, you'll have it before noon," says Donny.

He hangs up the phone next to the register.

"Damn," he mutters to himself.

He walks back to the office and stands for a moment. Robert does not look up. Donny clears his throat. Robert sighs, and without taking his eyes off of his paperwork says, "Yes, Donny?"

"Um, I'm gonna load one of the trucks for deliveries once Ramo…I mean Mrs. Pastor gets back from Office Depot. Um, I might need you to make the deliveries."

Robert looks up giving Donny an intimidating stare developed during years of meetings with lawyers, judges, criminals, and even killers.

"Isn't that *your* job?"

At that moment, Ramona walks in with a couple of bags of supplies. She places them on the desk on top of Robert's paperwork.

"What job?" she asks.

"Donny was suggesting that I do some deliveries for him."

Ramona is a bit surprised and turns toward Donny. He gives her a pleading look which jars her memory.

"Oh, yes," she says, "it's Monday, isn't it. Yes, Robert, I think that Donny is correct."

"What?" shouts Robert. "But look how I'm dressed."

"Um, we have coveralls hanging in the back," says Donny. "They just got back from the cleaners. Um, I'd better start loading."

Donny quickly moves off.

"What the hell was that all about?" asks Robert.

"Why do you insist on intimidating him?"

They are interrupted by the jingle of the customer bell and Ramona heads out to the front of the store.

About forty-five minutes later, Ramona comes into the office wearing coveralls and holding a piece of paper.

"Let's go," she says. "I have the route. I've decided to go with you."

"You still haven't told me why Donny can't go."

"Alright, he's expecting a delivery from the tree farm."

"So? They come every Monday. They unload the truck. We can handle that."

"Can't you just put on the coveralls and come with me? Look, you're spoiling the treat. I'm naked under this outfit. Will that convince you?"

"Well, I suppose I can't argue with that offer."

Robert returns in a few minutes wearing the coveralls. They head out to the truck and Robert gets into the driver's seat. He cannot start the truck and looks confused.

"You can't drive a stick?" asks Ramona.

"You mean a manual transmission? No, I never have. When would it have ever come up?"

"Ugh, switch places with me. Sometimes you are so useless, Robert. Here, maybe you can navigate."

She hands him the route and they switch places. After a few jerks and stalls, they get on the road.

"You don't appear to be an expert either," says Robert.

"We're going aren't we? I've never used one on the column before. I've got it now."

"Where did you learn how to do this? I wasn't aware of this hidden talent."

"I learned from my father before he died. He wanted to make sure I could take care of myself. I think he knew he was sick long before he told us."

"I would have liked to know him."

"Probably not. He likely would have prevented us from marrying."

"Damn. Oh, make the next left."

They make the first delivery and Robert gingerly returns to the passenger seat.

"You didn't get hurt, did you?" asks Ramona.

"No, I'm fine. So, can you tell me now, why you were so bent on leaving Donny at the shop?"

"Okay. It seems he has a thing for the girl who delivers from the tree farm."

"What? That spooky girl with the black makeup and the tattoos? She has rings in her face."

"First, I believe it is called Goth. Second, he likes her. He's been trying to work up the nerve to ask her out."

"How do you know all this?"

"I talk to him, Robert. You might want to try it. He's an intelligent and sensitive young man."

They make a few more deliveries and Robert seems to be moving more slowly and carefully at each stop.

"So what makes you so interested in Donny's love life?" asks Robert.

"I just want to help him out. Our kids are doing so well that I sometimes miss their problems. I am a mother, you know."

"Well now that we're done with the deliveries, maybe you can take care of my problem."

"What do you mean?"

"What do I mean? You told me you were naked under there. I was hoping for a peek, or maybe something more."

Ramona begins to chuckle.

"Oh, my," she says. "Did you really believe, I mean we're in public and do you think I would let my delicate skin touch this canvas material?"

"Wait, you were joking?"

"Well, I don't know about joking. It was supposed to be a little incentive. I cannot believe that you took me seriously. That's so funny!"

"If you think that's funny, you're gonna love this. You were right about the material. My nether regions are pretty badly chafed up."

"No! You didn't! Even your underwear?"

Ramona puts her hand over her mouth.

"Oh, yes I did," says Robert.

He unzips the front of his outfit revealing his bare chest. Ramona is now laughing uncontrollably.

"I'm glad that I can entertain you," he says. "I am quite sure that there is no longer any hair on my balls and may seriously be in need of medical attention on my upper thighs."

At this point, Ramona is nearly crying with laughter.

"Oh, my sweet baby. I'll take you home and apply some first aid. I'm sure I can find some lotion to rub on you."

"I trust that we can keep this between us?"

"Of course, Robert. My lips are sealed. Oh, one more thing."

"Yes?"

Ramona can barely get it out through her laughter.

"May I assume that you will not be joining me at the gym tomorrow?"

Monday, Oct 27th
~ Fiesta Mambo, Deck 9 ~

Elmo is standing on the balcony of their stateroom, in a pair of shorts with no shirt. He is holding onto the rail and leaning out to look at the side of the ship.

"Don't jump," says Grandpa. "Your father would kill me."

Elmo turns around, but is not startled.

"When did you sneak in?" he asks.

"Just now. I called you, but apparently you didn't hear."

"The wind going by is pretty loud out here. I have no idea how fast we're moving."

Grandpa steps onto the balcony, but does not get close to the rail.

"About seventeen knots, according to what I've learned, although, I have no idea what a knot is. Did you catch up on your sleep?"

"Enough. With the curtains drawn, it's as black as night in here. Great design."

"You should see the rest of the ship. The tour was quite impressive."

"Wow, look at you, Grandpa. You're turning into quite the tourist."

"Well, we can discuss that later, but now, I need a favor. It seems I need a pair of bathing trunks."

"Didn't you pack any?"

"I've never owned any."

"Never? In eighty-three years?"

"Well, possibly in Italy, when I was a boy. Did you ever see me at a beach or a pool?"

"Gee, I guess not. That just seems so weird. I mean, we had a beach house. Never?"

"Look, can you help me?"

"Well, I just packed the one. It will be big on you, but there is a drawstring assuming you have hips. Or did you leave those in Italy as well?"

"What will you wear?"

"Oh, I have several of these basketball shorts. They're elastic and would fall right off of you, but I've already gained five pounds in a day on this cruise."

They go back into the cabin and Elmo hands Grandpa the suit. Grandpa goes into the bathroom and comes out looking surprisingly fit, although a little pasty.

"Jesus, Grandpa. Did you last see the sun in Italy as well? I'll bring plenty of sunscreen. If you get burned, you might just turn to dust. I'm starving. Are we at least getting lunch first?"

"About that. I am meeting some of our tablemates in the Sol Siesta, the pool area in the front of the ship. They assure me that it is quieter than the main area with the band and the kids. Also, they seem to have some sort of scam that saved some deck chairs. We're meeting for lunch at the small deli there called Danza del Sol."

"Sounds exotic."

"You don't mind, do you, Elmo?"

"Not at all. I was looking at the activities in the Treasure Map before you arrived. There is a basketball court on the Sports Deck and they're having some sort of contest. I plan to have a big shit, followed by a big lunch. I will then try to get some exercise, which I hope to follow up with more shitting, although vomiting is still an option."

"I wish you luck with all of that. Do I look okay?"

"You look so great, that I need to take another picture. Stand by the curtains so I can get the room in."

Elmo reaches for his phone on the dresser, but it is not there. He looks around, but sees that Grandpa is growing impatient.

"Never mind, I'll do it later," says Elmo. "Here is the sunscreen and take my cap. It's adjustable. You do not want to get burned. The sun is much stronger down here in the tropics."

"How do I use this?" asks Grandpa, holding up the spray can.

"Jesus, Grandpa. Your friends will show you. You can get a towel on deck. When do you want to meet back up?"

"It's formal night. How about if we shower and change between four and five. The group wants to meet for a cocktail before dinner. You may join us for that."

"Gee, thanks. Okay, you go have fun playing with your friends now."

Elmo pushes Grandpa out of the room and watches him head down the hall. He winces when he notices that Grandpa is still wearing black socks and wingtips.

Elmo shouts after him, "And remember to wait a half hour after eating before you go into the water, young man!"

Grandpa waves without turning around. Elmo returns to the room and does a quick search for his phone, to no avail.

"Fuck it," he says, under his breath. "178 square feet, and I can't find it."

He pulls on a t-shirt, grabs his Dance Card, and heads to the Embarcadero.

Monday, Oct 27th
~ Fiesta Mambo, Deck 1, Crew Quarters ~

Olivia hears a knock at her door. She rubs her eyes and squints at her clock. She throws back her sheet and stumbles out of bed. Without turning on the light, she opens her door. Standing in the doorway, silhouetted by the light, stands a tall Indian man in a security uniform.

"Are you alone?" he asks, as he squeezes past a yawning Olivia.

He hits the switch for the overhead light.

"Come in and make yourself at home, why don't you," she says. "Yes, I am alone. Yasmine is at the infirmary. What do you want, Vijay?"

Vijay closes the door.

"I need you to make a pickup tomorrow as soon as we dock."

"Get somebody else. I told you that I was done with that."

"You have a free morning, and it's too risky to get anyone else, and I'm *not* asking."

Olivia is trying to stand her ground, but is unconvincing.

"You security goons think you can push the rest of us around, but I told you that I was done with your little scam. I'm out of here in two weeks, so go get someone else under your thumb."

"You think that I can't make your last two weeks a living hell? If I want to, I can see that you never see New Zealand again."

"How? If I go down, I'll take you with me."

"Good luck with that. I'm the only one you know in the hierarchy. And if I'm the one that fingers you, than everyone will think you are desperate. You think I'm running this operation? I only know the person above me. That's why it works. I'm at their mercy like you are at mine."

"Well, I'm not available. Yasmine tweaked her knee and we have an extra rehearsal to reblock Thursday's show in case she can't do it."

"You're lying."

"No I'm not. You can check with any of the performers, or wait until she comes back on crutches. Why can't you get someone else?"

"You know damn well why, because you work the art auction. Here's the information. You figure out a way to get it done or both of us are in deep shit."

He hands her a piece of paper with an address and a name.

"You need to be there at ten in the morning. If you get out when we open the gangway at nine, you'll make it with no problem. Just hand me the tube when you come aboard. I'll be working the aft gangway."

"Yeah, and what if I get caught? How do I know that there aren't police or agents looking for me?"

"Look, you said it yourself. You have two weeks left. I thought you were done, but this just came up. You'll have some extra money to buy Mummy and Daddy some souvenirs when you get back home. Just make it happen."

Vijay walks out as Olivia hangs on to her last ounce of resolve. As soon as the door closes, she falls onto her bed in tears.

Monday, Oct 27th
~ Fiesta Mambo, Deck 13, Sports Deck ~

A small crowd has gathered around the basketball court to watch the end of the three-on-three tournament. Jerry takes a jump shot for the game winner that bounces off the front of the rim. Elmo boxes out Will and snags the rebound. He quickly fires a bounce pass to his teammate Jerrell who is swinging toward an open space on the wing. Jerrell takes a jumper, but it caroms too low off the backboard and bounces over the front of the rim. Fortunately, Elmo is there for a tip-in to tie the score at ten.

Elmo, Jerrell, and Jerrell's little brother Duane huddle above the foul circle with the ball. Elmo is having a little trouble catching his breath.

"Way to climb back," says Elmo. "Their guy Ben is cheating off Duane to double team one of us. Jerrell, take it out and get it to me on the right. Instead of setting a screen, go to the hole. I will hit you with a bounce pass on the give and go and will roll to the corner. If Ben goes with you, get it to me in the corner. He'll come out on me with Will. Duane, I'm gonna snap the ball to you at the foul line. You'll be open. Stick it. Jerrell and I will crash."

A concerned look crosses Jerrell's face, but Elmo ignores him and holds his hand palm down in front of him. Both Jerrell and Duane do the same on top of Elmo's.

"Team!" they shout, in unison.

The play goes exactly as designed. When Duane receives the ball, he takes the jump shot. The ball takes two bounces on the rim, and nearly two full revolutions rolling around the rim before finally dropping through the net. After sharing high fives, Elmo and the boys shake hands with their opponents. A member of the Cruise Director's staff hands them each a gold, plastic medallion on a red, white, and blue ribbon. The medallions are decorated with the Fiesta logo and the name of the ship.

"Thank you for playing with us," says Jerrell. "All of our cousins are smaller than Duane."

"So you are with the big reunion group?" asks Elmo. "I've seen you around the ship."

"Yes, sir," says Duane.

"Hey, it's Elmo, not 'sir'. You guys can really play. They were bigger and have obviously played together."

"Naw, we had 'em the whole time," says Jerrell, elbowing his little brother. "I was worried when you set up Duane. I thought he was gonna choke like usual. You should be a coach."

"Well, just remember that the best players make their teammates better. In a few years when Duane is your size, you're going to be glad that you did. Thanks to both of you."

Elmo shakes their hands and heads off holding up his medal and pumping his fist. The boys do the same.

Heading toward the front of the ship, he stops to get a soft ice cream cone. Upon entering the Sol Siesta, Elmo stops suddenly. He is startled to see Grandpa standing in the pool chatting with a group of seniors including Paul, Larry, and Alice. It's an image of his grandfather that he cannot recall ever seeing before. He looks almost…happy?

Elmo turns and heads to the pool deck to watch the ice sculpting demonstration.

Monday, Oct 27th
~ Fiesta Mambo, Deck 9 ~

Elmo takes his tuxedo out of the closet and lays it down on the bed. The door opens and Grandpa walks in carrying his shoes. He's barefoot and has a towel draped over his shoulders. His hat and trunks are both two sizes too big. Elmo is struck by how incredibly small his grandfather looks.

"Did you have a good time with your new friends?" asks Elmo.

"To be honest, I'm not completely sure. It was certainly pleasant. I suppose I've had surprisingly little experience with 'pleasant'. How was your afternoon?"

"Actually, pretty cool. I won this in a basketball tournament. I met a few nice kids. I even watched how they carve ice. I can't believe that we've been here barely a day."

"Agreed. I decided to do this primarily to humor Milton. This is turning out to be much more than I expected."

"Don't forget, we still have a formal dinner tonight, as well as some sort of headliner singer performance."

Grandpa lets out a deep breath.

"I'll tell you what, Elmo. You shower first. I'm going to take a twenty minute nap. Wake me at 4:25, if I'm still asleep. We are supposed to meet some people for cocktails and something called trivia on Ortega Street, at five."

"It's Olvera Street, after some place in San Diego. Are you sure I won't cramp your style?"

"No, I may need your help. I don't want to look like a fool answering general knowledge questions."

"Stop it, Grandpa. You're the smartest guy I ever met."

Elmo goes into the bathroom and Grandpa lies down. Both are wondering why Tommaso is so concerned about making an impression.

~~~~~~~~~~

At 4:50, they are both putting the finishing touches on their ensembles. Elmo places his new medallion over his head and turns toward Grandpa.

"What do you think?" he asks. "Too much?"

Grandpa laughs.

"I think that our target is to be smooth rather than ostentatious. Maybe you should leave that behind."

Elmo is now wrestling with his sleeves.

"Grandpa, can you help me with these? I can't line up all of the holes on these French cuffs."

He hands Grandpa a pair of cufflinks causing him to smile broadly.

"I am touched, Elmo. When I gave you these last Christmas, I was hoping to send you a message. I can't even be sure what I was trying to say, but I am so proud of the man you have become. You honor me."

"Thanks, Grandpa. Maybe the message was just to show me what my life could be."

"Perhaps, but the best part of all is to still be around to experience it together."

Elmo looks at the cufflinks and hugs his grandfather.

"Okay, enough Elmo. If we walk out of here together all misty-eyed, people will take us for a couple. Are you ready?"

"Geez, Grandpa. Way to break the mood."

Elmo puts on his jacket and checks himself in the mirror.

"Smokin'!" he says.

Monday, Oct 27th
~ Fiesta Mambo, Deck 4, Olvera Street ~

Grandpa and Elmo exit the elevator and head down Olvera Street toward a piano bar called Fandango. They pass people in bathing suits and flip-flops as well as some dressed to the nines in gowns and tuxedos. Paul and Larry wave to them as they enter. They both are also wearing tuxedos.

"Alice and Sarah are in the ladies room," says Paul. "I'm ninety, and I still haven't figured out why they need to go in pairs."

Elmo slides another chair near them so they may all sit. A member of the cruise staff is laying out some papers and setting up a microphone on the piano. Just as Elmo sits, he sees the other men all standing. He is confused for a moment, but then sees Alice and another woman walking into the bar. He quickly stands as well.

Alice is wearing a long dress which consists of a white button-down top with sheer long sleeves over a long red skirt. Around the waist is a large sash in a bow, also red. This explains Paul's red tie and pocket square. Sarah is wearing a plum colored long dress with some beaded highlights running down her left side from shoulder to hem.

"My, you both look lovely," says Grandpa. "Sarah, I'd like you to meet my grandson, Elmo."

Sarah shakes Elmo's hand and smiles.

"It's nice to meet you, Elmo," she says. "You gentlemen all look so handsome."

Alice flips through the drink menu.

"These drinks are so colorful," she says. "I'm going to try an appletini. Is anyone else having anything?"

"None of us are big drinkers, but on a cruise, we splurge a little," says Larry. "I'm going to have a Manhattan. Paul?"

"I'm feeling like a vodka martini," he says.

"Since we'll be in Mexico tomorrow, I think I might try one of the margaritas," says Sarah.

"What do you think, Grandpa?" asks Elmo. "I'm leaning toward a rum and coke. You're a vodka Collins man, as I recall."

"Just ice water for me please," he says quietly.

A server comes by and takes the drink orders. He is Viktor from Ukraine according to his nametag.

"Are you sure I cannot get you anything other than water, sir?" he asks, looking at Tommaso.

For just a flash, Elmo sees a look from his grandfather that might have meant a painful death for Victor in an earlier lifetime.

"Not just now," says Tommaso.

The cruise staffer identifies himself as Rodolfo from Honduras, and a member of the Cruise Director's team. He explains the trivia game rules. Elmo gets up and grabs a few score sheets and pencils as well as some scrap paper. He distributes them among the group.

"Alice is our trivia expert," says Paul. "She was a travel agent for many years and is quite worldly."

"We make a good team," says Alice. "Larry is our resident historian, and Paul covers the sports and entertainment. Sarah is new, but we hope she can help us with the music questions."

The group is intermixing conversation among the trivia questions and sipping their drinks.

"This is so pretty that I hesitate to drink it."

"No, it's not Duke Ellington. I'm sure it was Count Basie."

"Didn't you get that pin on our last cruise?"

"Bismarck is North? So what's the capital of South Dakota?"

Tommaso seems to be sinking deeper into his seat.

"Question Twelve," says Rodolfo, "What was the name of George Harrison's last band? No shouting out, please. This one could be easy or tricky."

"George Harrison was one of the Beatles, right?" asks Alice, while looking directly at Tommaso.

He quickly glances at Elmo who gives a less than subtle single nod.

"I believe so," croaks Tommaso.

"This seems too easy," says Sarah. "I know he did solo work, but I don't recall another band."

Elmo leans in.

"It's The Traveling Wilburys," he says. "He formed a group with Jeff Lynne, Tom Petty, Bob Dylan, and some older dude, Roy something. Orson, maybe?"

"Dylan, I've heard of," says Larry.

"Orbison?" asks Paul.

"Yeah," says Elmo. "Roy Orbison. I think he was blind or something."

"He wasn't blind," says Sarah. "The heavy dark glasses were some sort of a trademark."

"And old dude? Give us a break, Elmo," says Paul. "Roy Orbison was actually *after* our time. Alice, write down what he said. With the kid on the team, we might actually have a chance."

The game continues amid laughter and a bit of arguing. Tommaso seems to be getting smaller and paler by the minute.

"This is the tiebreaker question," says Rodolfo. "The answer is a number, and whoever is closest gets the point. Okay, here it is. In what year, did the U.S government enact the Racketeer Influenced and Corrupt Organizations, or better known as, RICO Act?"

Rodolfo reads it again, but the group is already in deep discussion.

"They got Capone on that, right?" asks Paul.

"It was tax evasion, specifically," says Larry. "Maybe it came as a result of Capone."

"That was sometime in the thirties, I believe," says Alice.

"Either that or the late twenties," says Paul. "What do you think we should put down? I'm thinking sometime between twenty-nine and thirty-five. Any ideas?"

Elmo nudges his grandfather with his knee and gives him a questioning look. Tommaso hesitates and Elmo cannot ever recall him looking so unsure of himself.

"1970," says Tommaso.

"Pardon?" asks Alice.

"It was 1970," says Tommaso.

"Are you sure?" asks Larry.

Grandpa looks to Elmo who nods for him to continue.

"Absolutely. It was signed into law by Nixon. Most states created their own laws a couple of years later."

"Good enough for me," says Paul. "Alice, if you please?"

Alice writes down the answer and they switch sheets with another team for scoring.

"He's good with history," says Elmo. "It just took him a little while to get going."

"You might be surprised to learn that the RICO statute has been used against the Hell's Angels, police departments, politicians, Michael Milken, and even the Catholic Church," says Tommaso.

"Really?" asks Sarah. "Were you in law enforcement?"

Elmo nearly spits out the last sip of his drink. He gives Grandpa the evil eye.

"Not exactly," says Tommaso. "Just a hobby, I guess."

Rodolfo announces that the group has won the contest and gives out medals to each of them. They are the same medals that were given out for basketball.

"Congratulations," says Rodolfo. "I've never had anyone answer that tiebreaker exactly before."

When the waiter comes by, Tommaso says, "Allow me, please."

"We cannot let you do that," says Larry. "While I'm sure that everyone appreciates the offer, we've had problems in the past with that sort of thing getting out of hand. We have a standing policy of everyone taking care of their own on the ship. Please take no offense."

"Of course not," says Tommaso, holding up his medal. "I suppose I was carried away with the excitement of the victory. May I share a celebratory bottle of champagne at dinner?"

"That would be wonderful," says Alice. "We have no provision for that. We've actually never won before."

"Well it's all thanks to young Elmo and your encyclopedic knowledge of criminal law, Tommaso," says Sarah.

Elmo notices her lingering smile. He sees that his grandfather has noticed it as well.

As they get up to head for dinner, Elmo takes Grandpa by the elbow.

"We'll meet you in the dining room," says Elmo. "We need to make a quick stop at the Information Desk."

"We'll save you a seat," says Paul, laughing.

Elmo leads Grandpa away. After he is sure they are out of earshot of the others, he says, "What the hell is wrong with you? I've never seen you like this. First you are sitting there like a zombie, and then you're Joe Smooth. Are you okay?"

"Elmo, I apologize. Quite frankly, I have no idea what's wrong. It's as though I am outside my body. It's extremely uncomfortable."

"Should we go to the Infirmary? Maybe it's some sort of anxiety attack."

"I don't think so. Physically, I feel all right. I've never had high blood pressure."

"My experience is that you had *no* blood pressure. You were pale, but mostly it looked like you lost your confidence. This can't be about a trivia game, for God's sake. Is it a woman? Sarah seems to be digging you."

"Do you think so?"

"Did you just ask me that? I'll pass her a fucking note in geometry class. Look, we can talk about this after dinner. Can you hold it together for a few hours?"

"I'm feeling better now. Thank you, Elmo. I'll be fine."

"Good. I'm starving. Just stick to simple subjects. Avoid religion, politics, and most of all, your 'encyclopedic knowledge of criminal law'."

Monday, Oct 27th
~ Fiesta Mambo, Deck 3, The Ballroom ~

Elmo and Grandpa join the others at dinner. In a few minutes, Melody and Shana come in to complete the table. The men all rise to greet them. Melody is stunning in a shimmery off-white number, eliciting oohs and aahs from the men and women alike. Shana looks quite nice in a colorful long gown in a Native American motif, but is barely noticed next to her mother.

"Hubba hubba," says Paul. "That's quite an outfit."

Before Melody can respond, Shana chimes in saying, "The brighter the lure, the bigger the fish."

"Why thank you, Paul," says Melody. "Please excuse my daughter. What's the old adage about teaching someone to fish? She's been eating so well on handouts, that she doesn't realize that eventually, the ponds dry up."

After a moment of awkward silence, Shana says, "Maybe that's why I'm content to remain a vegetarian."

No one is completely sure what this all means, but they all recognize that this is an ongoing issue.

Handy comes by with the menus and compliments everyone on their appearance. Tommaso orders a bottle of champagne and Fabrice brings glasses for everyone.

"What are we celebrating?" asks Melody.

Alice removes her medal from her clutch and holds it up.

"It seems for the first time in two dozen cruises, we actually won something. With the assistance of Tommaso and Elmo we are the reigning trivia champions. A toast to the victors!" she says, holding up her glass.

They order, with Elmo choosing the escargots, the lobster bisque, the prime rib, and the lobster tail.

"I see you are a growing boy," says Handy. "Save room for special a dessert."

Lively conversation continues during the meal.

"Paul," says Elmo, "I learned during trivia that you were in the Navy. Did you see action?"

"Action? Did I ever. I was on an aircraft carrier for nearly two years in the Pacific. I spent almost all of it in the laundry room. My shipmates had plenty of action, including at Midway. Unfortunately, I fought the war with starch and a steam iron."

"Nonsense, Paul," says Alice. "Every contribution helped."

"Well, I certainly didn't defeat Hirohito single handedly. Larry, here was the real war hero. He even has a Purple Heart to go with that trivia medal."

"Really?" asks Elmo. "Were you on a ship as well?"

"I usually don't like to make a big deal about it, but I've been thinking about it more since my wife passed."

"I'm sorry---"

"No, it's fine Elmo. I fought for fourteen months in the infantry in France and Germany. I married my Sylvia just before I shipped out. Being a Jew, I hoped to save other Jews by defeating Hitler and the Nazis, but we had no idea until later how much damage they had done. I was really just a kid representing my country."

"I can't imagine doing that being several years younger than I am now. It must have been frightening."

"Oh, like you wouldn't believe. We were all in it together, but I also lost a lot of friends. I was in a truck that was flipped by mortar fire. I fractured a finger and had a little hearing loss in my left ear. Believe me, I was lucky. I made it home to my Sylvia and we had sixty-nine years together."

"She was a wonderful woman," says Alice, "and I miss her terribly."

"Wow," says Elmo, "I don't think I've ever met a war hero before."

"I learned later, that nothing is quite as simple as it seems," says Larry. "Do you mind if I tell you a story, Elmo?"

"Please do, sir."

"Larry is fine. Okay, several years ago, Sylvia and I went on a cruise, just the two of us. It was for an anniversary, maybe our thirty-fifth. I'm not sure. We get seated at a table for four with a German couple, about our age. Sylvia and I make eye contact. Of course we don't say anything, but we know that we're going to ask the Maître d' to move us to another table."

"I didn't know you could do that," says Elmo.

"Sure, you can," says Paul. "You don't even have to be stuck with us."

"Stop being silly, Paul," says Alice. "Let Larry continue."

"We had nothing specifically against these people mind you," says Larry. "Even though it was decades after the war, well, we were Jews and they were Germans, and---"

"You don't need to explain," says Melody. "It's perfectly understandable---"

"That's just it," says Larry. "As we're sitting through the meal, we're making conversation, you know, 'Where are you from?', 'What do you do?'. So this fellow, Dieter is his name, mentions he's from Nuremberg. Well, it turns out that I spent some time in Nuremberg as well. I don't want to make a short story long. In a nutshell, it turned out that he was a soldier at the same time I was, and that we even fought in the same battle."

"You mean that you could have possibly been shooting at each other?" asks Elmo.

"Yes, and may have killed each other's friends," says Larry.

"Awkward, to say the least," says Shana.

"That's just it," says Larry. "The more we talked, the less awkward it became. This man was no Nazi. He was drafted into a war and was handed a gun and told to shoot at those people, much as I had been. We both lived to become engineers, each had three children, and each even had a common interest in tennis."

"Remarkable," says Sarah.

"Wait until you hear this part," says Paul.

"Sylvia and I had such a nice time with these folks, Greta was her name, that we decided to stay at the table. We actually became such good friends that the next time they visited Florida, they stayed as our guests in our home. We remained friends for many years."

"Incredible," says Melody.

"You see, Elmo," says Larry, "while there is heroism in patriotism and even in war, you must never, ever forget about the heroism of forgiveness and the ability to learn about someone. Ignorance is *always* the enemy."

"Thank you, Rabbi for that wonderful sermon," says Paul, holding up his glass. "Who's ready for dessert and coffee?"

A photographer comes by and takes a series of table photos.

"Hey, does everyone have their medal?" asks Elmo.

The six trivia champs have a group picture taken with their prizes around their necks.

"So what's everyone doing tonight?" asks Grandpa.

"Mom will be trolling for my new Daddy," says Shana.

"Honey," says Melody, "did it ever occur to you, that I might be lonely and actually enjoy the companionship of a man? I'm not sneaking around or fleecing anyone. I am always completely up front with gentlemen, certainly more than most people are on their computer dating profiles. And what's with all the fishing references?"

"You're using the right bait," says Paul. "That's for sure."

Alice gives him a little slap.

"I'm sorry, Mom," says Shana. "I didn't mean it to come out that way. Between the jet lag and this not exactly being my element, I've been shabby company."

"That's the best thing about a cruise," says Alice. "It's never too late to get your 'groove' on, so to speak. The four of us are going to the headliner show. We've seen her before and she's really quite good. Since we're dressed, we may do some dancing or pub crawling after. Of course, you're all welcome to join us."

"You guys have a lot of spirit," says Elmo.

"When you get to be ninety, Sonny Boy," says Paul, "the last thing you're going to want to do is waste a lot of time sleeping. Besides, Larry and I are not going ashore tomorrow. We've been to Cozumel several times. I've already got enough maracas and sombreros."

"I would like to join you," says Tommaso. "Elmo, what about you?"

"Shana," says Elmo, "can I interest you in the show? Maybe I can show you around the ship. I've seen quite a bit of it already."

"Why not? Mom, is that okay?"

"It's fine with me. I'm going to do some exploration of my own."

"You should try the casino," says Larry. "That's where the high rollers hang out from what I understand."

"Thank you, Larry, but I've been at this for a while. I avoid gamblers. They make the worst husbands. I'm interested in a man who knows a sure thing when he sees it."

Alice nearly spits out her coffee and Sarah nudges her under the table. The men completely avoid eye contact.

"Oh, my!" says Melody, giggling. "I'm afraid that did not come out right at all!"

Monday, Oct 27th
~ Fiesta Mambo, Deck 4, Olvera Street ~

On the way to the show, Elmo makes an excuse about stopping by the cabin. He asks Larry to save him and Grandpa a couple of seats and directs his grandfather toward the elevators.

"What is this all about?" asks Grandpa.

"Just hang on a minute. That's kind of my question for you."

Instead of the elevator, they exit out onto the deck by the muster stations. Elmo turns to face Grandpa and places his hand on the rail.

"Grandpa, are you all right?"

Grandpa moves up to the rail and looks out over the ocean.

"I wish I knew, Elmo."

"They have doctors on board. I can take---"

"No, Elmo, it's nothing physical, I assure you. I just seem so…off balance, I suppose. I certainly have not been myself."

"I'll say. I don't get it. Is it the people we're with? If so, we can move. Is it Melody?"

"No, Melody was just a thing. That's done with and probably for the better. And I actually like the group. I just can't explain why. They're very much like the people at my condo back home, and I can't stand any of them."

"Well, no sex tonight, okay? I would like to get a good night's sleep."

"What about Shana, Shoshone, or whatever her name is? Be careful with her. She has some serious self-esteem issues."

"Thanks, Dr. Phil. As much as I love discussing my sex life with you, no, I'm not interested in her. She's not my type, and she kind of creeps me out."

"Who is Dr. Phil?"

"That's another thing, Grandpa. You go to the trivia thing, and all of a sudden, you're helpless. Jesus, you're literally the smartest guy I've ever known, but you don't know any *things*."

"I'll admit that it's not my game."

"Again, my point. You seemed totally bent on proving something to these people. When you were stumped, you looked like you wanted to cry. Then, when you got the RICO question, you were showing off like a blowhard tool. You're just not yourself."

"Thank you for your concern, Elmo. You are completely correct. You've given me some things to think about. Let's go to the show and discuss this more later, I mean since it does not appear that either of us plan to get laid tonight."

Elmo grins.

"That's my Grandpa."

Monday, Oct 27th
~ Fiesta Mambo, Deck 5, Teatro Real ~

After the house lights come on after the show, the group stays for a few minutes to discuss their plans.

"Alice and I are going to do a little dancing and possibly have a nightcap," says Paul. "Anyone want to join us?"

"I'll tag a long for a little while," says Larry, "but will probably slink off to bed before long. I thought that the singer was wonderful, although I liked her song choices better the last time."

"I obviously have never seen her before," says Sarah, "but I could not have been more impressed."

"Tommaso," says Alice, "I'll bet you didn't know that Sarah is a singer."

"Strictly in the shower," says Sarah.

"In that case, Grandpa would love to see you perform," says Elmo.

This is met with silence, and a particularly intense glare from Grandpa.

"Tough room," says Elmo.

Grandpa turns to Sarah.

"I apologize for the impertinence of my grandson," he says. "Please let me make it up to you by treating you to a cappuccino. I'd love to hear more about your singing."

"Why not? That sounds lovely, Tommaso."

Shana has remained silent and withdrawn throughout the conversation. Elmo takes a deep breath.

"Shana?" asks Elmo, "I'd still like to show you around the ship if you're interested. I can even show you the undercarriage of the bus my grandfather just threw me under."

This elicits a half smile.

They all file out of the theater. Tommaso and Sarah walk down one flight to Olvera Street. Again, there is a mix of formal wear and cruise wear.

"I'm amazed by the range of dress," says Sarah. "Alice says that sometimes they like to sit somewhere along here and just make fun of people's outfits. One of her favorite lines is, 'Just because it comes in your size, doesn't mean that you should wear it'."

"Ouch," says Tommaso. "I'll admit that I have a pet peeve about some of the dress."

"Let me guess. Is it when men on formal night wear their t-shirt *with* the sleeves, or turn their ball caps to face forward instead of backward?"

"So you noticed that as well. As much as I despise anyone not being able to present themselves in an appropriate manner, I recognize that these are the times we live in. What really gets my goat is when a man dresses two or more levels below that of his companion."

"What do you mean?"

"Take that couple over there getting their picture taken. She is dressed, if not formally, at least close."

"Long dress, nice shoes, fancy jewelry, and clutch. Okay, if a gown is level one, I'd accept this as level two."

"Alright, now look at her husband. Polo shirt, chinos, decent belt, and shoes. He's clean and neat, but still two levels below her."

"How so?"

"Level one would be formal wear, either a tuxedo or even a dark suit and tie. Level two would be jacket and tie minimum. Level three, you can ditch the tie or the jacket, but not both, and always with a button-down shirt."

"What about that guy with the fancy jeans?"

"Look, I know that some fools pay hundreds of dollars for these things. It doesn't matter. I've grudgingly accepted Dockers, Khakis, what have you, assuming they are pressed. Save the jeans and polos for the bowling alley."

"You're pretty serious about clothing, Tommaso."

"Actually, I'm not. What I'm serious about is respect. Dressing below your woman is not only embarrassing to her, but is additionally showing the world your contempt."

"I see. We've just moved into an area of my expertise."

"May we continue our discussion over coffee?"

"If you don't mind, Tommaso, I recall that the bar had some specialty coffees, if you catch my drift."

Tommaso points to Fandango.

"There is this place, where we met before dinner. It would allow us to continue to judge people's clothing."

"I am thinking of another place, if you don't mind the walk."

"Not at all. Lead on."

~~~~~~~~~~

"You seem to like to eat," says Shana.

Elmo joins her at a table for two at La Bamba. He has two plates filled with empanadas, churros, and flan.

"I thought you might like to try something. It's pretty good. The waiter is coming with our drinks."

A dark-skinned woman brings them a coffee and a tea along with some creamers and sweeteners. He can see that she in Nigerian, but her name seems to have no vowels. Shana shrugs and takes a churro.

"So, you're an artist?" asks Elmo.

"I suppose you could say that."

Elmo takes a forkful of flan as he wonders whether it or Shana is better company.

"What is your area?" he asks.

"Area? Oh, you mean medium. Mostly pottery, but I also paint and do a little sculpture. It's very hard to make any living at it. People would rather get cheap crap at Pier One or Target."

"I saw that there's an art tour on the ship. Some of the stuff in the stairways looks pretty good to me."

"I've seen a few things I like. I know I can come across as a bitch, but I don't want anyone to think I'm an art snob."

"An art snob?"

"Yeah, it's somebody who thinks only they know what's good. It's particularly offensive coming from an artist, since they only ever seem to like their own stuff."

"I never really thought about it."

"I also noticed that you did not make any effort to correct me when I called myself a bitch."

"Just to prove that I was paying attention, you actually said you can come across as a bitch, not that you were a bitch."

"Do you think there's a difference?"

"I do. I recently broke up with a girl who was like that. She has a good heart. She has some maturity issues and some self-esteem issues that she handles by being, well, bitchy."

"Ouch! That hit close to home. I do appreciate your honesty, however."

"My bad. No amount of honesty makes up for a lack of tact."

"That's profound. Is that a quotation?"

"I'm not sure. I've heard it more than once from my mother. Damn, she'll be pleased with herself when she hears about this."

"She should be. Maybe I should consider this maturity thing. Now let's go look at some of this art."

~~~~~~~~~~

Tommaso and Sarah bump into Alice and Paul by the elevators.

"Larry turned into a pumpkin," says Paul. "We're on our way to Hernando's Hideaway for a dance. It's down on Deck 3, I believe."

"Can you remind me where the jazz bar is located?" asks Sarah.

"Sure," says Alice. "It's way up on Deck 13 in the backside of the ship. It's called the Conquistador Lounge."

"Backside?" asks Sarah.

"After twenty cruises," says Paul, "she still can't get bow and stern. She calls them the 'backside' and the 'pointy end'."

"Well, the front *is* the pointy end, is it not?" asks Alice.

Paul nods in reluctant agreement.

"Well you kids be good, and don't stay out too late," he says, with a wave.

Tommaso and Sarah find the lounge with little effort.

"It looks as though they just finished a set," says Sarah. "It will be about twenty-five minutes before they return."

"Fine. We'll sit and chat over one of their specialty coffees."

They find a quiet table that still has a nice view of the small stage. After a brief look at the menu, they order. The waiter returns with two mugs slathered in whipped cream.

"Oh my, this looks delicious," says Sarah.

"I've learned so much about the others, including possibly more than I should have," says Tommaso. "Yet, I have learned very little about you. Please tell me about yourself."

"While I have no real regrets, I have had some tough times. I left college to marry a man that I thought I was in love with. He expected me to stay home and take care of him and a houseful of kids. I had three miscarriages, all somehow my fault, of course. He made a decent living, but soon the anger came out, which got worse with his drinking. I should have known. Both of his parents were alcoholics."

"You seem much better, now."

"I am better. One day, I decided to go back to school. I put all of the bitterness behind me and earned my degree in education. I found a job teaching second grade and fell in love with it. Other than the grief in dealing with the loss of my partner, I've been quite content."

"This is where you are losing me. I lost my wife over thirty years ago, and I still grieve every day. It is wonderful that you found happiness, but it seems that it was in spite of your husband. Did he become sober? Did you find a way to forgive him?"

Sarah looks lost for a moment.

"Oh my, Tommaso! How could I have been so foolish! Somehow, I thought you knew more of the story. You think that my partner and my husband are the same person, don't you?"

"They're not?"

"Oh, not at all. My husband killed himself while driving drunk several years ago. Thankfully he didn't hurt anyone else. I had considered divorce, but I was just too afraid. As difficult as it was, it may have been the best thing to ever happen to me."

"So you remarried, then?"

"Wow! How did we get so far off? Not exactly. While at college, I met a woman named Meg working in the Library. It turns out that she was the Assistant Librarian. I used to go to her for research help often. Remember, I had been out of school for nearly twenty years. We were about the same age and we just hit it off."

"Your partner."

"Well, that's how I refer to Meg, now. We never really had a name for it. It wasn't really a sexual thing, but in many ways, we were soul mates. We eventually spent so much time together that we just moved in together. I had a nice house. She was the most supportive person I had ever met. I can't say I ever really had a close friend of any kind before, and this was more. Do you understand any of this?"

"Some, I do. My wife and I were as close as you can be. I've had many women since, but never any more than sexual. I just could not imagine meeting anyone I could be so close to."

"So you found yours early, and I found mine late."

"So it would appear. While I envy Larry for the length of time he had with, Sylvia, was it? I wouldn't trade a second of my time with Marie for anything."

"I'm so glad you understand. I lost Meg to cancer nearly a year ago. I'm so embarrassed that I had conveyed the story so poorly at first. You must have been so confused."

"It was a bit of a shock, I must say. Look, they're about to start."

~~~~~~~~~~

Elmo and Shana are walking down one of the cabin corridors looking at the artwork.

"Maybe it's a circus theme," says Elmo, "although that's still only about a third of the pieces. Maybe they ran out."

"Wait, stop here and look just at this one," says Shana. "What words come to mind?"

"Okay, I see wheels and ladders, and of course the buildings, which appear to be tilted off center a bit."

"Balance."

"Balance? Yeah, I guess I can see that."

"I think that's the theme. Some are super literal, like the tightrope and trapeze, and some are more subtle, like this."

"Maybe. I guess so. But why put up art that you have to be an artist to figure out?"

"Elmo, I can't be sure that this was their plan, although it shows more sophistication than I expected. For all I know it's a subliminal way to make people feel balanced since they are on a moving vessel."

"Sounds awfully complicated, but if you're going to spend a few billion on a ship, you might as well put some thought into it."

"I took a few courses in art therapy. You'd be amazed at how art can affect the subconscious. I've actually considered going into the field. Many hospital systems are embracing the concept."

"Well, I kind of like the clowns."

As they discuss their backgrounds, Elmo learns that Shana grew up relatively poor and has had trouble adjusting to a higher lifestyle.

"I guess I'm the opposite," says Elmo. "I've always had it pretty easy, and slacked off as a result. I feel that I'm making up for it now. It's hard, but I like it."

"It sounds as though your parents support you. That must be nice."

"They always have, even when I was a lousy prick to them. I'm very fortunate. I'm sure your Mom has done her best."

"Probably, I mean, I can't imagine leaving home and being on your own at eighteen, and then raising a child. We're just so different."

~~~~~~~~~~

"Thank you for listening. You've been a wonderful audience. My name is Darcy Blake and aside from playing this sax a bit, I also lead the orchestra here on the Mambo. Please keep your eye on the schedule for all of our shows and performances. Thanks, and have a great night on the Mambo!"

Tommaso and Sarah applaud before heading for their cabins.

"Thank you so much, Tommaso. As you can tell, I'm quite a jazz fan, particularly from the forties and fifties."

"I recognized a few Louie Prima pieces, but I am not nearly so versed as you."

"It is secretly my life's dream, to sing with a combo like that."

"So you are a singer, then?"

"As Alice said, pretty much in the shower. There's not much call for this type of music in Iowa."

"I imagine not."

"Tommaso, do you mind going out on deck with me for a bit as we head toward our cabins?"

"Not at all. I could use some fresh air."

They go down to the twelfth level and walk out toward the rail.

"I expected it to be windier," says Sarah.

"We've slowed down considerably. You can see land on the other side. I assume that is Mexico."

"I can't wait to see it tomorrow. Tommaso, may I ask you a question?"

"Of course."

"When we finally got on the same page about my background, you seemed to take it in stride. I was so embarrassed that I had not made myself clear. Also, you seem quite 'old school' to me. My type of relationship was far from accepted by many in Iowa. Is it that different in New Jersey?"

"Hmm, let me think for a moment. I'd like to phrase this correctly."

They move over toward the rail.

"Like many people," says Tommaso, "I'm in a period of transition, only unlike many, this is a first for me. For example, you mentioned earlier that you considered singing to be a dream of yours. I believe that you specifically said, 'a life's dream'."

"So I did. I guess it's common to have a bucket list."

"I never had."

"Tommaso, that's not possible."

"Actually, it is. I have spent nearly every waking moment of my life doing what I felt needed to be done. I've had plenty of adventures as a result. I've had success and failure, triumph and tragedy, but no dreams."

"Really? I'm not sure I can imagine it."

"Now I'm not making any judgments about reality versus fantasy or even doing versus desiring. I've just never been wired that way. Even this trip was more of a favor to a friend. He died suddenly a few days ago, so I brought my grandson in his place."

"Well I'll be. And what about my 'lifestyle' choice?"

"I'll admit that I was quite shocked and embarrassed, both by my completely missing a significant part of your story, and by the story itself. Thankfully, I am sufficiently versed in etiquette to not let it show."

"You should give lessons. I've had several people spit out their food. So you are not offended?"

"First, it is not my place to have offense or not. I did grow up in a world where such behavior was considered immoral, even though I imagine that it was as common as today. My grandson has helped me to alter my views."

"Elmo?"

"No, his younger brother Peppino is gay, and I could not love a person more. I thought it would be a more difficult transition, but love is indeed a powerful thing."

~~~~~~~~~~

"I'm down on Deck 2 in the bilge," says Shana. "We're in the least expensive cabin."

"I assume there is a hole in the wall for the oar," says Elmo.

"I don't get it."

"You've never seen Ben-Hur?"

"I don't think so."

"You'd remember it. It's on every Easter. Reserve four hours, though. Let's make a quick stop on Deck 3. That's where the Art Studio is."

The studio is closed, but there is a fair amount of art outside along with information about the big auction on Saturday.

"Now this art is shit," says Shana.

"How can you tell? Some of it, I like."

"I mean that as an investment, it's shit. These are primarily prints and lithographs by semi-famous commercial sellout artists to turn a fast buck. Snooty people with a few bucks think they're getting a deal. These 'limited' editions are the biggest scam in art."

"Hmm, good thing I'm not in the market."

"Elmo, thanks for showing me around, but I'm exhausted. My cabin's just down the stairs. I'll be fine from here."

"Okay, I'll see you at dinner tomorrow, I suppose."

Elmo turns toward the elevator. When it opens, Olivia is standing there.

"Oh, my God. I'm so glad I found you!" she says. "I was on my way to rehearsal, but needed to check something in the studio. I need a giant favor."

She unlocks the studio and leads him in.

"What can I do for you?" he asks.

"Are you going ashore, tomorrow?"

"I hadn't planned to. I actually have no plans."

"Tomorrow is usually a shore day for me, but we have an extra rehearsal due to an injury. I want to know if you can go into town and pick something up for me."

"Pick something up?"

"Yes, it's really simple. You just get off the ship with the first group. They open up at about 8:30 on Deck 2 up in the front of the ship. You get in a cab---"

"Whoa, a cab? I don't speak Spanish."

"You don't need to. I'll write down the address. It's less than two miles. You'll still be able to see the ship. The driver will wait. You go to the address and ask for Cortez. He will give you a package, and you just get back in the cab. I'll give you the proper amount of money for the fare and a generous tip."

"You don't have to---"

"I insist. When you get back to the ship, you need to go through one of the security checkpoints. Go to the one closest to the rear of the ship. A guy there will be looking for you and will take the package. You'll be back an hour before lunch even opens."

"I guess I can do it. I'm not going to get kidnapped or murdered by a drug cartel, am I?"

"No, silly. That's not here on the Yucatan. That's across the gulf. I just have this emergency rehearsal and it's a special gift for someone back home."

"Okay, why not? I'm on vacation and it will give me an excuse to at least see a little of Mexico."

She hands him a paper with an address and a small stack of Mexican currency. She gives him a kiss on the lips.

"Thanks, Elmo. You're a lifesaver. I've got to run to the theater now."

"Okay, I'm off to bed. I look forward to the next show."

On his way back to his cabin, he wonders why he is such a sucker for women. He's relieved that there is no tie on the door, but now recognizes that he comes by it honestly. He opens the door to find Grandpa sitting on his bed in pajamas, reading a book about the ship.

"Good evening, Elmo. Do you think I could have been an engineer?"

"Grandpa, you could have done anything you wanted, maybe you still can, but why an engineer?"

"I don't know. I find everything about this ship to be a marvel. Not just the design and the size, but the efficiency. Do you know that there are over one thousand crew members aboard this ship? And this is not one of the bigger ones."

Elmo is getting undressed.

"Grandpa, I've gotta ask, what's going on with you? You don't seem like yourself."

Grandpa puts down the book and looks at Elmo.

"In a minute. How was your evening with the girl?"

"Oh, it was okay, once she relaxed. I guess she's just trying to find her way. We weren't so different in that respect."

"Transition."

"What about it, Grandpa?"

"That's what's going on with me, I believe. I just didn't do it when I was your age. I was forced into a life as a boy and just ran with it. I think that I might finally be ready to try something new."

"At eighty-three? You sure you don't want to take a few more years to think about it?"

"I'm serious, Elmo."

"What I mean is that most people envy you. Transition is hard as shit. You can take my word for it."

"And look how much stronger you are as a result. Your sister is also always testing herself. Peppino may be the strongest of all of us."

"He's pretty tough for a faggot."

"I hope that you enjoyed your little joke. That is absolutely the last time you will ever refer to your brother that way."

Elmo's smile fades quickly as he looks at his grandfather.

"I understand," he says. "Never again."

"Thank you. I am having breakfast and sitting by the pool with Paul and Larry in the morning. What about you?"

"I've decided to take a short trip into Cozumel in the morning. You're welcome to come."

"No thanks. It seems that making friends and socializing is part of my transition."

"And what about Sarah?"

"An intriguing woman, to be sure. There's no sexual attraction, yet I find myself drawn to her in some way. I must admit that I am somewhat off balance."

Elmo lies down and turns off the light.

"Let's meet up for lunch," he says. "Oh, and about the balance thing, try the artwork on Deck 7, starboard side."

Tuesday, Oct 28th
~ Fiesta Mambo, Port of Cozumel ~

"Elmo, get up," says Grandpa. "They just announced that they are opening the doors to Cozumel in a half hour."

Elmo shakes the cobwebs out of his head as he figures out where he is.

"Oh, thanks, Grandpa. I usually set my phone alarm, but I can't find it. I was hoping that Jameson would have picked it up by now. What time is it?"

"About eight. I'm going up to meet the fellows. It's our turn to save seats."

Elmo jumps out of bed.

"Shit, no time to shower. You want to meet at the Embarcadero for lunch? Pick a time, Grandpa."

"It's too crowded to meet there. I'll meet you here at one. Does that work?"

"Perfect. Have a good time."

Elmo throws on a shirt and shorts and opts for his running sneakers. He grabs his wallet and the note from

Olivia. While opening the door, he stops for a moment to collect his thoughts. He goes back into the cabin for his Dance Card and a baseball cap with the Mets NY logo on the front.

Arriving on Deck 2, there is a line waiting to go out onto the dock. A security officer takes Elmo's Dance Card and puts it in a slot. Elmo nods and takes back his card. He leaves the ship and walks with the crowd along the pier.

About halfway down the pier, there is a person wearing a sombrero and a serape. They also appear to have a large fake moustache. A photographer from the ship is stopping the tourists and snapping their pictures. Elmo tries to decline, but gives up after a few seconds.

"When in Mexico…," he says, to no one in particular.

Many of the tourists are also taking pictures of each other with the ship in the background. Elmo is asked by a few families to snap the photos for them so they can all get in the picture together. Again, Elmo regrets the loss of his phone.

At the end of the pier there are several shops and restaurants. People are already drinking at Senor Frog's and it's not even nine o'clock. There are also people with signs gathering cruisers for a variety of excursions. Elmo spots the taxi stand off to the right.

Several of the drivers are offering rides, and Elmo immediately chooses the guy who seems to be most versed in English.

"Do you speak English?" asks Elmo.

"Yes I do, mister, at least well enough to beat my *muchachos* to the first fare of the day."

"I have an address here," says Elmo. "I need to go there to pick up something. I'll need you to wait for me and return me back here. Understand?"

The cabby opens the back door of a 1995 Chevy Impala.

"I understand, mister. That will be $20 American."

Elmo pulls out the Mexican currency.

"Will this do, including tip, or do I comparison shop among your friends over there?"

"This will do just fine, sir. If you please?"

He holds out his hand directing Elmo to get in. Elmo slides into the back seat and reflects more on the art of female persuasion.

"Where did you learn English so well?" asks Elmo.

The driver looks in his mirror and says, "Some in school, mostly from TV. I figured in this line of work, it would help to speak the language of the people with money."

"Smart."

"It's the Mayan blood. Most of the craziness you hear about Mexicans are to the North and West. You will notice the people here are a little shorter than average. Those are the Mayans. We are also smarter and more resourceful as a people."

"Interesting. I never knew any of that. We barely learn our own history in the States anymore."

They pull down a side street between some colorful apartment buildings. The driver comes to a stop.

"It's the yellow building," says the driver. "You want the one with the blue door. You see it, mister?"

"Yeah, thanks. You're gonna wait, right?"

"Yes sir, and please use caution. While this is not Mexico City, we still have some bad neighborhoods. If there's any trouble, just come running and we can get out fastly."

"I think you mean quickly."

Elmo gets out and walks toward the blue door. A woman is watching him from an upstairs window, and a couple of kids playing out front stop to watch him as well. Elmo steps up on the slab in front of the door and knocks.

In a moment the door is opened by a dark man wearing blue jeans and no shirt. He has multiple scars on his chest that very well could be the result of being stabbed.

"Cortez?" asks Elmo.

"You trying to be funny, Gringo?" asks the man.

"Funny? Uh, no. I'm just here to pick something up from Cortez."

"What happened to the Chiquita, the redhead?"

"She got tied up. She asked me to pick up a package for her."

"Hang on."

The man eyeballs Elmo for a few more seconds and goes inside. A minute later he comes back carrying a black tubular container with a strap.

"Here it is."

Elmo takes it and looks at the man.

"Is there something else, Gringo?"

"Uh, yeah. What was funny about Cortez before?"

"Read a history book, Gringo."

The man slams the door. Elmo turns and heads for the cab which is idling in the same place as before. He gets in.

"Could you see that guy from here?" asks Elmo.

"I didn't see anything, but he may have been in several knife fights."

"I thought you didn't...Oh, I get it. I suppose it could've been one really bad knife fight. What can you tell me about Cortez?"

"You mean the Cortez who wiped out the Aztec Nation in Mexico in the sixteenth century?"

"That must be the guy. I guess it was kind of funny."

They get back to the dock. Elmo gets out with his package, hands the money to the driver and thanks him. He heads back toward the ship. The boarding area is pretty sparse as it is early. He easily maneuvers toward the line closest to the rear of the ship.

A rather large woman in a big hat is several places in front of him. She places two large bags on the conveyor belt at the security checkpoint. When the guard sees the outline of bottles in the first bag, he reverses the belt. This causes the second bag to tip, spilling several more bottles onto the deck. Some of them break on contact sending a cloud of capsaicin into the air.

The heavy woman screams and starts yelling at the security guard. The security guards are arguing. Several passengers are covering their eyes, noses, and mouths.

"You broke my hot sauce!"

"I thought it might be alcohol."

"My eyes are burning!"

"Please, madam, let me help you."

"It's like tear gas!"

The security guards from the other line rush over and immediately divert the incoming passengers away from the spill. Elmo quickly gets passed through and picks up his tube on the other side of the belt. He looks for someone to take the package, but is quickly carried with the flow of people to the stairs.

Elmo shrugs and takes the package back to his cabin. He figures he'll just catch Olivia after the show. Who knows, she may be grateful enough to pay him back in a more intimate manner.

He enters his cabin and is amazed to see that the beds are already made. He checks the Treasure Map and decides to hit the gym to make room for lunch and to possibly take a quick dip in the pool. It's not even eleven o'clock so he won't have to meet Grandpa for over two hours. After a quick change, he heads out to the gym.

Tuesday, Oct 28th
~ Fiesta Mambo, Deck 11, Sol Siesta ~

"So what do you think of your first cruise?" asks Larry.

Larry and Tommaso are lying on a pair of deck chairs overlooking the pool. It is sparsely populated as many passengers are off exploring Cozumel.

"I'm fascinated," says Tommaso. "It is much more pleasant than I expected."

"How about the food?"

"Again, unexpectedly good. I've obviously had better, but never in such a large venue. It's as good as most restaurants, at least in the U.S., and you can't argue about the variety. I'm most impressed by the implementation."

"How so?"

"While obviously, this morning is especially pleasant due to most people being off the ship, I am amazed by how they manage the flow of people. It just never seems overly crowded. There are three thousand people jammed into a single venue for seven full days. They are eating, playing, sleeping, and sightseeing. Yet nothing seems overly rushed or crowded. Compare that to any single trip to the Post

Office or a doctor's office. And these are places everyone goes for basically the same function."

"I agree, Tommaso. You also get more bang for your buck on a cruise. Sylvia and I travelled extensively, but we always agreed that a cruise was our favorite."

"I can't even imagine if my Marie would have liked this. She was so young. We never really travelled. I worked a lot. Once my son started school, she was alone a lot."

"That's not uncommon. Sylvia and I were deeply in love. We got married and love quickly became responsibility. For the next twenty-some years, we were soldiers, workers, parents, cooks, repairmen, seamstresses, you name it. Family was our identity."

"Yet it seems that you remained in love."

"It wasn't so easy. When the kids left, we were different people. We barely knew each other. We were more like co-workers. Luckily, we fell in love all over again."

"It seems that you were quite fortunate."

"I'll say. Do you know how hard it is to find a good seamstress these days?"

"I was just at the same crossroads with my Marie when the cancer came. I spent nearly all of the last year with her, but I would change anything for one week more."

"That's the problem, my friend. We just don't get to make those decisions."

"I suppose not."

"Tommaso, do you mind if I ask you a question?"

"Not at all."

"What type of work did you do?"

"I suppose that you could say that I was a business manager."

"I thought as much. Problem solving, conflict resolution, that sort of thing?"

Tommaso props himself up to look at Larry.

"Oh, don't worry, Tommaso. You're secret's safe with me."

"Have we met before?"

"No, nothing like that. I'm an engineer by trade, but spent nearly my entire career in high-level construction. I've dealt with every level of your kind of 'management' over the years. I just wanted to verify that the old sniffer was still working. I actually had you pegged ten minutes into the first dinner."

Larry taps the side of his nose. Tommaso nods and lies back in his chair.

"You'll be happy to know that your sniffer is spot on. I assume I can rely on your discretion?"

"You don't reach our age without discretion. I just find it amusing."

"How so?"

"What portion of your business was illegal? I don't care what it was, just a proportion."

"Okay, Larry, I'd say between twenty and thirty percent."

"It was at least forty in the construction game. One point for me."

"Did you hurt people?" asks Tommaso.

"I suppose we did. We wiped out other contractors financially. Foreclosures were not uncommon. There were certainly bribes and blackmail. We rarely resorted to physical violence, but certainly caused several union battles. We may have even encouraged a few suicides."

"Is there a point to this?"

"Have you killed anyone?"

Tommaso exhales, realizing that he's going to have to wait for Larry to get to his point.

"No, not personally, but my list is similar to yours. My hands are unclean."

"I have, you see. I killed at least a half dozen men during the war. I don't know if they were all soldiers."

"We all do some reckoning, particularly at our age, Larry. War is all about killing."

"You're missing my point, I think. I am considered a hero, you, a criminal. I meet you, and I see myself."

"You didn't go to war to be a hero. Neither of us went to work to be a criminal. We are all patriots or at least loyalists to somebody. Other than money, what would you say was your greatest motivation for your life choices?"

"The protection and security of my family and other loved ones."

"See, I would have the exact answer, and would either of us respect a different one? Forget the titles. We made our choices in spite of them, and would you change any of them looking back?"

"That's what frightens me. I don't think I would. Yet, when I think of a hero, I think of Paul and not me. He sold electronics and still had a wife and family. The worst he ever did to anyone was to sell them a bad TV or soaked them on a refrigerator repair. Nobody died. Nobody lost their livelihood."

"Many lost some dignity, and who's to say that's not as bad. I certainly can't absolve you. We paid our taxes, just like Paul."

"Taxes? Is that what you two lazy slugs have been yapping about while I was doing ten laps around the track?" asks Paul, as he walks over to his deck chair. "I beat the IRS like a drum when I was in business. C'mon, fellas, let's take a dip."

Tommaso and Larry end their conversation and climb up out of their chairs to join Paul in the pool.

Grandpa enters the cabin and immediately sees the tube on Elmo's bed. He cannot find a note so he checks his watch for the time. It is twelve-thirty, so he decides to change and wash up for lunch. Grandpa looks in the closet and sighs. He takes out a shirt, one of the flowered ones purchased for him by Ramona.

After getting dressed, he sits on his bed and looks again at the tube. He shrugs and picks it up. After unlatching the lid, he pops it open and looks inside. He slides out the object and unrolls it. It is a painting that appears to be original. While he is examining it, Elmo comes into the room.

"Hey, Grandpa, I'm starved. You ready for lunch?"

"Elmo, what is this?"

"What is it? How should I know? It looks like a painting and a pretty shitty one if you ask me."

"Where did you get it?"

Elmo sees the open tube and realizes that the painting came from inside.

"Oh, is that what was in the tube? I never opened it. I picked it up for a friend in Cozumel. Somebody was supposed to pick it up at security but no one did, so I brought it back here. I figured I'd find Olivia and give it to her later, maybe after the show tonight. Is something wrong?"

"I'm sure it's nothing, but something seems odd here. You'd better tell me the whole story, and don't leave out any details."

"Gee, Grandpa, anything you say, but can we discuss it over lunch?"

"I don't see why not, but first, I need you to get Jameson."

"There's a call button on the phone for the room steward. I'll call."

Elmo picks up the phone and hits the appropriate button while Grandpa returns the painting to the tube and closes the latch. In just a moment, there is a knock on the door. Elmo opens it and a steward other than Jameson is standing there.

"How may I help you?"

"Is Jameson available?" asks Grandpa.

The young man hesitates for a moment seeming unsure.

"He is just now going off duty," he says. "I may be able to catch him."

The young steward runs off down the hall. A moment later, he comes back with Jameson.

"Please excuse my young assistant," says Jameson. "Louis is only on his third sailing. He is here to assist you when I am not available. How may we serve you?"

"I need only you at the moment," says Grandpa.

Jameson nods to Louis, who immediately scurries off to other duties. Jameson comes in and Elmo closes the door.

"I need this put in a safe place for a little while," says Grandpa. "I will consider this a personal favor. Do you know what I mean?"

"I do, and no one including myself will know the contents."

"Thank you, Jameson. That's all for now."

Jameson takes the tube and leaves.

"What the hell was that all about?" asks Elmo.

"I know what he is, just as he knows what I am."

"What the hell does that mean?"

"Elmo, what's with all the questions? Didn't you say you were starving?"

Elmo begins to speak, but just shrugs and closes his mouth as they head for the Embarcadero.

Tuesday, Oct 28th
~ Fiesta Mambo, Deck 5, Teatro Real ~

Vijay walks toward the dressing area underneath the stage at the back of the theater. He is startled by the loud start of a motor, as the lift controlling the movable center of the stage engages. Vijay has to hop out of the way as the scissoring mechanism begins to slide open allowing the stage to drop.

"Hey, watch out!" shouts one of the stage techs. "You trying to get crushed?"

Vijay makes some sort of gesture that would be offensive in India. As he turns back toward the dressing room, he runs smack into Olivia.

"I just got off my shift," he says. "Where the hell were you? You'd better have my package."

"You should already have it. Like I told you, I sent somebody else. Like I also told you, they were to give you the package when they reboarded."

"Well they didn't. Are you sure they went? Are you sure they came back?"

"Look, Vijay, I can't be sure of anything. I was here all morning and I need to get some sleep."

"Who did you get to do it? Who else besides the dancers got shore leave today?"

"The passengers."

"What? You sent a passenger? What the hell were you thinking?"

"I was thinking about getting you off my back once and for all. I'm sure he did what I asked. I told him to go to the aft screening line like I always do."

"Well, no one showed…wait, damn! There was a problem. Maybe he came in when the old lady spilled her fifty bottles of hot sauce. What was the name of the passenger?"

"His name is Elmo."

"Elmo? Seriously? Elmo what?"

"I don't know his last name."

"How about a cabin number?"

"Sorry."

"Do you have any idea what's at stake here? You're going to get us both killed. Elmo's not a common name. If I can access the passenger database in security, I can find his room. Maybe the package is there. Go back to your room. If I can't find this guy, I'll come find you. Think about how you can find him. Wait, this had better not be some kind of double cross."

"Double cross of what? I don't even know anyone in the scam but you. I just want to go home."

Tuesday, Oct 28th
~ Fiesta Mambo, Deck 11, The Embarcadero ~

Elmo places his hand under the hand sanitizer dispenser as he and Grandpa leave the buffet area. A mechanical buzz precedes a squirt of Purell into his palm. He rubs his hands together and shakes them to dry.

"That's absolutely everything?" asks Grandpa. "You left no detail out?"

"No, Grandpa, you got it all, three times! Now can you explain your obsessive interest in this? And what was that thing with Jameson?"

"In my business, or at least my former business, you constantly assess people. You can take my word for it. Jameson is involved in illegal activity and is quite high up in the chain."

"That's insane. I'm not saying that you don't have special insight, but a Jamaican cabin boy?"

"I can also assure you that he knows the same about me."

Elmo stares at him for a moment.

"Okay, whatever," he says. "What about the painting. I told you it was a gift. It's a picture of watermelons, for God's sake."

"It appears to be real," says Grandpa.

"So?"

"The story is suspect. You say it was a gift because you were told it was a gift."

"Yeah, so why would she lie about that?"

"I'm not saying she is lying. I'm just saying that if she were, it is the best lie to tell. It's simple, credible, and cannot be refuted."

"The same could be said of the truth."

As they turn the corner onto the corridor toward their cabin, a young blond man in an officer's uniform purposefully strides passed them down the hallway. Elmo jerks a thumb in his direction.

"Want me to get you an ice cream?" he asks.

Before Grandpa can even crack a smile, they see the young man stop at their cabin door and knock vigorously.

"May I help you?" asks Grandpa, as they walk up to the cabin.

"Are you Mr. Tommaso Pastor?" asks the officer in a thick Scandinavian accent.

Elmo notes from his nametag that he is 3rd Lieutenant Kjell Brekken from Norway.

"Yes, I am," says Grandpa.

"May I see your Dance Card, sir?" asks the officer.

Grandpa hands him the card. The officer checks to see that he is indeed speaking with Tommaso Pastor and hands him back the card along with an envelope.

"This is from the Captain," he says, before giving a quick nod and striding away.

Elmo and Grandpa enter the cabin and Grandpa tosses the letter onto his bed.

"Aren't you going to open it?" asks Elmo.

"In a moment. First things first. The painting escapade is in a word, 'fishy'. If it is nothing, than we have only placed someone's property into safekeeping. If not, then someone has involved my grandson in a criminal enterprise without his knowledge."

"All I did was pick it up. I didn't even know what it was."

"Will that convince the feds? Art theft is federal. Actually, we are not in the states. This could involve Interpol or worse."

"Worse?"

"Yes, much worse. Local authority. If you think American law enforcement is corrupt, you should try the foreigners, particularly Mexico and the Caribbean countries."

"Gee, Grandpa, I'm sorry."

"It's okay, Elmo. We're cautious and we go step by step. We never panic. It might still be nothing."

Grandpa reaches for the envelope and opens it.

"Well this is an unexpected surprise," he says.

"What now?" asks Elmo.

"It seems that we've been invited to dine with the Captain this evening."

Elmo throws up his hands.

"Who the hell *are* you?" he asks.

"Sometimes I'm not sure myself."

"Maybe I shouldn't go."

"Why not?"

"I'm Milton Spiezle, remember?"

"Oh my, yes. Going alone might raise curiosity, too."

"What about Sarah? She'd probably love it."

"She might at that. Are you sure you don't mind? More importantly, can you stay out of trouble?"

"I can't even tell when I'm in trouble."

Grandpa laughs and pats Elmo on the shoulder. He then picks up the cabin phone.

"Then it's settled," says Grandpa. "Show me how this phone works."

Olivia is awakened by someone banging on her door. She turns on the light, slips on her robe, and opens the door. Vijay pushes his way in and closes the door behind him.

"You never got the package, you lying bitch!"

"Vijay, I swear, I sent this guy Elmo to get it. I thought you could look up his room number."

"I did, bitch. There is nobody named Elmo on this ship."

"He's definitely on board, I can assure you. He's a young guy with bright red hair. I know he's traveling with his grandfather."

"Do you know his name?"

"Why would I know that?"

Vijay grabs Olivia by both arms and throws her roughly on the bed.

"Ow! Keep your hands off me. I know what he looks like. Can't we look at the pictures of the people who got off the ship this morning?"

Vijay thinks for a minute.

"I can, but you can't. I can't get you into the security area. And I don't know what he looks like."

"What about the photographers. They get everyone as they exit the ship. If we got to the photo area---"

"We can go through them together. Once I have his face, I can match it with the database. Get some clothes on. We've got to go right now, before my next duty."

"The only reason I'm doing this is to be done with you, prick."

Olivia grabs some clothes and goes into the bathroom to get dressed. Soon they are walking up to the service counter at the Photo Shop. A rather severe looking woman is operating a computer.

"Svetlana," says Vijay, "I need to look at the photos taken of the passengers getting off of the ship this morning."

Svetlana looks around to make sure there are no passengers within earshot.

"Why don't you go fuck yourself? If this was official business they would send someone important."

"Look, I'm not the one giving you Russians any grief."

Svetlana points to her nametag.

"No Russia. Belarus. Since you Indians take over security, you give everybody grief. Why should I help you? You can push around little girls like this one, but not me."

"It will just take a minute."

"What's in it for me?"

"What do you want?"

"You have access to sat phone, no? Next week is my son's birthday. I want one hour call to home. It cost too much from port."

"Okay, deal. Can you queue up the pictures of the people getting off the boat this morning?"

She hits a few buttons on the keyboard.

"Just first two hours. The rest are not loaded, yet."

She pulls up the information and motions them to the screen.

"Just click here to scroll through," she says.

Almost immediately Olivia grabs his arm.

"Stop, go back! Right there. That's him. See, he was one of the first people off the ship. I told you he did it."

Vijay stares at Elmo's picture for a moment.

"All right. He should be easy to find. I'll match him up to the people getting off. That will give me a name and a cabin number, assuming you're telling me the truth."

Vijay heads toward the stairs leaving Olivia behind. She gives Svetlana a smile and small wave. She receives only an icy stare in return.

Tuesday, Oct 28th
~ Fiesta Mambo, Conquistador Lounge ~

"I'm so excited, Tommaso," says Sarah. "I really appreciate your asking me. Are you sure that I'm dressed alright?"

"You look lovely, Sarah," says Tommaso. "The invitation said cruise casual, whatever that may be. I'm sure we'll be fine. Have any of you ever dined with a Captain before?"

"I have a couple of times," says Paul, "and Larry has, too. It used to be more common. Just like in the Love Boat, the Captain had a large table in the dining room, mostly for friends, high rollers, and muckety-mucks."

"In more recent years," says Alice, "the Captains tend to stay in their cabins, since being in the dining room was such a distraction. Now, they can add two tables for more passengers times two seatings."

"From what I understand, this is pretty rare," says Larry. "Do you have any idea why you might have been invited?"

"None whatsoever," says Tommaso. "Maybe I won some sort of a lottery."

"Are you absolutely sure that Elmo doesn't want to go?" asks Sarah. "I feel awful taking his place."

"He absolutely insisted," says Tommaso. "You can ask him yourself in a few minutes. I think you got him hooked on the trivia contests. He's doing the Sports Trivia contest right now."

"Why do you think we came here for our cocktail?" asks Paul. "We don't know enough about sports."

"Tommaso," says Alice, "the four of us are going on an excursion tomorrow in Grand Cayman. It's a bus tour, so there is very little walking. Are you sure you don't want to come with us? I'm sure that you can still get on the tour."

"Thank you for the invitation," says Tommaso, "but I promised my grandson that I would spend some time with him, at least until he gets a better offer."

At that moment, Elmo comes into the bar followed by four young boys. Each of them is wearing one of the cruise ship medallions. The boys are excited and full of energy, but are also being quiet and respectful of the other patrons.

"Hey, folks," says Elmo. "As you can see, we won! Hey, come over here, guys."

The boys, who were all looking out of the windows from this highest vantage point on the ship, come over. Elmo begins the introductions.

"This is Jerrell and this is his brother, Duane. They are my basketball partners from the other day. These are their cousins, Earl and Desmond. These guys know a lot about sports. Guys, this is my grandfather and his friends."

"It's a pleasure to meet you," says Jerrell, apparently representing the group. "Elmo got all the old questions."

"Yeah," says Elmo, "real old, like anything from before 2005."

"Elmo, dear," says Sarah, "are you sure that it's okay that I go with Tommaso?"

"Absolutely," says Elmo. "The boys and I are hitting the buffet tonight. I'm giving their parents a chance for a nice quiet dinner in the one of the specialty restaurants. Come on, dudes, it's time for dinner. High fives!"

The boys all give Elmo a slap on the hand as they hurry toward the stairs.

"I guess we'd better mosey on down as well," says Paul. "You two have fun with the Captain. The ship docks at nine-thirty and we have to be off right away for our excursion. How about if we meet in the Embarcadero for breakfast at eight? I want to hear all about your dinner."

"That sounds perfect," says Tommaso. "Elmo, have a nice dinner with your friends. Can you meet me back in the cabin around nine?"

"Sure, Grandpa, assuming you're not steering the ship."

Tuesday, Oct 28th
~ Fiesta Mambo, Deck 9 ~

Vijay looks both ways down the corridor before entering stateroom 9368. He systematically begins searching Grandpa and Elmo's cabin for evidence of the painting. Having no luck in the closet or bathroom, he drops to his knees to look under the beds.

He hears a voice say, "Can I help you find anything?"

Vijay jerks his head up suddenly, nearly knocking himself unconscious on the bed frame. He rolls over and in between seeing stars, makes out the silhouette of someone standing in the doorway. Jameson is leaning against the doorframe with his arms folded.

Vijay awkwardly staggers to his feet rubbing his head. Jameson coolly looks at his fingernails.

"Get lost, Jameson. I'm on official business."

"I'm sure you are, but I am as well. Do you think that those towel animals fold themselves? It's bunny night. The ears can be quite tricky, you know."

"I told you to get lost."

"If you tell me what you are looking for, I may be able to assist you. A steward is always ready to assist."

Vijay stops to think for a moment. Maybe Jameson knows something.

"One of these two passengers is about twenty-five years old. His passport says he's eighty-one. He may also be using an assumed name."

"I have seen very little of Mr. Pastor and Mr. Spiezle."

Jameson is giving nothing away, which further angers Vijay.

"I'm looking for a package. It's a black tube about this big with a strap on it."

He holds his hands a couple of feet apart.

"A tube you say? What is in this tube?"

"None of your fucking business. That's what's in the tube. Have you seen it or not?"

"If I do not know the contents, how will I be sure it is the correct tube?"

Vijay already regrets mentioning the tube to Jameson. He rubs his head some more. This time, he looks at his hand to verify that he isn't bleeding.

"Just forget it, alright?"

"I do not believe that I have seen such a tube. Should I come across it, of course I will immediately inform your superiors in security."

"Look, I said to forget it. Just forget you ever saw me. You might need a favor from me someday, understand?"

"I suppose we could all occasionally use a favor. How are you at making towel animals?"

Vijay glares at Jameson. He pushes by him and storms out of the door. Jameson takes two of the towels and begins folding.

Tuesday, Oct 28th
~ Fiesta Mambo, Deck 11, Captain's Cabin ~

Tommaso knocks on the door marked Private – Crew Only. It is opened by a man in uniform. Tommaso shows the young officer his invitation and is led through some passageways to the Captain's quarters. Upon entering, they are greeted by a steward, and led to what can best be described as a living room. It is well appointed and has a surprisingly non-nautical theme. There are three others present.

"Hello, my name is Stewart Baskin, and this is my wife, Helen. We are celebrating our fiftieth anniversary and were fortunate enough to be invited to dinner by the Captain."

"I'm sure that being in the El Dorado Club didn't hurt," says Helen.

My name is Tommaso, and this is my friend Sarah," says Tommaso. "I am unfamiliar with the El Dorado Club."

"It's the highest level of the Fiesta Line's loyalty program. It means that we have been on over one hundred cruises."

"Wow," says Sarah, "this is our first."

"Really?" says Stewart. "You must be somebody pretty important, then. Few El Dorado members get to dine with the Captain. Oh, let me introduce you to Ted Pratt. Ted, this is Tommaso and Sarah. Ted's on the Fiesta Board of Directors."

"It's a pleasure to meet you," says Ted. "I'm just here checking on my investment."

"Funny guy," says Stewart. "Ted here sold his tech company for several millions of dollars and now cruises around in the VIP suites on all of the ships. Not a bad gig, if you ask me."

Tommaso is glad that the conversation has shifted to Ted since he has no explanation as to why he's here. A moment later, the Captain comes in wearing a casual version of his uniform.

"Welcome to my home," he says. "For those of you who have not previously met me, I am Captain Stefano Bacigalupo. You may call me Stefano, but I would prefer Captain, outside of my home, if you don't mind. I have been Captain of this ship for nearly six years."

Everyone shakes hands, although it is evident that he has previously met the others.

"Please join me in my dining room," says the Captain.

They move to a small, but elegant dining room which is beautifully decorated. The table is set much as the tables in the dining room, other than a much more expensive centerpiece. It is a rectangular table for eight that is set for six. Sarah sits to the Captain's left with Tommaso next to her. Helen sits to the Captain's right with Stewart on her other side. Ted takes the remaining seat across from the Captain.

The waiter pours champagne and slips out of the room.

"Mr. and Mrs. Baskin," says the Captain, "I believe that we are celebrating a very special occasion. I would like to make a toast to commemorate your fiftieth anniversary and you're loyalty to the Fiesta Cruise line. *Cento di questi giorni!*"

"Salute," says Tommaso, as everyone takes a drink.

Sarah leans in toward Tommaso and whispers.

"What did that mean?"

"May you live a hundred years," says Tommaso.

The waiter deftly delivers each course in the traditional Italian dinner style. While they eat, there is lively conversation.

"No, this is actually quite rare," says the Captain. "On most voyages, I do not have any meals with the passengers. I use this room mostly for meetings with my officers."

"I really love your artwork," says Sarah. "Did you choose it yourself?"

"Sadly, no. Most of it is chosen by the same cabal that decorated the ship. It's fine, as I'm not much of a connoisseur. I do have a few personal pieces in the next room."

"Such as the bust on your divan?" asks Tommaso.

"Ah, you noticed that. Yes, I do have a bust of Benito Mussolini. I assure you, that I am no fascist, nor do I purport to be a dictator even though there are certain parallels to a ship Captain. I am a student of Italian history, and Mussolini's success as a leader has been somewhat lost to his political failings."

"They were pretty big failings," says Stewart.

"Perhaps," says the Captain, "but he would not have gone headlong into world war at the speed of Hitler and the Germans. Much of his movement was positive domestically. I'm not sure what might have happened if the Axis showed more restraint. Hitler forced his hand. But let's not speak of politics."

After another delicious course, Ted discusses his good fortune in business.

"The downside is that I spent a lot of time working, so much so that I never took out time for a family. When I turned fifty, I cashed out and started living my life. That was a little over twelve years ago. I've had many adventures."

"But what good is it, if you're all alone?" asks Helen.

"Oh, I've had plenty of romantic adventures as well, including a couple of marriages. I'm just between them at the moment."

"You should visit the casino," says the Captain. "Our stock has been a little sluggish as I'm sure you know. We could use the money."

"I wish I could help you, Stefano," says Ted, "but gambling is one vice I stay away from."

"Interesting," says Tommaso. "I have a friend that you should meet."

"Normally, I would politely decline, but I am intrigued by someone who makes it to the Captain's table on his first cruise. Perhaps we can meet for a drink at some point."

"I would like that, Ted," says Tommaso.

After dessert, the Captain raises his wine glass.

"I have a surprise for you. My second officer is going to escort you on a special tour of the restricted areas of the ship, including the bridge. Tommaso, if you do not mind, I would like you to remain here with me for a few moments."

Tommaso looks to Sarah, who nods.

"That would be an honor," says Tommaso.

"I am going to pass on the tour," says Ted, "as I was present during the construction of the ship. Tommaso, here is my cabin information. I'd like to invite you and Sarah for a drink tomorrow evening. If you give me your stateroom number, I will leave you a message with the details."

"Of course, and it was a pleasure meeting you, Ted."

Ted shakes the Captain's hand and heads out. Sarah, Stuart, and Helen are led away by an officer for their tour.

The Captain leads Tommaso into his living room and pours two glasses of Limoncello. Tommaso nods in approval as the Captain hands him a glass. They touch glasses and take a drink.

"I know who you are," says the Captain.

"I suspected as much, but you, are unfamiliar to me, Stefano."

"We have never met. You knew my father. You would know him as Frank Bacigal. His name was Americanized at Ellis Island."

"From the docks."

"Yes, you have a good memory. He went to America shortly after my birth to find work. My mother received letters from him almost daily. She saved them all. I actually still have them in storage."

"This must be fifty years ago."

"More. He told my mother of you preventing him from getting involved in crime and how you got him a job on the docks as a stevedore. He said that you saw something in him."

"I most certainly did. Some people are not cut out for certain things. I could tell this of your father. If I recall, he proved me right by moving up quickly and became important in the union."

"Indeed. He was able to send us enough money for me to go to good schools. I joined the Navy and moved up quickly. He was able to use his connections to get me started on the crew of a cargo ship."

"You must have been very talented to have achieved this."

"I suppose that I was, but my father always mentioned in his letters his debt to you for getting him started. He met many others of our countrymen over the years that were not so fortunate to have such a benefactor."

"Grazie, grazie, but how did you know I was on board?"

"Like you, I imagine, part of my success is a result of attention to detail. I usually peruse the manifest before a cruise. No real reason, as it contains thousands of names. I'm not sure that I ever caught an individual name before. Through some level of serendipity, I just caught the name of Tommaso Pastor. Quite frankly, it is more of a thrill to me than if Mussolini himself were on board."

"I am honored."

"If there is anything you require while on my ship, you only need to name it. My entire senior crew will be so informed."

Sarah and the others return from their tour, and she is grinning from ear to ear. Everyone says their goodbyes and are led out by a junior officer. Once in the hall Sarah stops Tommaso and gives him a kiss on the cheek.

"I drove the ship!"

"I'm sorry I missed it."

"You are a most unusual man, Tommaso. What did the Captain want?"

"It seems that I knew his father many years ago."

"And you didn't know that when you picked this cruise?"

"I had no idea who the Captain was until just a few moments ago. That is the honest truth. An amazing coincidence to be sure."

"Well, you have proven to be pretty amazing. I hope that Elmo won't be upset when he hears about it."

"Elmo will be fine."

They head toward Olvera Street to see if they can find the others.

"Helen said that Ted is staying in the nicest suite on the ship," says Sarah. "It's two stories and has a grand piano in it. Do you think that we might get to see it?"

"I am concerned that your next cruise will be quite a letdown from this one."

"Why would I ever need to go on another cruise?"

"I was expecting it to be more restful, but I am having a wonderful time."

"Hey, Grandpa!" shouts Elmo as he runs up to them. "I just got rid of the kids. Their parents were very grateful. The others are down at the other end in the bar. I just ran into them."

"I am going to go sit with them, Tommaso. I just can't wait until morning to tell them all about it. Would you join me?"

"Actually, I'm going to call it a night, Sarah. I have some business to attend to with Elmo. I will see you at breakfast, however."

"I'm looking forward to it. Thank you again so much, Tommaso."

She heads aft toward the bar, and Elmo and Tommaso head toward the elevators.

"She seemed awfully excited," says Elmo. "I guess you guys had a good time."

"It was interesting, to say the least."

Tuesday, Oct 28th
~ Fiesta Mambo, Deck 9 ~

Elmo opens the cabin door and turns on the light.

"Hey, Grandpa, we got two animals tonight," he says.

On Elmo's bed sits a bunny made out of folded towels. On Grandpa's bed, lies a snake.

"Jeez, Grandpa, you make friends everywhere you go, don't ya?"

"There appears to be a note in its mouth," says Grandpa.

Elmo picks up the note and hands it to his grandfather.

"Maybe it's a cottonmouth," says Elmo. "Get it?"

"Yes, I get it. Am I expected to laugh now?"

"It wouldn't kill you. Why are you always so serious?"

Grandpa hands him the note. It simply says 'Call 1134, J'.

"Jameson?" asks Elmo.

"Hand me the phone."

Grandpa calls and Jameson is at their cabin in ten minutes carrying the tube in a rolled up bedcover. He describes his encounter with Vijay, the security guard. He also lets them know that Vijay is aware of the discrepancy in their ages.

"And there's no possibility that this could be any sort of standard security practice?" asks Grandpa.

"Absolutely not. The security *batty creases* will push around the crew, but are very strict in their dealings with the passengers. Vijay is definitely up to something."

"Batty what?" asks Elmo.

"What you call an asshole," says Jameson.

"Speaking of which," says Elmo, "why did you bring the tube back here?"

"That was the right move," says Grandpa. "It's not Jameson's risk and they've already searched here, so they have no reason to come back. Worst case, we can always throw it overboard. We have to assume it has some value."

"Why do you assume 'they' and not 'him'?" asks Elmo.

"I cannot be sure, but this Vijay doesn't sound smart enough to be in charge of anything."

"You've got that right," says Jameson. "How can I help you?"

"I'm out of my element on this ship. I need an explanation of ship's protocol among the crew."

Jameson explains the various factions on the ship. Security is mostly controlled by the Indians. Food service is more of a mixed bag, but has a high percentage of East

Asians. The Russians and Eastern Europeans control most of the bar services and photography. Africans and Caribbean Islanders do most of the cleaning and housekeeping. The performers and Cruise Director's staff are mostly from Canada, England, and Australia, but are not a factor in the ship's hierarchy.

"Jameson, I need to go off the ship tomorrow and make some inquiries. Do you know where I can get a secure telephone line to the U.S.?"

Jameson grabs a pad and pen from the side of the combination vanity and desk. He writes down some information and hands the note to Grandpa.

"Go to this address. It is a grocery store. Read exactly what is on the paper to the proprietor. He will get you what you need. The minutes are expensive, but he will not take advantage of you. You'll need American dollars. Five hundred will be more than enough. You can get it from the Purser's office before you leave the ship."

"Is this number the best way to get a hold of you?"

"That, or you may pass anything through Fabrice at your dinner table. He is loyal to me."

"I still have no idea if I have anything to be concerned about. I hope to know more tomorrow. Thank you for your help, Jameson."

Jameson leaves and Tommaso sits down on his bed.

"How do you find such interesting people?" asks Elmo.

"Hand me the tube, the pad, and the pen. I have some work to do."

"What can I do?"

"Stay out of trouble. Do you have plans for tomorrow?"

"I told Melody after cocktails, that I would accompany her and Shana to the beach in George Town. I figured I might as well go to a Caribbean beach if I came all this way. I'll just cancel."

"No, Elmo, you should go. This may get more intense. I don't need you yet, so you may as well relax."

"Sure, relax. No problem."

Grandpa ignores him. He unrolls the painting and begins to study it carefully. Elmo turns to get into bed and sees the terrycloth bunny.

"What the fuck are you looking at?"

Grandpa and Elmo meet their group for breakfast. They each relate their previous evening's events in the Dining Room and in the Captain's quarters. Tommaso, of course leaves out any personal details.

"You should definitely go visit this fellow Ted," says Paul, "if for no other reason than to see the VIP suite. Alice, Larry, and I have seen some on other ships. Talk about fancy!"

"I notice that you did not mention Sarah," says Tommaso, with a sly smile. "I hope that you can join me if the opportunity arises."

Sarah smiles broadly.

"Only if it won't be an imposition," she says. "I thought you might bring Melody."

"It's still a thought. I expect that Ted might be just her type. Speaking of which, aren't she and Shana meeting us this morning?"

"I believe that they are meeting us at the debarkation deck at nine-fifteen," says Alice. "It seems they do room service for breakfast on most days. I'd guess we'd better get going."

When they arrive at Deck 2 to debark for George Town, Melody and Shana are waiting. Melody is dressed for the beach, but Shana is dressed like the others, wearing shorts and a blouse. Elmo can't recall seeing her in a bathing suit. Maybe they don't wear them in New Mexico.

As they are heading off the ship, both Elmo and Grandpa are surprised that they are getting onto a smaller boat rather than onto a pier.

"We don't dock at the island?" asks Elmo.

"No," says Paul. "We're taking what's called a tender. Some ports aren't deep enough for cruise ships. You really are new at this."

"The water looks a little rough," says Alice. "Let's sit in the lower level if possible. I wouldn't want any of us to leave our breakfast behind."

When they get on board the tender, the bottom is nearly full, so Elmo and Larry go up top.

"I like it better up here," says Larry. "I like the sun and wind."

"You're not worried about your breakfast?" asks Elmo.

"Damn the burritos, full speed ahead," says Larry, with a flourish of his hand, "although that joke might worked better after lunch."

"No, it was good, Larry. I almost lost *my* breakfast."

About five minutes into the ride, Elmo slides over on the bench seat to speak to Larry.

"Larry, if you don't mind me saying so, you look a little down. You didn't say a word at breakfast."

"Thank you for noticing, son. I mean that in a good way. This is my first cruise without Sylvia. Everyone has been great, but sometimes, well, it's just not the same."

Elmo is now unsure that he should have said anything. He pats Larry on the shoulder and Larry gives him a smile and a nod. Soon the tender is pulling up to the pier. Once the crew secures it, they head for the stairs.

After they all get off of the tender vessel, they make their way to the end of the port. Alice, Sarah, Paul, and Larry meet up with their bus tour group, while the rest head for the taxis. Grandpa bids Elmo goodbye, arranging to meet on board for a late lunch. He briefly speaks with a driver who opens the door of his cab. Grandpa gets in and they leave.

Melody goes up to a different driver and says "Seven Mile Beach?"

Melody and Shana get into the back seat and Elmo gets in the front. After they head toward Bay Road, Melody gets the driver's attention.

"I'd like you to stop at the National Gallery along the way."

Elmo notices a moment of frustration on the cabby's face. He looks in the mirror for a moment to size up his passenger.

"Dat is very out of the way," he says.

"No it's not," says Melody, in a strong tone. "It's a short detour onto Esterly Tibbetts Highway just ahead."

The cabby knows that he has missed his opportunity and lets out a small grunt.

"Yes, ma'am," he says.

When he pulls in front of the museum, Shana gets out.

"I'll see you back on the ship," she says, and heads toward the museum.

"Driver, is there still nothing in between the Avalon and the Harbour Heights?" asks Melody.

The cabby smiles.

"Just trees, ma'am, and the beach."

"Take us there."

"If I may say so, it is easier to access the beach from the Avalon."

"Then the Avalon it is. Will I be able to get a cab back from there?"

"Not a problem, ma'am. You can ask in the lobby, but there is usually somebody hanging around."

The cabby turns and smiles at Elmo, who is too confused to respond.

They arrive at the Avalon, which appears to be a nice complex of beach villas. Melody pays the driver and adds a healthy gratuity. She and Elmo walk down a path along the side of the property to the beach.

Elmo is stunned by the beauty of the beach. The sand is nearly pure white and the blue of the water defies description. The beach to their left is sparsely populated and has several green umbrellas up next to chaises with matching green cushions. Melody leads Elmo toward the right where there is a completely empty stretch of beach backed by a stand of trees. A few hundred yards ahead is another resort beach, presumably, the Harbor Heights.

~~~~~~~~~~

Grandpa exits his cab and pays the driver. He walks toward a ramshackle building which is supposed to be a market. He goes in, completes his transaction and walks out with a cell phone. It is not new, but it is untraceable and is loaded with enough minutes to make the calls that he needs to.

Grandpa finds another cab and goes to a park near the pier. He finds a bench in a quiet spot and sits down. He punches in the code and number necessary to call his son's home.

Robert is reading the paper when the house phone rings. He's on the couch in his robe with nothing underneath. He's sitting on a towel and has an ointment applied to his still raw inner thighs. They rarely get calls on this phone other than phone solicitors, but Robert shrugs and picks it up.

"Hello?"

"Robert, it's your father."

"Papa? Why are you calling on the house phone? Wait, are you and Elmo all right?"

"Robert, you need to listen. I have limited time. Elmo and I are fine. I am on a secure line, and only remembered this number. I'm fortunate to find you at home."

"I had a minor, um, injury. I'll be back at the nursery in a few days."

"Nothing serious I hope."

"No, nothing a little Neosporin won't fix. What do you need?"

"This may sound odd. Do you know anything about art?"

"Not really, but I assume this is about something more than aesthetics."

"Yes. I'm not yet sure, but we may have stumbled upon something involving stolen art. I need to talk to an expert."

"We?"

"Elmo is fine, but I want to keep it that way. Can you help me?"

"I can't think of anyone…wait, Ramona just told me about someone Tommy just met while visiting Pep. I can call her on my cell and find out. Can I call you back?"

"No, Son, but I can call you in ten minutes."

"Can you call on my cell?"

"Yes, but you'll have to give me the number. I do have a pen and paper."

Robert gives him the information and verifies that it was received. He hangs up and calls Ramona who is at the nursery.

"Yes, Robert. Let me call Tommy and get more information. I'll call you right back."

Ramona calls Tommy, but gets no answer. She thinks for a moment and calls Scotty. Scotty answers almost immediately.

"Mrs. Pastor? Is everything all right?"

"Yes Scotty, I'm sorry to call you at work, but I need to reach Tommy."

"It's okay, I just started a free period and I'm in the most secluded place in the building, the school Library. Let me try her and I'll connect you in the call."

After about a minute, Ramona hears both of their voices.

"Your mom just called me looking for you, Tommy."

"I know. I didn't feel like dealing with her. I'm sure it was nothing important."

"I guess you'd never know unless you picked up, would you?" asks Ramona.

"Mom? Jesus, sorry about that. What do you need?"

Scotty already knows that he is in for some serious shit when he returns home.

"I need to get your father on the line. How do I do that?"

"This is Scotty. Is Donny there? It would be easier if he showed you."

"Yes, he's here. Good thinking. Tommy, you said something about meeting an art expert in Boston."

"Yes, Brad, a friend of Pep's. I don't know if he's an expert, but he's minoring in it at Harvard."

"Good enough. Bring in Pep while I connect with your father. I'd call him myself, but apparently not all of my kids pick up when I call."

"I said I was sorry, Mom."

Scotty knows that he's going to be sorry.

Ramona calls Donny over and he shows her how to call her husband and link him to the call. Robert says his father will be calling in about three minutes and Donny walks him through the process to add Grandpa.

"Pep?" says Ramona, "Can you reach your friend Brad, the art expert?"

"What? I guess I can call him. Should I ask what this is about?"

At least four different people say 'no'.

"Okay, hang on," says Pep.

Pep calls Brad, who thankfully picks up.

"Do you have a few minutes?" asks Pep. "This is going to sound weird, but someone in my family has some urgent art related questions."

"I'm not sure I ever heard an urgent art question," says Brad, "but I have a half hour before class."

Pep connects the calls and says, "Everybody, this is Brad. He's studying Art History at Harvard. Please identify yourselves in reverse order of this call."

"This is Tommy in Manhattan. We met last week."

"Scotty, the boyfriend in Newark."

"Hi, Brad. This is Ramona. I'm Pep's mother in Cedar Grove, New Jersey."

"This is Robert, Pep's father in Glen Ridge."

"Thank you for your time, Brad. My name is Tommaso. I am Robert's father and Pep's grandfather calling from George Town in Grand Cayman."

"Wow!" says Brad. "I thought this was a gag. How can I help?"

"In a nutshell," says Grandpa, "I have a painting that I believe to be authentic. I need to verify this."

"Um," says Brad, "that's not much to go on. What else can you tell me?"

"It is signed, but not completely legible. There is a first initial of 'R' with no period. The front leg of the 'R' sticks out somewhat horizontally. The last name begins with a 'T' and appears to end with a 'Y'. The intervening letters are few and none go above or below the line like 'h' or 'g'. If I had to guess I'd say that the name was rather short with the second letter being an 'a'."

Grandpa gives Brad the approximate size and describes the texture. He also mentions that it was obtained in Mexico.

"Alright, I can't think of who, so let's work on real vs. fake. Is there any border around the edge that's not painted?"

"Yes, about an inch, all the way around."

"Prints tend to be full canvas, so someone probably painted it. Oh, duh, what's it a picture of?"

"Watermelon slices."

"Like wedges? Does it look almost like a child's painting?"

"Yes, this helps?"

"Maybe. There's an artist named Rufino Tamayo, T-A-M-A-Y-O, but he usually leaves the 'O' off his signature in script, but not when he prints."

"It is signed."

"He also always does his 'R' with the leg sticking out."

"I don't believe this," mutters someone.

"Can I tell if it's real?"

"Hmm, maybe. He's copied a lot, since his work is not complex. He is Mexican and was big in the middle of last century. He died, I think in the nineties, and he was also in his nineties. His stuff has sold for more than a million. I sure hope you didn't steal it."

Brad laughs, but no one else makes a sound.

"I'm very impressed, Brad. You seem quite knowledgeable. Can it be authenticated?"

"You're more lucky that I am knowledgeable. I did an internship in Mexico, and even have been to the Rufino Tamayo Museum. There has also been an increase in stolen Mexican art as of late. As for authentication, I'm assuming an expert is out of the question."

"You would be correct."

"Okay, here's one thing you can try, but be very careful."

"Go on."

"Take a glass of water. Dip the unpainted edge of the canvas in and DO NOT get the paint wet. After about fifteen seconds, remove the canvas from the water and let it drip off. Wait one minute. Then smell the wet part of the canvas."

"Smell it? What am I smelling for?"

"If it's a fake, or recent, or a print, it will smell exactly like you would expect, probably either no odor, or like musty wet canvas. If it has a strong odor, kind of like cedar, it might be authentic, or at least old. The canvas used in Mexico back then was made of a different set of materials. If you get the odor, it's very old, and no one would have likely copied Tamayo that far back."

"You have been very helpful, Brad. I am in your debt. Now, can everyone get off the line except for Robert?"

Everyone disconnects in the middle of the call leaving only Brad and Pep on the northern end.

"Pep?" asks Brad, "are you still there?"

"Yes, Brad, and my grandfather was not kidding about being in your debt. I have no clue as to what that was all about, but he will find a way to make this up to you."

"Pep, I don't know what to say. Prior to this, I was really looking forward to dating you and getting to know you."

"And now?"

"And now, you had better be as cool as I think you are, because you have the most badass family ever and I want to marry them."

Back in the Cayman Islands, Grandpa continues his call with Robert.

"Robert, I'm going to need some money transferred to the account I'm using on the ship. I assume we have some accounts here in the Caymans."

"You watch too many movies, Papa. Everything's electronic now. What account are you using?"

Grandpa reads him some numbers.

"No problem, Papa. I can access that today. How much do you need?"

"One hundred thousand, no, make it one-fifty."

"Papa, do you need me to come down there?"

"No, Son. It's just a precaution."

"Please take care of my boy, Papa."

"You can count on me, son. Now I need one more thing. I need you to get the phone number of someone for me."

~~~~~~~~~~

"I thought Shana was coming with us," says Elmo.

"She's not much for the beach being from New Mexico. I'm glad you came with me. I wouldn't be able to do this alone."

"The cabby seemed irritated by the extra stop."

"He was just pissed off that I didn't tell him about the stop until we were underway. He'd have tried to scam me otherwise."

"Smart."

Melody picks a spot near the water that is equidistant from the two resorts. She lays out her towel and Elmo does the same. He sits down and looks out at the water. It is considerably calmer than the sea was in the tender. He remembers something about the word 'leeward' is his SAT studies.

After placing down her bag, Melody moves to the front of her towel into Elmo's periphery. She pulls off her long beachcover revealing a white bikini that Elmo is sure that he has seen on a Sports Illustrated cover. Melody is in AMAZING shape for a woman at any age.

She turns to face him and bends forward to reach into her bag. Elmo flinches as he fully expects Melody to fall out of her suit. She pulls out a can of sunscreen as Elmo reflects on the magical powers of Lycra. Melody liberally sprays herself and is glistening when she holds the can out to Elmo.

"Can you do my back, please?"

Elmo stands and takes the can. He sprays her back and neck.

"Thanks," she says. "Would you like me to do you?"

Elmo tries to come up with an appropriate response.

"Oh, just turn around," she says. "I'm not Mrs. Robinson."

"Huh?" asks Elmo as he turns around.

"Ugh, youth," she says as she sprays him. "Here, you should spray the rest of you. The sun is stronger here than where you live."

Elmo takes the can and applies the spray. He drops the can back into her bag and sits back onto his towel. Melody lies down on her back. She reaches for a string on her top and gives it a gentle tug. Her top pops open revealing a pair of surprisingly round and firm breasts.

"Can you hand me the can, please Elmo? I seem to have forgotten a couple of spots."

Elmo turns to reach for the can and sees her lying there. For a moment, he is too shocked to move. He reaches into the bag and fumbles for the can. He holds it out to her while diverting his eyes.

"Christ, Elmo. You're not going to tell me you've never seen a woman's breasts before. It's not like I'm asking you to rub it in. Be an adult."

She sprays herself to a high sheen and then tosses the can into the bag.

"No, it's not that," he says. "It's just that I've never been to a topless beach before."

"This isn't a topless beach. Why do you think we schlepped all the way here?"

"What do you mean, not a topless beach? I may be an amateur, but I'm pretty sure you're topless."

"It's illegal here."

"Illegal?"

"Yes, and highly frowned upon."

"Really? Do you mind telling me why you are flouting the law?"

"Mostly, to get an even tan, but I also am annoyed by the provincial attitude, particularly from the most corrupt bankers on the planet. You don't mind do you? It's not as though I had much covered anyway."

"I can't argue with that. I'll keep an eye out for the *Federales*."

Elmo lies down.

"Do you like what you see?"

"I'm assuming that we're not talking about the white sand or the blue ocean."

"No, silly. These were a gift from my third husband. I just want to be sure he made a wise investment. Oh, never mind. I can see that you approve."

"Jesus, Melody."

They lie undisturbed for about an hour. Melody sits up and begins to reassemble her top. She stands and looks out to the water.

"Come with me for a swim, Elmo."

Elmo opens one eye and sees that she is at least moderately covered.

"Aren't you a bit overdressed?"

"I can cover quickly on the beach. I don't want to tempt fate in the water."

"Fair enough."

Elmo gets up and they walk into the calm surf.

"It looks pretty safe out here," says Elmo.

"What if there is a shark or a sting ray?"

"What am I supposed to do if there is, punch it?"

"My hero."

"I can't believe how warm and clear this water is," says Elmo.

When he turns around, he sees that Melody is holding a piece of material with strings. He is about to ask why she removed her top when he realizes that she did not. He is confused for just a moment.

"Oh, shit," he says, as she reaches into his shorts.

"Help, shark!" she says.

Wednesday, Oct 29th
~ Fiesta Mambo, Port of George Town ~

Melody stops off for some shopping at the pier, so Elmo hops on the tender to return to the ship. He's wearing a t-shirt and basketball shorts. His hair is stiff and he smells of sweat and sunscreen. He asks a fellow passenger the time and knows that he will not have time for a shower or even to change before meeting his grandfather for lunch. At least he's hungry.

When he gets on the ship and goes through security, he sees an Indian officer staring at him. Assuming this is Vijay, his first reaction is to grin at him. Fortunately, the thought of sex with a woman in her sixties allows him to keep his grim façade.

Upon arriving at the Embarcadero, he finds Grandpa with the dinner crowd finishing their dessert and coffee.

"Hey there, Elmo," says Paul. "How was the beach?"

"I can only say that you should have been there," says Elmo.

"Did you see any wildlife?" asks Alice.

"Surprisingly wild, I'd have to say."

"These folks are heading off in a few minutes," says Tommaso. "Some are napping and some are going to a towel folding demonstration. Go get yourself some food, and I'll sit here with you while you eat. I want tell you about my day."

Elmo loads up a few plates with food and asks a waiter for three glasses of fruit punch. The waiter brings them over and is looking for the third party.

"These are all for me. Thank you."

The waiter leaves and Elmo turns to Grandpa.

"So what's up?" he asks.

"I'm ninety-five percent certain that we have stumbled onto something, although I'm still not sure what. From this point forward, we act as though nothing has happened. We give away nothing and continue to gather information."

"I understand that this is for my protection, but can you remind me why we just don't either throw the thing overboard or just give it back to them?"

"Either may be fine, and both options are still in play. On the other hand, we still do not know if you are in jeopardy and the object is the only real leverage we have."

"We're pretty vulnerable here at sea."

"I'm quite sure that so far, we are only dealing with underlings who are in a panic. They are motivated to work this out on their own. If the organization is set up correctly, then they aren't even sure of who to be afraid of. They may even suspect us of being part of the cabal."

"Jesus, didn't you retire? I think you love this shit."

"I don't need the stress any more than you, however I am good at this, so I compartmentalize it better."

"What if we just get off the ship in Jamaica in a couple days and fly home?"

"Also still an option, but the game is afoot until then anyway, so we mustn't be careless. By the way, your parents both say hello."

"You spoke to them?"

"And Tommasina and Peppino as well."

At this moment, Olivia walks up to their table.

"Elmo, I've been looking for you. We need to talk."

Elmo turns toward his grandfather who is staring off into space.

"Sit down," says Elmo. "This is my grandfather."

Grandpa turns to look at her and turns back to the window without a word. Elmo gets the hint.

"We can talk in front of him. He's profoundly deaf and can barely remember anything anyway. Do you want something to eat?"

She looks again at Grandpa, who is gazing through the window.

"No food. I need to know what happened with the package."

"That? I did exactly what you said. That Cortez was a hard looking dude."

"So you did get it? What happened when you returned?"

"Just like you asked, I went through security and left the package. I went through the screening and just left it on the conveyor."

"You didn't take it with you?"

"Why would I? You said security would take it. Maybe you'd better tell me what's going on. You seem frightened."

Olivia thinks for a moment. At this point, she is not even acknowledging Grandpa's presence.

"Oh, I have to tell somebody. You remember that I have less than two weeks left on board, right?"

Elmo nods.

"Well as a dancer, my schedule allows me to get off at most ports. Somebody asked me once to do just what I asked you to do."

"Pick up a package?"

"Yes, only these packages contain something not quite legal."

"Wait, did you have me transport drugs or something?"

"No, nothing like that. It's some kind of art."

"Art? What's illegal about art?"

"I'm not sure. I think it's either stolen or fake."

"How does this work, if you don't mind me asking?"

"I'm not sure. A security guy got me to do it once. Then he told me he'd rat me out if I didn't keep doing it."

"Blackmail."

Grandpa begins to cough. Elmo places a napkin in his hand and Grandpa goes back to staring out of the window.

"He said I'd never see my family or home again. It can happen. Sometimes a crewperson just disappears."

"So what do they do with the art?"

"I peeked in the package once. It looked like a cheap art print. But later, I saw it again at the art auction."

"The art auction?"

"Yes, I host it. I don't think Vijay knew that when he recruited me. The item was in the auction, but not on the original manifest. I look it over before the auction. It was inserted later."

"And?"

"And it sold. What was odd was that it didn't say reproduction or limited addition like the other items. It sold for a typical price."

"So what's unusual about that?"

"You see, the art auction is kind of a scam in itself. They sell copies, reprints, and limited edition prints, which are basically worthless. The auctioneer never lies about what something is, but polishes the apple so that cruisers with money think they're getting an investment. There are even known artists who allow their work to be copied to make the whole thing seem legitimate."

"Interesting. So who's in charge of this scam?"

"That's the problem. I only know the security guy. It's not clear that he knows any more than the person above him. Somebody from the auction house must be in on it, but that's only two people on the ship."

"And they are?"

"Claude Gireaux is in charge. He also has an assistant named Alison. I don't know her last name. She might be the only American working on the ship."

"You don't suppose I'm in any danger, do you?"

"Oh, Elmo, I'm so sorry to have involved you. I really was in a jam and they threatened me with never getting home. I thought I was done with them. I can't see how you are in danger, but I really have to find that package."

"Well, let me know what happens."

"I'll try, Elmo. I really will. I've got to get to the theater, now. Thanks so much for listening. I feel a lot better."

Elmo watches her leave and turns to Grandpa. The Embarcadero is nearly empty and workers are already preparing for the next meal.

"You can stop the drooling routine, Grandpa," says Elmo.

"We need to get back to the cabin," says Grandpa.

Wednesday, Oct 29th
~ Fiesta Mambo, Deck 9 ~

"You did an outstanding job, Elmo."

Elmo and Grandpa have returned to their cabin and Grandpa is removing the painting from the tube.

"I'm still not sure we should have that here," says Elmo.

"If we put it anywhere else, there's a greater chance that more people will know about it. Now that I am convinced that this is contraband, no one can implicate us for having it without implicating themselves. Please get me a full glass of water, Elmo."

"You always have a plan, don't you?"

"Why shouldn't I? My only advantage is to be smarter and more organized than everyone else. If I can avoid panic and error, I am in a better position to succeed."

"You sound like Bill Belichek."

"Who?"

"He's the coach of the Patriots, a very successful football team. Maybe that's why Tom Brady always seems so relaxed."

"You will have to accept the fact that I have absolutely no idea what you are talking about. Put the water on the counter, please. Pick up my watch and count off fifteen seconds after I dip this."

Elmo shrugs and picks up the watch.

"Go," he says.

Grandpa picks a corner of the painting and carefully dips it into the water and holds it in place.

"Five…ten…fifteen," says Elmo.

Grandpa lifts the painting from the water and lets it drip off.

"Sit next to me, Elmo. I need you to smell this."

Elmo shakes his head in disbelief but is long past asking his grandfather for an explanation. He sits down while Grandpa flips over the canvas. Elmo takes a deep sniff.

"Mulch. It smells like mulch."

"Not mold or mildew?"

"Grandpa, I work with mulch every day."

Grandpa gives it a sniff. It is a strong odor.

"Would you say it smells like cedar?"

"Yeah, it should. A lot of mulch is cedar, also it is colored and scented to smell like cedar. Now can you explain what we're doing?"

"First, I want to get back to your performance at lunch. I was quite impressed, particularly your recovery from your one error."

"The blackmail thing?"

"Yes, it was a little too aggressive. She was really opening up to you. She's the one from the first night?"

"Yes, Grandpa, and thanks for sharing. I can really pick 'em, can't I?"

"Don't be hard on yourself. She wouldn't open up unless she both liked and trusted you, and considering that you were lying---"

"Don't remind me. I felt like shit hanging her out there."

"That's the hardest part."

"What, having no conscience?"

"Quite the opposite. You allowed her to prove that she is an innocent dupe in all of this."

"How can you be sure?"

"I've been at this a long time. Basically it's about what she did not say."

"Then why couldn't we take her into our confidence?"

"Then the others in the scam would know. That's both the beauty and the danger of involving innocents in a criminal enterprise. I cannot promise anything, but I will try to protect her if it does not endanger you."

"I appreciate it. I tried to follow your mantra of giving away nothing."

"As I said, you were quite brilliant. As happy as I am that you are not in this business of mine and your father's, I am now convinced that you would have been quite good at it."

"Thanks, but I'll stick to mulch. It's stressful, but it's a different kind of stress. So what have you learned?"

"Two big things today. One, the painting is almost certainly real. I spoke to an expert from Harvard who told me of the sniff test."

"Harvard? Who the hell do you know at Harvard?"

"It was actually a friend of your brother."

"Pep? Forget I asked. What else did we learn?"

"We definitely are looking at a criminal enterprise. I have it mostly figured out, but I'm still working on a few things. Even though you were brought into this quite accidentally, at least one of the conspirators knows of your involvement, so we must keep moving forward. Oh, and of course that Olivia appears to be in the same boat as you."

"Olivia! Of course!"

"What is it?"

"My phone. That's where I must have lost it. I had it the first day, but couldn't find it after that. It must have fallen out of my pocket while we were---"

"I get the picture. We'll need to recover it. Let me think about it over a nap while you shower. Good work today. I really mean it."

~~~~~~~~~~

Grandpa steps out of the bathroom after showering and gets dressed for a casual dinner. He walks over to Elmo, who is sleeping on top of the made bed and shakes him on the shoulder.

"Wake up, Elmo. It's nearly time for dinner. We already missed the cocktail hour."

Elmo rolls over and squints up at his grandfather.

"I'm not sure I should go, Grandpa."

"Is something wrong, Elmo?"

"I kind of had an incident with Melody today at the beach."

"Some sort of disagreement?"

"Not exactly. More of an awkward situation."

"Awkward? What could be so awkward at the beach?"

Elmo remains silent.

"Oh, my," says Grandpa. "You don't mean to say---"

"Yup. Right there in the ocean."

"I…I don't know what to say."

"My point exactly."

"She is a lady. I'm sure you can count on her discretion."

"You mean while I sit between her daughter and another one of her conquests who just happens to be my grandfather? I'm more concerned about my discretion."

"Maybe I should be warning Paul and Larry."

"A joke? Seriously? That's the best you got?"

"You must admit, it is a great story."

"Who would I tell? It's not like we're going back to the frat house after this. And what about your story? What's with you and Sarah?"

"It seems that I like her."

"Not to be indelicate, but isn't she playing for the other team?"

"That's what I'm finding so odd. I really like her as a friend. I enjoy her company."

"What's so unusual about that? You seem to like women just fine."

"Of course I like female companionship. This is different. Sarah does not 'turn me on' in that way, but she makes me feel good. I've never had a woman as a friend other than your grandmother, of course."

"Jesus, aren't we a pair."

"I actually am enjoying the company of the entire group. It's very new to me, but I am intrigued by the change. Do you know that Sarah likes to sing? I actually want to hear her."

"Why don't we go to karaoke after the show?"

"That sounds swell, Elmo, but first you'll have to tell me what or who karaoke is."

"Do you live in a cave? It's…um…you know what? I'll just take you there. It's too hard to explain."

"Fair enough. Alright, let's just go to dinner and try to enjoy ourselves."

"Okay, I guess I'm slightly more hungry than embarrassed."

They leave the room and head for the stairs.

"You must admit," says Grandpa, "that Melody has the tits of a twenty-five year old."

Elmo looks at him and shakes his head.

"Ten, actually," he says.

"Ten?"

"Yeah, her tits are only ten years old. They were a Christmas gift from her third husband in 2004."

Wednesday, Oct 29th
~ Fiesta Mambo, Deck 3, The Ballroom ~

Elmo and Tommaso enter the dining room. Elmo heads to his seat, while Tommaso stops to talk to Fabrice for a moment.

"We missed you at cocktail hour," says Larry.

"Yeah, we were pretty wiped out," says Elmo.

"I find the salt water to be quite invigorating," says Melody.

Elmo takes a drink of water.

"Tonight, the show is called 'Havana Nights'," says Sarah. "I'm really looking forward to it. Are you boys attending?"

"I wouldn't miss it," says Tommaso. "Also, Elmo has suggested something for after the show. Are you game?"

"As long as it doesn't involve basketball," says Paul. "I'm wearing the wrong shoes."

Dinner continues with everyone describing their day.

"We learned how to make a sting ray and a dog out of towels," says Alice. "The sting ray was a new one for me. The fellow running the class also made the cutest monkey. It hung by its tail from a hanger. It was very impressive."

"A useful skill to be sure," says Larry.

"Well I'm looking forward to a day at sea tomorrow," says Paul. "I can use a little pool time. Is everyone up for breakfast at the Siesta Sol?"

"Count me in," says Tommaso.

Fabrice is serving the after-dinner beverages just before Handy comes along with the desserts. He clears his throat as he places an espresso in front of Tommaso. Tommaso looks down and sees a folded note on the saucer. He deftly palms it and puts it in his pocket.

There is much sharing and tasting of the desserts.

"I can't believe that no cruise ship has tried adding lazy-susan technology to their tables," says Larry.

"It won't work," says Paul. "No matter which way you spin it, someone will be sitting next to a kid who eats like Elmo. They'd starve to death on a cruise. Could you imagine the lawsuits?"

"You're hilarious, Paul," says Elmo. "Larry, I loved your idea. Let's talk business later."

"Remember everyone," says Alice, "tomorrow is a formal night. I, for one, plan to put those Neanderthals behind us to shame."

"That reminds me," says Tommaso. "I would like to invite all of you to cocktail hour at a small gathering given by a new friend that I met during the Captain's dinner. It is taking place in the Montezuma Suite near the rear of the ship."

"The Montezuma Suite?" asks Alice. "Tommaso, you never cease to amaze me. That's the best suite on the ship. I hear it is quite incredible."

"Then," says Tommaso, "I insist that you come and verify this for yourself at five o'clock tomorrow."

"You're God damned right I'll be there," says Alice. "Sarah, we'd better get dressed tonight!"

"Melody," says Tommaso, "I really would like you and Shana to attend. There is someone I'd like you to meet."

"That is too curious of an offer to refuse. Shall we all meet somewhere?"

"Let's see," says Tommaso, "I believe the entrance is on Deck 8 near the rear of the ship."

"How about the Library?" asks Paul. "That's pretty much where the Library is."

"Wait," says Elmo. "Something's not right. I've got it! How would Paul know where a library would be?"

"Funny, Kid," says Paul. "All right, we're even for now, but it's a long cruise."

"Then it's settled," says Tommaso. "Tomorrow at 4:45 in the Library."

They all get up to head for the theater. Tommaso pulls Elmo aside. He slides the note out of his pocket.

"I need to meet Jameson in the room at ten. It's about your phone. Can you bring the others to that thing later?"

"Yeah, I can handle that. You sure you don't need me?"

"Yes, Elmo. Thank you, but I'll be fine. I'll see you when you get back to the room."

Wednesday, Oct 29th
~ Fiesta Mambo, Hernando's Hideaway ~

"Where is Tommaso going?" asks Sarah.

"He had to run back to the room for something," says Elmo. "I expect he'll be along. How did you like the show?"

"It was more of a music montage, like 'Smokey Joe's Café', but I loved the music. The singers were wonderful."

"Speaking of singers, I heard that you are one yourself."

"Strictly amateur, I assure you."

"Well, here is your chance to prove otherwise."

He holds out his hand toward the entrance of Hernando's Hideaway.

"Isn't this the Discotheque?" asks Alice.

Elmo considers saying that it's just 'Disco' in this century, but decides against it.

"Not until eleven o'clock," he says. "Until then, it's used for karaoke!"

"*Oy vey*," says Paul. "This ought to be interesting."

They go in and get a table off to the side. There is a couple on stage butchering some country duet. Elmo decides that they are either too drunk or not drunk enough to pull it off. He goes along the side of the crowd near the DJ and picks up a binder. He returns and sits next to Sarah, hands her the book, and leans in to talk to her.

"Look up a song in here. When you find it, we write down the number and I give it to the DJ. He'll put you in the queue and when your song comes up, you go up there and sing."

"I've seen it, but I've never done it before. I think I'm too nervous."

"Nonsense. This is the perfect time. You're among friends and you'll never see any of these others again. I'm learning that that's what cruises are for."

"Well, I guess it doesn't HURT TO LOOK…Oh, my!"

The song had stopped just as Sarah was shouting at Elmo to be heard. Her last three words came at an awkward volume, bringing stares from some of the neighboring tables. Everyone in the group begins laughing, including Sarah. She opens the book to find a song.

"My, I don't even know any of these artists," says Sarah. "I assume that this is all new stuff. I was trying to find something by Keely Smith."

"Try looking under Oldies or under Louie Prima," says Elmo.

"So you know Prima and Smith? I would think that's before your time."

"When I was little, my grandfather had a big Cadillac and used to take me for rides. It drove my parents' nuts, because he let me sit up front without a proper child seat. They'd install it in the back, and he'd let me ride up front. He had a tape of their greatest hits that he would play on the ride."

"That's sweet...Oh, here we are, 'I've Got You Under My Skin'. Write down the number."

Elmo delivers the paper to the DJ and returns. It is between songs.

"The good news is that they have it, and it is the Keely Smith version. The bad news is that you are fifth in the queue, so we'll have to endure some of these other hacks."

"I thought the black woman was quite good," says Alice.

"I can't believe that I brought twenty extra hearing aid batteries on this trip just to be safe," says Larry, "and now I'm forced to turn it off."

After a mixed bag of songs, the DJ announces, "All the way from Iowa, I'd like to introduce Sarah."

"Wish me luck," says Sarah, as she heads for the stage to a smattering of applause.

"Break a leg," says Paul, "but not a hip."

Larry turns on his hearing aid.

Sarah begins to sing and the room immediately becomes quiet. People are stopping in the middle of their conversations and shushing their friends. Elmo is stunned. Sarah is an amazing singer. Not only can she carry a tune, but has perfect timing, and a smoky, sultry tone.

When Sarah finishes the song, there is a startling burst of applause and even some people standing. A woman to Elmo's left lets out a whistle and shouts, "You go, girl."

The DJ shouts into his mike, "That was Sarah from Iowa. Let's give it up for her."

Sarah returns to the table with a massive grin.

"Where the hell did that come from?" asks Alice.

"God, I love this cruise," says Sarah. "Elmo, give me that book!"

As the evening continues, the singing gets worse, but Sarah does two more songs, 'Over the Rainbow' and 'Summertime' from Porgy and Bess, both which are as well received as the first.

Elmo has lost track of the time when the DJ announces that they are closing up shop to switch to disco mode.

"Thank you so much, Elmo," says Sarah. "I never would have tried this at home."

"Well it's their loss in Iowa. You are an amazing singer."

"Do you really think so? I wish Tommaso could have heard it. Do you think he's all right?"

"I'm sure he's fine, but I'm going to check on him now. Good night, everybody and thanks for coming."

Sarah is just standing there, grinning at the stage as Elmo heads out. Alice grabs her shoulder.

"Come on, Cinderella. Ball's over, time for bed."

Wednesday, Oct 29th
~ Fiesta Mambo, Deck 9 ~

Elmo unlocks the cabin door to find the lights out. He turns on the light and is momentarily startled. Hanging from the air conditioning unit in the ceiling is a hanger from the closet. Hanging from the hanger is a monkey made from towels; only this monkey is not hanging from its tail. This monkey is hanging from a noose and has black paper X's for eyes.

"Elmo, is that you?" asks Grandpa, rolling over in his bed.

"Did you see this? Is this another message?"

"Do you like it? Jameson was here. I had him make it for you. Pretty funny, don't you think?"

"Grandpa, you are one sick fuck, you know that?"

Elmo grabs the monkey and throws it on the floor. Grandpa is clearly pleased with himself. Elmo picks up an outfit that is folded on his bed.

"What is this?" he asks.

"Also from Jameson. He was here to help us to recover your phone. Would you like the plan now, or in the morning?"

"Will in keep me from sleeping?"

"Possibly, no, make that probably."

"Then I'll wait until morning. It's too bad you missed the karaoke. Sarah is an amazing singer. She got the most applause by far."

"This was some sort of competition?"

"Sorry, I forgot that it was your first day on earth. Karaoke is the playing of musical tracks without lyrics allowing someone to sing along like they are a real singer with real accompaniment. I think it's Japanese."

"That makes sense. *Kara* is the Japanese word for 'empty' and *oke* is the first syllable in their word for 'orchestra', hence karaoke, or empty orchestra."

Elmo stops getting undressed and turns to stare at his grandfather.

"You speak fucking Japanese, but never heard of karaoke? You're a demon, right? I must be fucking dreaming."

"You probably need some sleep, Elmo. You've had a rough day. It will all make sense in the morning."

Elmo shakes his head and gets into bed. He reaches to turn off the light.

"Good night, demon."

"Good night, Elmo."

Thursday, Oct 30th
~ Fiesta Mambo, Deck 9 ~

Grandpa slides open the curtain covering the door to the balcony. The burst of light wakes Elmo who covers his eyes with his pillow.

"Are we still on the ship?" he asks.

"Yes, and you need to get up. I ordered you breakfast."

"What?"

"Room service. You need to stay here to meet Jameson a little after nine-thirty. I need to leave in a few minutes to meet Paul, Larry, Alice, and Sarah."

Elmo sits up and rubs his eyes.

"What time is it now?"

"Eight-fifteen. I'm meeting them at eight-thirty."

There is a knock at the door. Grandpa opens it to a waiter carrying a tray.

"Thank you, just place it here on the counter," he says.

"Enjoy your breakfast, sirs."

The waiter leaves and Elmo lifts the cover off of one of the plates.

"There's a lot of food here," says Elmo.

"I didn't know what you wanted, so I ordered two plates. I need to run, so let me tell you the plan."

"Can't I just eat and jump off the balcony?"

"That's Plan B. Now listen. Jameson will be here between nine-thirty and ten. He can get you to Olivia's room and open it, but cannot go inside. That is too risky for him. The dancers give lessons on sea days at ten, so the room will be empty."

"And the outfit?"

"You must wear it. There is a security guard at the crew entrance to steer away nosy passengers---"

"And terrorists?"

"Pay attention. Jameson said that they don't check carefully so if you walk in with him, you should be fine."

"Unless it's Vijay or someone else in the chain."

"We'll have to take that chance. Jameson seems to think that it's remote. Go in the room, find your phone, and get out. Jameson said that security doesn't even look at anyone going out, so just keep walking and come back here. Do you think you have it?"

"I have it. Enjoy your breakfast. Make sure you ask Sarah about last night."

"Good luck, Elmo."

Grandpa heads out the door. Elmo sits in the vanity chair to have his breakfast.

~~~~~~~~~~

At nine-forty-five there is a knock at the door. Elmo opens it and peeks around the edge to hide the fact that he is in a crew uniform. Jameson is standing there and Elmo lets him in.

"You know the plan, Mr. Elmo?"

"Yes. It seems simple enough."

"If anything goes wrong, just walk away, take off the jacket and disappear. There are many cameras, so move to Olvera Street or the pool area where it is crowded. This ship is my livelihood."

"You've got nothing to worry about. My grandfather will see to it."

"When you get back here, just leave the uniform on the bathroom floor under some towels. I will get it when I do the room later. Let's get started."

Jameson leads Elmo to the elevator and down to Deck 2. They head toward the rear of the ship and take the stairs to the crew level. The security guard gives them a cursory glance as they walk by. They head down the corridor leading to Olivia's room. When they arrive, Jameson looks up and down the hall to verify that they are alone. He takes a card out of his pocket and slides it into Olivia's door slot. There is a click and he turns the handle.

"In and out," says Jameson, as he walks away.

Elmo goes inside and closes the door. The light is already on and he makes a mental note to leave it that way.

He looks at the unmade bed and can't believe that he was in here less than four days ago. It seems like a year. He looks under the bed and sees nothing. He then slides the bed away from the wall and hears a light thump. Elmo peeks back under the bed and sees his phone leaning against the far wall. Deciding that he won't be able to reach it, he slides the bed out another three or four inches. He climbs on top and reaches down to grab his phone.

Elmo gets up and slides the bed back with his knee. He holds up his phone and gives it a kiss.

"It's about time something went smoothly," he says to no one, while putting the phone in his pocket.

Suddenly, the door opens. A beautiful girl wearing a spandex workout outfit and a knee brace is standing in the doorway.

"And who might you be?" she asks.

"I'm Eddie. I'm new on the ship. Olivia let me in to pick up something."

"Well, Eddie, I can give you one piece of advice. Walking around in uniform without your nametag can get you into hot water."

"Oh, yeah. Damn, I'm not used to it, yet. Thanks for the tip. I'd better go get it."

"In a minute," she says, as she closes the door. "You're from Canada, I'm guessing, since I don't detect an accent."

"Yeah, um, I'm from Toronto, eh."

"I'm Yasmine. I was just in the gym doing some physical therapy. I'm a dancer, but I tweaked my knee and I'm off of dance lessons for a week."

She pulls off her top revealing a sports bra. She pulls that off as well. Elmo cannot place her accent or her exotic look. Her skin is nearly golden. He really wishes he could see her nametag, rather than her bare chest.

"I'm part of the welcoming committee among the crew, Eddie."

She sits on the bed and grabs him by the belt. She pulls him close to her.

"I might be able to help you find that nametag. It may have fallen in here."

She unhooks his belt and slides down his pants. Elmo just stares at the ceiling.

"Oh, my," she says, "now this is a surprise. We don't get too many of these on the ship. No wonder Olivia grabbed you up first."

~~~~~~~~~~~~~

Elmo walks into the Siesta Sol and sees his grandfather in the pool with the group. He waits for eye contact and waves the phone to let him know that he was successful. Grandpa excuses himself from his friends and gets out of the water. He picks up his towel and walks over to Elmo.

"Good work, Elmo. No trouble, then?"

"Hard to say. We got down there fine. I found the phone right away and then, oh yeah, her roommate shows up."

"What did you do?"

"Me? Nothing. She, however, initiated a new crewman from Toronto named Eddie with a quite competent blowjob."

"I believe the appropriate expression here is 'Who are you?'."

"Funny, Grandpa, very funny. I got out fine and left the uniform as Jameson directed."

"Well at least we recovered the phone. That helps us."

"Great. I just hope they don't test for DNA. They'll think that someone's testicles exploded in that room."

"I don't think we have anything else happening until cocktails. I'd like to have lunch with Sarah. Let's meet at four to shower and dress. I just want you to relax and enjoy yourself today."

"Relax? I guess I can try."

"That reminds me. Your friends, the black boys came by looking for you. They said there was another sports competition today. It was, I believe, 'throw shooting'."

"Throw shooting? I have no idea what that is."

"Neither do I. I only know that it doesn't cost anything."

Elmo stares at him for a moment.

"*Free* throw shooting?" he asks.

"That sounds about right."

Elmo shakes his head and says, "Yet he speaks Japanese."

Thursday, Oct 30th
~ Fiesta Mambo, Deck 11, The Embarcadero ~

Elmo walks into the buffet area and spots the group of cousins.

"Hey, Elmo!" shouts Earl.

Elmo walks to their table and greets them.

"Do you mind if I join you for lunch?"

They all agree once he promises to join them for the tournament at one o'clock. Elmo heads to the buffet to gather his lunch. He returns with several plates.

"Are all of you going to compete?" asks Elmo.

"All but Desmond," says Duane. "He's chicken."

"I just get tired of losing," says Desmond. "You guys are all older than me."

"Our grandpop says it's how you learn to lose like a man," says Jerrell. "He says sometimes how you lose is more important than how you win."

"I have to agree with him," says Elmo, "although it's not always that simple. I have a little brother about the same distance in age from me as you two. He never wanted to compete. I don't think it was about losing. He just wasn't by nature a competitive person."

"Sounds like a wuss," says Earl.

"I used to think so, too, but now he's one of the toughest people I know. Competition isn't for everybody. That being said, I do plan to walk away with that medallion today."

After lunch, they all head up to the Sports Deck and sign up for the competition.

"It looks like the wind might be a factor, men," says Elmo. "We're moving about seventeen knots. Make your adjustments."

The competition goes on for several rounds. Desmond decides to compete and makes it to the second round to the chagrin of Earl and Duane, who bow out earlier. Elmo and Jerrell are the last two left in the final and are tied at the end.

"We are going into sudden death," says Rodolfo, from the Cruise Director's staff.

Elmo is contemplating clanging one off the front of the rim to allow Jerrell the victory when Jerrell approaches him and extends his hand.

"My cousin won't learn anything if you take a dive, Elmo."

Elmo shakes his hand.

"I understand, Jerrell. Of course you know that this means that I must bust your ass."

"I do and I would expect nothing less."

The two exchange shots for an amazing eight more rounds before Jerrell has one roll out giving Elmo the victory. Rodolfo informs the crowd that this is a record since he's been on the ship and hands Elmo his medallion.

"We should both get one of these, you know," says Elmo.

"It's just plastic," says Jerrell, "and besides, it's only worth something when you earn it."

"Well, plastic or not, this one is the most important to me since I had to work the hardest to get it."

When Elmo returns to the cabin, he finds Grandpa in conference with Jameson.

"Congratulations, Mr. Elmo. Mr. Pastor informs me that you have received one of the bonuses of working on a cruise ship from Yasmine."

"I hope I made the crew bulletin board and newsletter," says Elmo. "What are you two working on?"

"I have been in consultation with some outside assistance," says Grandpa. "I am including Jameson in the planning since he requires my help as we need his."

"*Your* help, as opposed to *our* help?"

"It's not completely legal so I cannot permit you to be involved, something that Jameson has agreed to respect as a father himself."

"Jesus," says Elmo.

"If we are to allow the auction to go on as planned," says Grandpa, "we must find a way to return the painting without raising suspicion. I still would like to keep Olivia in the dark and I still would like to maintain our leverage."

"That sounds pretty impossible."

"This is where Jameson comes in. Fortunately, being Jamaican, he has his shore leave tomorrow, where his family and business interests reside. It seems that he has an uncle who is an accomplished artist. You will accompany him to his studio and attempt to make a copy of the painting."

"In a day?"

"Actually in five hours," says Jameson. "He is quite talented and has done this sort of work before. Your grandfather has shown me the painting. I think that he can do a credible job."

"But we don't know how much the inside man knows about art. What if he's an expert? He works in the Art Studio."

"I didn't say that it wouldn't be a problem," says Grandpa. "That's why we need you. Three heads are better than two."

"Okay," says Elmo. "I'll give it some thought. You said there was a possibility that none of this may turn out to be necessary."

"That is Plan A. No risk is always best. If I found a painting missing after three days, I'd be paranoid about a scam. I'd check it more carefully than normal. That's our biggest liability at the moment."

"This stuff gives me a headache. I don't know how you people do this all the time."

"It takes a special constitution," says Jameson. "It runs in my family. I'll bet that it is in you."

"I hope not. Anything else, Grandpa?"

"I am going to have to confide in some of our friends. I'm going to need some help at the auction. I need to do some more planning, but we will finalize the plan tonight. Jameson will be getting off with the crew and get a car at about seven-thirty. You and I will get off the ship at eight. I have to meet someone, and you will get picked up by Jameson near the taxi stand."

"I will beep three times," says Jameson. "We have a bit of a ride."

"I will meet up with our friends at nine-thirty and we will do some exploring. I will meet you two near the pier at three o'clock."

"I must go now," says Jameson. "I will return at ten to finalize the plan."

Jameson leaves the cabin and Grandpa heads for the shower.

"Grandpa, if you ever hear me bitch about the stress of owning a business again, I want you to shoot me."

"This will be over soon, Elmo. I'm actually a bit excited."

Elmo laughs and opens the closet for his tuxedo.

Thursday, Oct 30th
~ Fiesta Mambo, Deck 8, The Library ~

Paul and Larry are already in the Library when Grandpa and Elmo arrive. Paul is in a standard tux but has accessorized it with a vest, tie, and pocket square in a red tartan plaid. Larry is even more ornate in a navy tux with black lapels and stripes. The tux has a paisley print. His shirt is powder blue.

"Wow, you guys look sharp," says Elmo. "Where are the ladies?"

"Where do you think?" asks Paul. "They're in the bathroom. Apparently there's one on this deck that they haven't visited, yet. I think they're spies taking samples for the EPA."

While they are kibitzing, Melody arrives in an absolutely stunning iridescent cobalt blue gown. It is showing a dangerous amount of cleavage, yet still seems stately. Elmo runs to grab the door for her.

"This is the first time since I've been on board that I feel the ship moving," says Larry.

Sarah and Alice return from the bathroom and have to manage the doors for themselves as the men are preoccupied looking at Melody.

"It's like some sort of optical illusion," says Elmo, moving his hand back and forth in front of his eyes.

"Ahem," says Alice, "the chopped liver is over here."

"Oh, good evening, ladies," says Tommaso. "Melody was just telling us the most enchanting story."

"I can see how enchanted you all are," says Alice.

She is wearing a long white gown that is gathered into a small flower on her left hip. The bottom is pleated and draped perfectly.

Sarah is wearing a deep emerald gown with sheer sleeves. It has a sash around the waist that hangs about halfway down the side.

"This had better be worth the effort, Tommaso," says Melody. "I spent half the day in the spa and salon, and I'm more spanx than flesh."

"Are we waiting for Shana?" asks Paul.

"No, she decided that this wasn't her 'scene'. She'll meet us at dinner."

"Then I'd guess we'd better be on our way," he says.

They leave the Library and head through a door toward the starboard side and head aft. They exit onto a small covered section of decking at the rear of the ship. Some of them peek over the rail and are looking directly into the wake left by the engines.

"I'd hate to fall into that," says Paul.

They move along around until they reach a door with a doorbell. There is a small sign above the peep hole that says Montezuma Suite.

"Here we are," says Tommaso, as he pushes the bell.

In a moment, a steward answers the door. Tommaso shows him a note and the steward welcomes them in. The suite is absolutely incredible. It is two stories high. There are large windows everywhere and a balcony that curls around the corner of the ship. There appears to be a small upstairs balcony as well.

In one corner, there is a fully stocked bar with a bartender and in the other is a baby grand piano. There is a pianist playing softly. The center of the room contains an ornate chandelier over a dining table.

"Please, come in and use the bar," says the steward. "Your host is upstairs showing some guests the residence."

"Did you hear that?" asks Paul. "The *residence*. We called ours the attic."

"In Iowa we refer to it as 'the hayloft'," says Sarah.

Everyone heads for the bar, except Tommaso, who moves toward the windows near the bottom of the curved staircase.

Ted walks down with a couple and greets Tommaso.

"Tommaso, these are the Howreys, Mary and Jim. Jim's a former associate from the Chicago area."

"Pleased to meet you," says Tommaso.

"Is that the one, in blue?" asks Ted.

"It is indeed," says Tommaso. "Come and I'll introduce you."

They walk across the room.

"Allow me to introduce---"

Melody turns around and shouts, "Ted!"

"Melody?" says Ted. "I can't believe it's you."

Everyone else is standing around stunned, particularly Tommaso.

"Oh, I'm so sorry. Ted, these are my friends and tablemates. This is Paul, Larry, Alice, Sarah, and Elmo. You already know Tommaso apparently."

"Everybody, this is Ted Pratt. Ted was my second husband!"

"Best hookup e-ver," says Elmo.

"I must admit to a bit of embarrassment," says Tommaso.

"Nonsense," says Ted. "First of all, it will make a great story. It's also a testament to your matchmaking skills. We're so compatible that we've already been married! I must say, Melody, that you look spectacular."

"I did have some help in that area. These were a Christmas gift," she says, pointing at her breasts. "What do you think?"

"Well, I am certainly thinking that I made a big mistake getting you that Jet Ski."

Elmo, who had been trying to keep a little distance between himself and Melody, is now leaning in to get every word of this incredible turn of events.

"If you don't mind me asking, why are you no longer married? You seem to fit quite nicely."

"In a nutshell," says Melody, "I wasn't adventurous enough for him."

Elmo begins choking on his drink and runs to the bar for a napkin. He is able to spit the drink back into the glass, but not before a significant amount of his seven and seven exit through his nose. The searing combination running through the delicate veins of his sinus cavity bring a flood of tears to his eyes.

Grandpa walks over and hands him a few more napkins.

"I think we should give them some space, now."

Elmo mutters something unintelligible with napkins over his eyes, nose, and mouth.

"I'll take that as a yes," says Grandpa.

Thursday, Oct 30th
~ Fiesta Mambo, Deck 3, The Ballroom ~

Everyone is sitting around the table except for Shana, who is as usual, fashionably late. Ted is sitting in her seat and cannot take his eyes off of Melody. Elmo has already asked Fabrice twice for paper napkins as he cannot get his nose to stop running.

"We were just in the wrong place at the wrong time," says Melody. "Ted was a former workaholic who needed to spread his wings. I was a free spirit who needed to settle down with a daughter in school. It was all very amicable, other than the sadness. Oh, here she is now."

As Shana gets closer, she sees that someone is in her seat. She looks confused for a minute when Ted turns around, smiling.

"Ted? Is that you?"

"Shoshone, that's exactly what your mother said. Let me look at you all grown up."

Handy offers to set an extra place, but Ted is meeting some people at the later seating. He invites the group for dinner tomorrow after the ship leaves Ocho Rios, but everyone begs off so that Ted can reunite with his former family.

"I go by Shana, now, not Shoshone, but I like to hear it when you say it. I've missed you, Ted."

"And me as well," says Ted. "This has been a most incredible coincidence."

Elmo tries to figure if it even makes his top five.

"Tommaso," says Paul, "I must make a toast to you. Most of us have cruised many times, but something about the presence of you and young Elmo here, have made this the most interesting one, yet."

"Here, here," says Alice.

"L'Chiam," says Larry.

Sarah rubs Tommaso on the shoulder with her free hand.

"While we're on the subject," says Tommaso, "I'd like to ask each of you a favor, a big favor."

"What do you need?" asks Paul.

"May we discuss it over dessert?"

"Sure," says Larry. "There's no show tonight, just one of those silly game shows. We can also get together afterward."

"As long as Paul doesn't miss the juggling show tomorrow night," says Alice.

"I'm telling you," says Paul, "I've seen this guy before. You'll definitely want to see him. He's amazing."

"You can relax, Paul," says Tommaso, "This will not affect the show tomorrow night in any way."

"Then I'm in," says Paul.

Grandpa tells them that he needs to meet with them later, a little bit after dinner. He needs to find a quiet and private spot where they can all be comfortable.

"The Library was quiet, and it certainly was empty," says Larry.

"Good idea," says Grandpa. "After dessert, I'd like to take a walk with Sarah for about a half hour. Can the rest of you meet me in the Library at say, eight o'clock?"

He turns to Melody.

"This includes you and Shana. It's important."

"Sure, Tommaso," says Melody. "We'll be there."

As planned, Tommaso and Sarah head out leaving the other's behind.

"Elmo," asks Paul, "do you have any idea what's going on? This is all so strange."

"I'll bet he's going ask Sarah to marry him," says Melody. "He seems quite taken with her."

"If that's the case," says Larry, "I think he's in for quite a surprise."

"Yeah, Mom," says Shana. "Haven't you been paying attention?"

"He knows all about that," says Elmo. "He is very fond of her just the same."

"I truly have no idea what you are all talking about," says Melody.

"Sarah's a lesbian, Mom."

"A what? Are you sure? This was discussed? At this very table? How could I have missed that?"

Handy leans in to refill the coffee.

"Even I knew this," he says.

~~~~~~~~~~

Tommaso holds the door near the library and he and Sarah go back to the secluded deck near Ted's suite.

"It is time for me to be honest with you, Sarah. I have lived my entire life in secrecy, but there is something about you and your party, that has brought about a change in me. Please allow me to get through this without questions or comments first."

"Absolutely, Tommaso. Fire away. After the cocktail hour, I doubt I could be much more surprised."

"Until recently, I have lived my entire life as a criminal. I came to this country from Italy as a young boy all alone..."

Tommaso continues with the condensed story of his past and recent 'retirement' due to a desperate effort to save his family. He tells her about Milton and the last minute addition of Elmo to his travel plans as well as the shenanigans needed to make their way on board.

He explains Elmo's accidental entry into the art ring and his need to protect his grandson. Tommaso includes the coincidental parts of the story relating to the Captain and Ted.

"I have manipulated people in the past to help me with bigger problems than this. However, I respect you, Paul, Larry, and Alice, and your intelligence and forthrightness. I no longer wish to continue to add lying to my sins. I still cannot, however trust anyone who might be involved. I only have this group to rely on."

"This cruise gets more incredible every moment," says Sarah. "First of all, I appreciate your honesty. It is important to me, although I must admit, I don't you recall you actually lying to me. You do tend to leave quite a bit out, however. I am all in for helping you protect Elmo, and I understand why you can only give each of us a limited part of the plan. This does not explain why you missed my singing yesterday."

"I truly wanted to be there. Elmo said that you were incredible. Unfortunately, I ran into one of my minions, if you will, and needed to plan something that Elmo took care of this morning."

"What about the sudden change. How do you know that you don't have dementia or a brain tumor?"

"Because I know that it is you."

"Me? How so?"

"I'm less sure of that. I loved one woman in my life and had one female friend. Both of them were my wife Marie. When I lost her, I grieved, and I moved on to many women, all empty physical relationships, the less talk, the better. I got close to no one. I just was not interested, and I have never have been subject to infatuation."

"So again, I ask, how am I different? Do I remind you of your wife?"

"That's the odd part. You are in no way comparable to Marie. I do not mean that you don't measure up. You are just very different people. There is only one similarity. I have a compelling need to see you happy. There is also an odd side effect that you make me happy. I cannot explain it at all. It's very frustrating."

"Clearly, romance it ain't. Tommaso, I'd like to talk about this some more, but the others should be in the Library by now. You can count on me for whatever you need."

~~~~~~~~~~

Everyone is in the Library when Sarah and Grandpa arrive. There are also a couple of other people looking at the books. Tommaso holds the door for Sarah and they enter. About a minute later, the other couple finishes their business and leaves.

Tommaso is about to speak, when Elmo turns to Shana.

"Shana," he says, "I am going to an authentic art studio tomorrow to meet with a somewhat well-known Jamaican painter. Would you be interested in coming with me?"

Shana looks surprised, but not as much as Tommaso. Elmo gives him a quick glance to let him know that he has an idea. Tommaso lets him run with it.

"That sounds interesting, Elmo," says Shana. "Mom, do we have any plans?"

"I, I mean we, were planning to go on a jeep trip with Ted. I completely understand if you have other plans."

Shana gives her mother a slight eye roll.

"Well, I seem to be available, Elmo. What do I need to do?"

"Grandpa, do you mind if Shana and I take off, so that I can tell her all about it?"

"Not at all, Elmo. You seem to have everything under control."

Once they leave, Alice says, "Okay, Tommaso, enough stalling. The suspense is killing me."

Tommaso goes on to explain that he needs some help with the Art Auction taking place on Saturday at three o'clock in Hernando's Hideaway. He explains Elmo's involvement and his need to see this through. Tommaso convinces them, with Sarah's help, the need for secrecy and the inability to trust anyone other than each other.

The plan will be for each of them to go to the auction as regular bidders. Once any lot is bid on, one of them must bid. Anyone who continues to outbid them beyond a reasonable value of an object will implicate themselves. After the cruise, authorities off of the ship will take over.

"Questions?" asks Tommaso.

"Okay," says Paul, "here's one. What if we win a painting?"

"It's yours to keep. I recommend going to the pre-auction and at least finding the pieces that you like. Again, it will be important that you do not communicate in any way during the auction. It has to look seamless."

"How do we pay for the items?" asks Alice.

"I have that taken care of," says Tommaso.

"What if someone is bidding that is not a suspect?" asks Larry.

"Larry, everyone is a suspect. It is assumed that the buyer is using an agent. There is a lot of money at stake here. The assumption is that this syndicate, for lack of a better word, has found a way to fence stolen artwork with clean documentation. This would be a service for very wealthy people who have no intention of dirtying their hands. This is why I need your help. An agent could look just like you. They may actually not be aware that they are doing anything illegal."

"But that would be unlikely," says Sarah.

"Very unlikely," says Tommaso.

"My daughter won't be in danger, will she?"

"No," says Tommaso. "She will be with Elmo and my people at all times. She will not be needed at the auction."

"I cannot speak for anyone else," says Sarah, "but I am in. I'll do whatever you need, Tommaso."

"Me too," says Alice.

"Count me in," says Paul. "This may be better than the juggler."

"Yes," says Larry.

Everyone is looking at Melody.

"You will not be able to discuss this with Ted, I'm afraid."

"Is he a suspect?" she asks.

"Not at all. It's for his own protection. We have no suspects, yet someone on the ship is involved, maybe several people. It could be the steward in his cabin, or the guy on the next exercise bike. The only thing we can be sure of is the trust of each other."

"No wonder crime doesn't pay," says Alice. "They can't by nature trust their confederates."

"It is a big problem," says Tommaso. "I do not do this lightly. I simply will not permit anything to happen to my grandson."

"I'll do it," says Melody.

Grandpa and Elmo are finishing their breakfast and finalizing their plans to go ashore.

"You haven't asked me about Shana, yet," says Elmo.

"I trust you."

"That's it? Just like that? 'I trust you?'"

"Why not? You're smart. You know what we're up against and you have the most to lose. Why shouldn't you take part in planning the operation? You'll let me know when I need to know."

"Maybe this shit is hereditary."

"I don't agree. Take your father for example. His intelligence is what protects him. He was quite the crybaby as a child. Actually, it's your mother that has the nerves of steel. She has protected him more than you could imagine."

"Wow, that really surprises me. He seems so even and she seems high strung."

"That's why the right partner is so important. She makes him even. I'm actually glad he's out now. I'm not sure the stress was doing him any good."

"Well they're like a couple of teenagers now. Since Scotty entered the picture, things have really been different. I hope I haven't screwed it up with this mess."

"We'll be fine. When are you meeting Shana?"

"I'm picking her up on the way down. I'd like to reassure her mother if needed."

"Well, I guess we'd better get going. Do you have everything?"

Elmo holds up a beach bag with two long rolled beach towels sticking out.

"Yup, what's all that stuff in your bag?"

"Just treats from Jameson for our tour. Apparently no one cares what you bring into Jamaica, only what you bring back."

"Good luck, Grandpa."

"And you, Elmo."

Friday, Oct 31ˢᵗ
~ Port of Ocho Rios, Jamaica ~

Elmo and Shana walk off the ship without incident. They head to the cab stand, but walk toward the back of the line rather than the front.

"I think we need to go this way," says Shana.

A small car rolls up behind the last cab and the horn beeps three times. The cabby in front of Jameson makes some sort of a rude gesture in his mirror. Elmo opens the front door and ushers a confused Shana into the seat. Elmo gently places his bag onto the back seat and climbs in. Jameson nods and pulls away from the curb. He returns the gesture to the cabby that was in front of him as he drives by.

"Um, Elmo, what is going on here?" asks Shana.

"Exactly as I said. We are going to a hands-on painting demonstration at the studio of a well-known Jamaican artist. I'm hoping that you will be able to do some painting as well. Oh, and this is Jameson. The artist is his uncle."

~~~~~~~~~~

Tommaso goes to the front of the cab stand and gets in the first car.

"Where can I take you, mon?" asks the driver.

Tommaso hands the driver slip of paper with an address. The cabby pulls from the curb.

After a short ride, Tommaso sees a café with some outdoor tables.

"May we stop here for coffee, Agent Velez? I hear that Jamaican coffee is special and I'd like to try some."

The diver stares into the mirror in shock. He jerks the car to the curb and angrily looks over the back of the seat at Tommaso.

"What gave me away?" he asks.

"Several things, actually. Let's go sit and I'll tell you. I wasn't lying about the coffee. I'd really like to try it."

~~~~~~~~~~

After a half hour of winding over narrow, hilly roads at dangerously high speeds, Jameson pulls off down a dirt pathway and pulls up near a ramshackle house. There is a large outbuilding as well with a severely bowed roof. Two young boys come flying out of a screen door and jump on Jameson before he can completely exit the car.

He yells something at the boys in a dialect that neither Elmo nor Shana can make out. A woman comes out of the house and looks at all three of them.

"I see you bringin' dem white people to my house wit no warnin'," she says.

"Don be givin' me nonna your lip, woman," says Jameson. "I'll have no one orderin' me about in my own home."

He walks up and gives her a hug and a kiss. Elmo gets his bag out of the car and he leads Shana over to Jameson's wife.

"Thank you for your hospitality, Mum," he says. "This is Shana and my name is Elmo."

"We don have much, but what's ours is yours," she says.

Jameson leads them over to the other building.

"Uncle Rohan! We have visitors!" says Jameson.

Shana tugs on Elmo's arm.

"You call this a studio?" she asks, in a low voice.

~~~~~~~~~~

The proprietor brings a Jamaican coffee for Tommaso and a bottle of water for Agent Velez.

"All right, let's get started. I'm Miguel Velez of the F.B.I. on loan to Interpol. I am assigned to art theft in the Caribbean, particularly a recent rash of thefts in Mexico. You can call me Mickey. I received your call a few days ago and have no clue as to how you reached me without contacting any other agencies or their switchboard, anywhere."

"It's a pleasure to meet you. I am Tommaso Pastor. Tommaso will do."

He takes a sip of his coffee and his eyebrows immediately pop up.

314

"Strong," says Tommaso.

"I came here primarily to see if you would actually show up. I considered that this was a gag by one of my co-workers."

"But you could not resist the possibility of a lead in your case."

"Exactly. I have several questions for you, first."

"In the interest of time, let me see how many I can answer in advance. You've obviously had me checked out extensively. Everything you found is true. I held a high position for decades in organized crime. I am now retired. I am not here to make any deals or rat on anyone. That part of my life is over."

"You're perfect so far."

"My grandson stumbled into this mess purely by accident. I have one goal and that is to protect his interest at all cost, including my life. I know that you have investigated him as well. He was a mildly troubled youth who is now a legitimate business owner and taxpayer. Any harassment of him by the government would prove to be a waste of those tax dollars."

"Fair enough. I'm only interested in the art ring."

"Just to make sure that we understand each other, I don't give two shits about the art ring. I am only assisting you as it accomplishes my goal."

"Understood."

"I have found the middle of the chain, which does neither of us much good. I can definitely implicate the pick-up person which will lead you directly to one or more buyers. Hopefully you can recover enough material to make your bones at the bureau. The other end of the chain is trickier, but we have a chance there as well. I will try to implicate as many in the chain as possible in exchange for your leaving Elmo alone."

"What makes you think I need to 'make my bones' with my superiors."

"Several reasons. First, you just gave it up when I mentioned a quid pro quo with my grandson before offering anything concrete in exchange. Also, as a minority agent, if you were any good, you'd be into drugs or weapons. My guess is that you were a highly educated minority who was recruited by the bureau, only they could not 'untrain' you enough for the street. Harvard, perhaps?"

"What about the cab ride?"

"If I must. A Jamaican would say 'mon' to a peer, but not a white customer. You should have said 'Sir' due to the British influence. The Jamaican hat is unlikely for a cabby at the port. Your accent stinks, but worst of all, I gave you an address about five blocks into the ocean. You gave me the address over the phone and I intentionally changed it. Only someone who already knew where we were going would not have questioned it."

Mickey tries to maintain a shred of dignity, but finally drops his head in disgust.

"Damn. It was that bad? At least you missed one thing. I went to Princeton. I'm Dominican, but grew up in the South Bronx. I was the highest ranking agent on every test, but I have thus far not been successful in the field."

"So you need a win. I can help you with that."

"Did I do anything right?"

"You almost had me stumped being first in the taxi queue. You had your hood up until you saw me, correct?"

"You're good, I'll give you that."

"You are not dealing with the typical criminal imbecile. I have a plan and I will know if it's moving forward at about three o'clock. In any case, you need to get on the ship without alerting anyone."

"Are you sure that I can't just use my credentials?"

"I will not risk alerting the conspirators. I must insist that you follow my instructions. I will take your belongings onto the ship when I return this afternoon. You will need to wear this."

He hands Mickey a bag.

"It is a uniform and you must wear the nametag. It will allow you to get on the ship. You must go to the area were supplies are being loaded at eleven-thirty. I have people who will be looking for you. When you get on board, go right to room 9368 and wait there. There is a key card in the bag. Feel free to nap, shower, order food, or whatever. I will meet you there at four o'clock. At that point, we will either have a plan, or you will get a free two day cruise."

"And what will you be doing while I'm stowing away?"

"I'll be sightseeing with my friends."

Mickey lets out a breath.

"Okay, let's do it. I'll take you back. My bag's in the trunk. And when this is over, you're going to have to tell me how you picked me out."

"And to think that you are the one with the Ivy League education."

~~~~~~~~~~

Uncle Rohan is much younger than Elmo had expected. He looks barely older than Jameson. Elmo unwraps the towels in his bag and shows Rohan the painting. Rohan smiles and nods.

"Easy," he says.

Rohan sets up his work area with two chairs and three crude easels. He carefully clips the painting to a board and places it on the center easel. He rolls a cart filled with paints and brushes between the two chairs.

"Can you tell me what this is all about?" asks Shana.

Elmo holds up his hand indicating that she should wait. She shrugs and waits as Rohan walks out of the rear door of the shack. In a moment, they hear an engine starting. Soon several overhead lights hanging from the rickety-looking rafters begin to glow.

Rohan returns and says, "We need a generator for this much light."

Shana finally figures out what Rohan is doing.

"Why is he copying that painting?" she asks.

"We believe that this was stolen from a Mexican museum. It is being fenced, or illegally sold through a group of criminals on the ship. We are going to catch them."

"We?"

At that moment, Jameson and his two sons walk in and each pick up a stack of what appear to be wooden tubes from the along the far wall.

"I will be working in the house on my part of the project," says Jameson. "My wife, Peta-Gaye will bring you drinks and lunch. In a moment, my cousin will be here to take you to find what you need."

"Thanks, Jameson," says Elmo.

"What do we need?" asks Shana.

"*We* don't need anything. *I* need something. You're going to be here."

"Alone? Doing what?"

"You're an artist, right? Come sit over here. Here's what I need you to do."

~~~~~~~~~~

Tommaso is waiting at the dock when the others arrive. He directs them to a large open jeep with a driver wearing a Captain's cap. He holds out his hand to help Sarah into the vehicle. She sees a small bandage on one of Tommaso's fingers and pulls her hand back.

"Tommaso, I don't want to hurt your finger."

"It's nothing, Sarah, just a small cut. I want to avoid germs."

They all pile into the Jeep.

"This is Glenmore," says Tommaso. "He will be our guide today. He is going to take us on a driving tour of the area and tell us some of the history as well. We will then be stopping for lunch at a nice place by the water, my treat. Finally we will visit Dunn's River Falls."

"I'm sure that you know that I don't plan on walking up a waterfall at my age," says Larry.

"I do not expect that any of us will be so adventurous," says Tommaso, "but I understand that there is enough to see to make the trip worthwhile."

"I can't wait," says Sarah.

"Glenmore, if you please," says Tommaso.

~~~~~~~~~~~

"Thanks for the ride," says Elmo to Jameson's cousin, as he exits the car.

He is carrying a bag and walks up to the house. Peta-Gaye greets him and walks him around back where a kettle of water is boiling over a wood fire. Elmo opens his bag and dumps the contents into the kettle.

Elmo walks over to the studio and sees everyone hard at work.

"Boys," calls Jameson, "go inside and help your mother bring out lunch."

After about ten minutes, the boys come out carrying plates and cups. Peta-Gaye is following them with a tray of food.

"You are in for a treat," says Jameson. "Peta-Gaye is the best cook on the island."

"How can you tell wit dat stink from out back," she says. "What is you boilin' dem wood chips for?"

"It's to help authenticate the painting," says Elmo. "Once it's boiled down, we'll apply it around the edge of the canvas."

Rohan and Shana come over and the boys hand them each a plate. Peta-Gaye gives them each a serving.

"What exactly are we eating?" asks Elmo.

"Goat curry," says Jameson.

"Tastes like chicken?" asks Elmo.

"Tastes like goat," says Jameson.

"It tastes amazing," says Shana.

"I thought you were a vegetarian," says Elmo.

"Usually, but I'm willing to try new things, occasionally," says Shana.

After lunch, everyone finishes their work. Elmo scoops the remaining liquid from the kettle and gives it a sniff.

"That is some pungent cedar," he says.

He brings a bowl with the substance to the studio. Shana has finished her project so Elmo asks her to use her trained hand to apply the liquid. While Rohan puts the finishing touches on his masterpiece, Shana carefully works around him to brush the cedar-scented liquid around the edges.

"Now, an hour in the sun for drying," says Rohan. "Jameson, where is dat rum?"

After enjoying some rum punch, they carefully pack up their things, including a dozen ornately decorated rain sticks, and a colorful painting of a Jamaican scene in a crude frame. The people in the scene look a lot like

Jameson's family. Jameson kisses Peta-Gaye and the boys goodbye and waves to Rohan, who appears to be sleeping at the base of a tree.

They drive back through the hills to the cruise port. Elmo and Shana get out of the car with all of their belongings.

"I will return the car and return to the ship," says Jameson. "I will see you later."

Almost the moment that he drives off, Glenmore pulls up to the curb. Tommaso and the others begin to climb out.

"Perfect timing," says Elmo. "Jameson just dropped us off."

"How did it go?" asks Grandpa.

"Could not have been better. We're all set. I think we should do it."

"Okay, let's get started."

Elmo gives three rain sticks each to Larry, Paul, Alice, and Sarah. He hands Shana the framed painting and everyone compliments her on her art skills. Grandpa receives a bag with Elmo's belongings. Finally, Elmo grabs the strap of the original painting tube and throws it over his shoulder.

"Elmo, what are you doing with that?" asks Grandpa. "I don't recall that as part of the plan."

"It's a present for Vijay," says Elmo.

Grandpa looks at him for a moment and smiles.

Friday, Oct 31st
~ Fiesta Mambo, Deck 2 ~

The group spreads out at the embarkation point. Shana goes first carrying her bag and painting. The security guards don't give her a second look. The four carrying the rain sticks go next.

"Did you have to get one for every grandchild?" asks Alice.

"Remember when my father bought that drum set for our son?" asks Paul. "This is a rite of passage for grandparents."

"Alice, you married one twisted individual," says Sarah.

During all of this show, the noisy toys are being fed through the x-ray machine via the conveyor belt. Afterward, they each pick up their three tubes and head onto the ship.

Tommaso passes through without incident. He waits around the corner to see how Elmo fares.

Elmo sees Vijay as he approaches the line. He makes sure to choose Vijay's station and just walks up as though nothing has ever happened. Vijay is momentarily stunned to see Elmo putting the tube on the belt. He turns for a moment to look for the guard who is directing the passengers to the elevators and waves him over.

"Cover me for a few minutes. I have a suspicious entry."

The guard takes Vijay's place and begins scanning the items. Vijay takes off after Elmo and follows him to the elevator bank. Elmo waits for a door to open and steps inside. Before any other passengers can join him, Vijay hops into the car and holds up his hands.

"Next car, please," he says, as the doors close.

Elmo pushes the button for Deck 9, but Vijay takes a key from his pocket and sticks it into a keyhole on the elevator panel. He turns the key causing the elevator to stop. He turns to face Elmo.

"What is in that tube?" he asks.

"A painting," says Elmo.

"That does not belong to you."

"You're not calling me a thief, are you?"

Vijay stops for a moment to think about how to handle this.

"Where did you get this painting?" he asks.

"Some souvenir stand. What do you care?"

"I must recover it for its rightful owner."

"I already have it."

Vijay is confused by this. Elmo can't believe that this idiot was entrusted with any part of this scam.

"I know that you received this in Mexico. Why did you bring it to Ocho Rios?"

"I told you, I bought it in Ocho Rios."

Vijay nearly asks to see the painting, but realizes that he has no idea what it looks like. Elmo wonders if he's going to have to help Vijay along.

"If I call the Jamaican authorities, they will take you off the ship. You won't get back to Fort Lauderdale."

Elmo is relieved that he has finally received a threat.

"Okay, okay," he says. "You got me. Some dumb red-headed slut asked me to get it for her in Cozumel. I figured it might worth something, so when it didn't get picked up at security, I just kept it. I assume you're the security guy who screwed up."

"Why did you take it off the ship?"

"I figured I'd try to sell it. I couldn't even get ten bucks for it. I didn't want to take it through customs so I figured it's now or never."

"Give it to me."

"Okay, you take it. It was either that or throw it overboard. How about we just call it even?"

Vijay tries to decide if this is sufficient. He is happy to have the painting so he can set things right with his contact. He turns the key and hits the button for the fourth floor. The elevator starts to move. When they reach Deck 4, the door opens and Vijay strides away holding the tube.

Elmo continues up to his cabin. When he arrives, he sees Mickey sitting on Grandpa's bed looking at Shana's painting. The rain sticks are lined up on Elmo's bed. Grandpa is in the shower.

"You must be Elmo," says Mickey.

"You must be the agent," says Elmo.

"Mickey, Mickey Velez."

He puts down the painting and extends his hand. Elmo shakes it.

"How do you like Shana's artwork?"

"I've seen worse," says Mickey. "You know your grandfather is putting a lot on the line for you."

"We're family. That's the way he rolls."

"I hope you're worthy of his efforts."

"It's a process. I could do a lot worse than to be like him."

"I can see how that would be a mixed message. I've already showered. Tommaso invited me to dinner."

"Good. I could use a shower myself about now."

"What's in the tubes?"

Elmo picks one up and flips it over. It makes the sound of hundreds of seeds running through the inside.

"I think they're seeds."

"Man, Princeton was easier than this."

Friday, Oct 31st
~ Fiesta Mambo, Deck 3, The Ballroom ~

"This is my new friend, Mickey Velez," says Tommaso. "Mickey, I'd like you to formally meet Larry, Paul, Alice, and Sarah. Melody and Shana have other plans this evening, but are part of the team as well."

"How exactly did you get on the ship?" asks Alice.

Mickey looks at Tommaso.

"We are all completely open and honest in this syndicate. Feel free to speak or not as you are comfortable."

Mickey shrugs.

"Alice, is it? It worked exactly as Tommaso planned. I went to the loading dock where the ship takes on supplies. I wore the uniform and nametag I was given and two of his people met me and led me aboard. The security was disturbingly lax."

"How do you feel about juggling?" asks Paul.

"Will you give that a rest?" asks Elmo. "Mickey, Paul has been humping the juggler doing the headline show all week. He'd better be at least half as good as you say, Paul."

. As they reach the end of their meal, the waiters all seem to disappear.

"I'd guess we'd better get down to business," says Tommaso.

Suddenly, the lights in the dining room dim and a fanfare comes over the loudspeakers.

"Good evening, ladies and gentlemen. I am your Ballroom Maître d'. Our dedicated staff of servers has a special thank you presentation. As this is Halloween, we have added some additional flair to their performance. Remember to attend our Halloween inspired midnight buffet up on the pool deck. The festivities start at eleven-thirty and we will show off the talents of our chefs and food artists. And now, allow me to introduce, your dining staff!"

Elmo leans toward his grandfather.

"That's my cue to go back to the room," he says. "I wish they had served dessert first. I'll see you at the show."

The wait staff performs two corny song and dance numbers to recorded music. The homage to Halloween seems to consist of the wearing of masks and funny hats. During the second song, several of the wait staff are carrying jack-o-lanterns and intricately carved watermelons.

After the festivities, Handy and Fabrice return to serve coffee and dessert and everyone praises their performance.

"Hey, I have a question," says Larry. "Where is Mickey going to sleep, being that he's a stowaway?"

"He will bunk with me," says Tommaso. "I have a key to Melody and Shana's room. I expect that they will stay in the suite with Ted. Elmo can use their room. I will confirm this at the buffet later."

Tommaso turns to Mickey and adds, "Ted is not part of our group."

~~~~~~~~~~

Elmo enters his cabin and finds Jameson and an associate working inside. The associate picks up a rain stick and removes the green, black, and yellow band from around the end. The band is made to resemble the Jamaican flag. He hands the rain stick to Jameson, who uses a flathead screwdriver to carefully wedge off the end of the tube.

The associate places a plastic bag over the end of the tube. Jameson then flips the tube over while holding the bag in place. The tube makes the familiar rain sound until all items have fallen into the bag. Jameson gives a few more shakes to be sure that the tube is empty. Jameson removes the bag and carefully seals it while his associate goes over to the balcony and tosses the empty tube overboard.

"Not seeds, I see," says Elmo.

Jameson holds up the bag which contains a few hundred yellow disks.

"I was expecting weed," says Elmo, "you being Jamaican and all."

"Not on the ship. It's too hard to find a place to use it, and it's too easy to get caught. OxyContin is where it's at. I got a cousin in Canada who gets me all I need and the crew can't get enough."

After the last tube is discarded, Jameson packs all of the pills into a bag and gives them to his associate.

"Take these downstairs," says Jameson. "I have one more errand to run."

After the kid leaves, Jameson picks up the painting done by Shana.

"You want it?" asks Jameson.

"Sure, why not. It will give me something to remember you by."

Jameson carefully dissembles the frame and removes the painting. He rolls it up and hands it to Elmo. He then rolls up another piece of canvas and taps Elmo on the shoulder with it.

"Okay," says Elmo, "you know what to do next."

After Jameson leaves, Elmo takes the pieces of the frame and tosses them into the sea.

~~~~~~~~~~

Vijay walks into the Art Studio. There are several passengers milling around looking at the items for the auction. He tries to get the attention of Claude Gireaux, one of the two art dealers on board. Claude is explaining the investment potential of limited edition lithographs to an elderly couple.

He sees that Vijay is carrying the tube and nods toward the back of the room. Once he gets rid of the couple, he tells his associate Alison to work the room while he heads toward Vijay. There is a small desk area that allows them a bit of privacy.

"Are you out of your mind," says Claude. "What are you doing here when we are full of patrons?"

"I've got it," says Vijay.

"Where has it been for the past three days?"

"There was a miscommunication. I took care of it."

"Give it to me."

Claude opens the tube and is relieved to find that it is the Tamayo that he was expecting. He is about to roll it back up when he hesitates for a moment. He looks at Vijay and then back at the painting.

"I'm glad you found it," says Claude. "I still have time to get it into the auction. You'd better get out of here."

~~~~~~~~~~

Elmo enters the Teatro Real and gets to his seat just in time for the house lights to dim and the orchestra to play a fanfare and vamp intro. The curtain opens and the Cruise Director comes bounding out carrying a microphone. On stage, is a mike stand next to a stool with a water bottle on it.

Elmo catches his grandfather's eye and gives him a thumb's up.

"Welcome to another great show aboard the Fiesta Mambo! Once again, I am Mack Daddy, your Cruise Director. I want to tell you all a story about something that happened to me while walking through Olvera Street last night..."

He goes on to relate an elaborate cruise joke involving two old ladies and a parrot. He continues by encouraging everyone to attend the midnight buffet.

"One more announcement, Ladies and Gentlemen. Tomorrow at three o'clock is our art auction. You can view all of the pieces in Hernando's Hideaway on Deck 3 at two o'clock. There are many special lots and this could be your opportunity to find a great piece at a great price."

Mack Daddy places the mike in the mike stand and steps up to speak.

"And now, without further ado, the comedy stylings of Max Durkin!"

"What?" shouts Paul, "Max who? Where the hell is the juggler?"

After the show, Paul is still steamed.

"Relax, Paul," says Alice. "Sometimes they have to make a last minute change. The comedian was pretty funny at least."

"He was alright," says Larry. "A little too much of the cruise schtick if you ask me. We all know that the toilets are loud."

"You don't understand," says Paul. "This juggler used like, eleven rings at once, and they were on fire."

Elmo pats him on the back.

"Maybe he got burned up while practicing," he says.

"We have a couple of hours before the buffet," says Sarah. "How about if we go up to the Conquistador?"

Everyone agrees with this plan except Mickey, who opts to go back to the room. Tommaso looks at Elmo who gives him a nod.

"I put together a bag for later and left it on your bed, Grandpa. I'll go back with you after the buffet and pick it up."

"Fine, Elmo," says Grandpa. "You escort everyone else to the lounge. I need to speak with someone here first."

After they leave, Tommaso walks toward the stage. He speaks to a crew member for a moment. The crew member nods and goes backstage. A few minutes later someone comes out to see him. They sit down in the front row and begin to chat.

~~~~~~~~~~

Claude is closing up shop, when a young dark-skinned man in a steward uniform comes in holding something. Claude sees that he seems to be quite nervous.

"What are you doing here?" he asks.

"I found this, and I didn't know what to do," says the steward, in a heavy African accent.

He hands Claude the rolled up object like it is burning his hand. Claude notices from his nametag that he is from Ghana.

"All right, calm down. Tell me what this is all about."

"I am in my first month, on probation. I only work in the crew area until I finish my apprenticeship. My superior tells me that there is a lot of bad things happening among the crew and that I should stay away from such things, but be aware."

This piques Claude's interest.

"What sort of bad things?" he asks.

"Mostly drugs, I think. I don't know anything else, but I found this in a trash barrel in a crew cabin."

"Maybe they were throwing it out."

"My father in Ghana is an artist. I think this may be too valuable to throw away."

"Let's have a look," says Claude.

He unrolls the canvas and is so surprised to the see the Tamayo that he nearly drops it. He takes a breath to regain his composure.

"You did the right thing. Have you told anyone else about this?"

"No sir, my supervisor frightens me. I cannot be sent home."

"This is a painting that was supposed to be delivered here and disappeared a few days ago. I am very pleased that you found it. Can you tell me specifically where you found it?"

The steward looks like he is going to cry.

"It is alright. I just want to thank whoever found it. If it turns out that they are among these people doing bad things, I think that the Captain should know. You're involvement will remain a secret between us. Is that fair?"

"You are most kind, sir, but these men are in security."

"Which, security?"

"I do not know their names, but they are in room 1474. One is from Malaysia. He has always been nice to me. The other, the tall Indian one frightens me."

"You have been most helpful. I think you were correct in not telling anyone. I will take care of this matter and leave your name out of it. Good luck in your new position and welcome to the Mambo."

Immediately after the steward leaves, Claude opens up the painting and compares it to the other one that Vijay had brought him earlier.

"*Merde!*"

He puts both paintings in a safe place and hurries out the door.

~~~~~~~~~~

Mickey enters the cabin and turns on the light. There is a towel animal on each bed. On Tommaso's is a shark and on Elmo's, now Mickey's, is a pig.

"I guess everybody on this ship is a comedian," he says to himself.

He notices a canvas rolled up on Tommaso's pillow. He unrolls it and finds Shana's colorful landscape. It is signed 'Shoshone'. Mickey wonders what happened to the frame and begins to look around. Suddenly, he realizes that the rain sticks are gone as well.

Mickey had planned to search the room, but decides against it. He tosses the towel pig onto the floor and lies down on the bed.

"What the hell have you gotten yourself into," he says.

He almost immediately falls into a deep sleep.

~~~~~~~~~~~~

Vijay enters his room after his shift in the video room. He is about to unbutton his shirt when he sees an envelope on his bed. He opens it and reads the enclosed note.

Extremely urgent that we meet. Eleven-thirty Deck 8 aft.

Vijay sits on the bed and rubs his neck and head. He checks his watch and sees that he has an hour before the meeting. He decides to go to the mess for a cup of coffee.

Before he leaves, he opens a drawer and takes out a small tin. He opens it and takes out a small yellow pill. He goes into the bathroom for some water to wash down the pill. Afterward, he twists his neck from side to side to release some tension.

He heads for the crew's mess.

~~~~~~~~~~~~

Tommaso enters the Conquistador lounge and finds his party. Alice and Sarah are looking out of the front widows down onto the pool deck. They are watching the crew setting up the buffet.

Tommaso stops by the bar and orders a drink. The bartender nods and gives a signal to one of the two waiters. A young woman named Lana from the Cruise Director's staff comes in and goes to a closet. She is pulling out a couple of microphones.

"Hey, Lana," says Larry. "Can you come over here for a second?"

She closes the closet and comes over.

"I only have a moment," she says. "I need to bring these for the show downstairs."

"I just wanted to hear your Welsh accent once more before we leave the ship," says Larry, "and my friend Paul, here has a question for you."

"What happened to my juggler?" asks Paul.

"Oh dear," she says. "It was quite horrid. The juggler was mugged in Jamaica this morning before the ship docked. He was hit over the head quite badly."

Tommaso turns his head with sudden interest.

"How did you get a replacement so fast?" asks Tommaso.

"That was the only fortunate part," says Lana. "He was already in Ocho Rios and was able to come aboard."

Tommaso turns to Elmo who turns up his hands.

"So now we have three thousand and one suspects," says Elmo.

In a little while, Alice and Sarah rejoin the group, and a moment later, Melody and Shana walk in.

"Over here!" shouts Paul.

Elmo gets up to slide over a few more seats.

"How is everything going with Ted?" asks Alice.

"It's been amazing," says Melody. "It's like we've never been apart. I don't want to jinx anything, but we might actually both be in the right place, now. He's always adored Shana."

"Good for you," says Sarah. "Where is he?"

"He had to conduct some business although I can't imagine what at this hour. He's going to meet up with us at the buffet. After that, he's invited us to stay in the suite. Wish me luck!"

~~~~~~~~~~

Vijay goes back to the deck by the Montezuma Suite. He walks up to the only other person there, who is looking out over the rail. Vijay leans next to him and looks down at the wake.

"I guess you want an explanation about what happened with the painting," says Vijay.

The man takes a stiletto and in a flash drives it into Vijay's back near his kidney. It one motion, he grabs the back of Vijay's pants and flips him over the rail and into the wake below. He still has the knife in his back as he hits the water.

~~~~~~~~~~

The group begins their stroll through the pool area. It is crowded, but still a fun lively atmosphere. There is a Mariachi band playing. Ted comes up to meet them and he could not look happier with an arm around Melody.

The tables are decorated to perfection. There are several ornate ice sculptures. Every vegetable and fruit known to man is carved into artwork and displayed in a variety of lighting. There is plenty of food as well, although no one can imagine eating another bite.

"Where is Larry?" asks Tommaso.

"He turned in early," says Paul.

"I think he was a little blue," says Alice. "I think this was Sylvia's favorite part of the cruise."

Tommaso notices that they are holding hands.

"Shana crapped out early, too," says Elmo. "I guess she had a busier day than expected."

They watch Ted and Melody walk off together and Paul and Alice head off toward the railing.

Tommaso looks at Sarah.

"I can't, Tommaso," she says. "I just can't."

She turns and heads away.

"Well that was awkward," says Elmo.

"Let's head back to our cabin and check in on our guest," says Tommaso.

~~~~~~~~~

When they enter the cabin, the light is on and Mickey is asleep on top of the covers. He stirs and covers his eyes until he can adjust to the brightness.

"Sorry to disturb you, Mickey," says Elmo. "I'm just getting my things and will be out of your hair in a minute."

"Where are the shaker things?"

"You mean the rain sticks? Gee, I'm not sure. Maybe we should call someone in law enforcement."

"Stop taunting him Elmo," says Grandpa. "We are on the same team today."

"Sorry, bro," says Elmo. "I'll see you guys at breakfast at nine-thirty."

After Elmo leaves, Tommaso gets ready for bed and lies down. Before he can turn off the light, Mickey turns to face him."

"Is this going to blow up in my face?"

"Relax Mickey. You've made the right play here. By Sunday, you will have recovered a valuable stolen piece of art. You will also have at least three people up the chain assuming you find the inside man in the studio and Cortez back in Mexico."

"At what cost?"

"At no cost, if you think about it. In exchange for my help, you have already agreed to leave the girl, Olivia alone. She was a dupe, like Elmo, and is of no value anyway. You have also have agreed to ignore Jameson and any activity he is involved with."

"Yeah, but drugs---"

"I cannot even be sure of that. Unlike you, I have no interest in anyone's criminal activities as long as they do not impact my family."

"It was in the tubes. How did they get on board? Where did they go?"

"I assure you that I do not know. You aren't DEA. If you let it distract you, you run the risk of blowing our operation."

"God, I hate the sound of that."

"Look at the upside. We still may catch more people up the chain. You might parlay this into a promotion. In any case, I need some sleep. We can talk about this more in the morning."

~~~~~~~~~~

Elmo walks into Melody's cabin and is relieved to see two freshly made beds. He tosses his bag on one and strips down to his shorts. Elmo pulls back the covers, lies down, and clicks off the light. Just before sleep comes he gets a whiff from the pillow. It's Melody's perfume. He is disturbed to find this has brought about an erection.

Before he can figure out how to deal with that issue, the door opens and there is a robed figure silhouetted against the light of the hallway. Elmo is momentarily too panicked to move. In this moment of paralysis, the figure takes off the robe as the door closes. She climbs onto Elmo and straddles him.

"Ooh, is this for me?" asks Shana.

She is naked and rubbing herself against Elmo.

"Shana?" he stammers.

"Were you expecting anyone else? Don't you want me?"

A dozen sarcastic answers fly through his head before he lets out a breath.

"Sure, Shana, why not? We're on a cruise, aren't we?"

Saturday, Nov 1st
~ Fiesta Mambo, Deck 2 ~

Tommaso awakens to an empty room. After showering and dressing for breakfast, he steps out onto the balcony. Looking out over the water, he reflects on the experiences he and Elmo have had on this cruise.

He wonders if traveling is for him. Still, he enjoyed the time with his new friends. Is this how it ends, living in a retirement community in Boca Raton? And what of Sarah? He cannot get his hands around their relationship. She evidently has similar feelings based on her reaction last night.

~~~~~~~~~~~~

Elmo awakens to find a naked Shana draped over him. He can't see the clock so he has no idea whether he is late for today's activities or not. He reflects on his cruise experience. How do these senior citizens keep up their pace? It makes his home life of six days and sixty-five hours per week as a business owner seem like a walk in the park. Still, some of it has been fun.

Elmo gives Shana a nudge and she begins to stir. Soon her eyes flutter open.

"Good morning," says Elmo.

"I hope I didn't scare you last night," says Shana.

"I think that I'm beyond fear at this point. I just want this mess to be over. You really helped me out yesterday, you know."

"I'll say I helped you."

"That was nice, too, but I'm serious about the help."

"It was exciting for me. I came on this cruise in a shell and tried to keep it closed. It feels good to live a little."

"Your part is done, but I still have your painting."

"I want you to have it."

"You sure?"

"Yes, it will remind you of our time in Jamaica."

"Well, I'm honored, truly."

"I can honor you some more."

Elmo lifts the covers and looks at her body.

"It's tempting. First, tell me what time it is."

She rolls over so she can see her travel clock.

"Damn, it's eight-thirty. I assume you have to run."

"Sadly, I do. Are you coming to breakfast?"

"No, I plan to roll over and sleep for about three more hours. I may stop by the auction just to watch."

Elmo gets up and starts getting dressed.

"You know we still have one more night here," says Elmo. "And we still have a houseguest in our cabin."

"Mom and I have to pack tonight. I'm not sure how things went with her and Ted. Maybe we should just leave it as it is. You know, ships in the night?"

"Hey, I could send Mickey over."

"Hmm, that might work, too."

"We'll talk at dinner."

He gives her a kiss and heads out.

~~~~~~~~~~

Mickey walks into the cabin as Tommaso is preparing to leave.

"I was just out for a walk to clear my head," says Mickey.

"Impressive ship, isn't it? Have you cruised before? This is my first."

Mickey stares at Tommaso with his hands on his hips.

"How do you remain so cool? I swear, my stomach is in knots."

"Mickey, this is none of my business, but you can learn something here. We'll talk more after the operation. For now, I know what I can control and what I cannot. I have assessed all risk and have put a plan in place. Now, we have no other options than to work the plan."

"It helps to be the smartest guy in the room."

"Thank you, but not as much as you think. Overestimating your opponent is as dangerous as underestimating. Since neither is in my control, I tend not to focus on such things."

"You should be teaching at the Academy."

"You don't pay enough."

They head for breakfast.

"Thank you for all joining me here for breakfast," says Tommaso. "I asked you to come to the dining room for two reasons. First, it allows us to get a table in relative seclusion. Second, I wanted to try it once before we leave the ship tomorrow."

"That's the spirit," says Paul. "You may become a cruiser, yet."

Mickey, Elmo, Larry, Alice, and Sarah are also at the table. Sarah and Larry both seem more reserved than usual.

After breakfast, they order another round of coffee and tea. Elmo asks for another serving of eggs benedict.

"Let us begin, shall we?" asks Tommaso. "Elmo will not be attending the auction as he is known to Vijay and possibly others. I might be in the same boat, no pun intended. I will be nearby in case there is a problem. You will each attend the preview and the auction independently."

"Mickey, too?" asks Alice.

"Yes, but he will not be bidding. He will be observing to identify our buyer. Each of you is to bring a pad. Mark the items that you'd like to bid on. You can wander away from the studio before the auction to compare lists. I'd prefer that we didn't bid against each other."

"You may be sitting where you can't see the rest of the team," says Mickey, "so bid out loud so we can all hear you. It will cut back on the eye contact."

"Try not to bid unless someone else bids first," says Tommaso, "and then keep at it until they stop. Don't worry about the money. Since Mickey is the art expert, he will bid if he is confident that you can stop."

"The girl, Olivia will be there?" asks Mickey.

"Yes, as an emcee type of thing," says Tommaso.

"And she's not in on this? Why?"

"There was no point. We could not allow her to give anything away. We don't even know if anyone other than Vijay is aware of her involvement. It is safer this way to everyone except her, and it is no more dangerous for her."

Mickey thinks about this for a moment.

"That seems right," he says. "Continue."

"We do know that at least one of the two people running the auction is involved, but not even Olivia knows who."

"You're sure?" asks Mickey.

"As sure as I can be. Otherwise, she would have to be the mastermind, and I know that's not the case. In any case, it will be up to Mickey to root out those conspirators using his incredibly extensive training."

Mickey winks and points his finger at Tommaso.

"What if we see something we want to bid on for ourselves?" asks Paul.

"I don't recommend it," says Mickey. "This type of art is typically a bad investment."

"Sure, bad when I'm paying for it. Not when Tommaso is footing the bill."

"Use your discretion," says Tommaso. "My expectation is that there will be one buyer interested in one painting, which is the Tamayo piece depicting watermelons. It probably won't be in the preview, but might be a last-minute addition."

"Once I am sure that I have my man," says Mickey, "I will leave the auction and you folks are done, other than picking up your art, of course."

"Wait a minute," says Elmo. "What if there are multiple bidders, and what if someone else from the chain shows up? Can you handle that?"

"Do I have a choice?" asks Mickey.

"I have an idea," says Elmo. "I have this group of young 'friends' on board. They can sit with you during the auction. They are African-American, so they will look like your kids."

"I don't want to involve children," says Mickey.

"There's no risk. They can act as runners. You'll have a pad, right? You can use them to pass updates to Grandpa. Also, if someone leaves and you need to stay, they can shadow them to see where they go. Remember, you won't know the cabin number of your suspect even if you mark them."

"Hmm, I'm not sure about the last part, but I like the runner system. Are you sure we can trust these kids?"

"Have you been disappointed with our plan so far?" asks Tommaso.

"I'm meeting them on the sports deck after breakfast," says Elmo. "I'll have them prepared."

"The sports deck?" says Paul. "After what you ate, you'd better bring a bucket and a mop, Kiddo."

"Any other questions?" asks Tommaso.

No one speaks.

"Alright then, Godspeed everyone. Oh wait, one more thing. After dinner tonight, I have arranged for a special treat in the Conquistador lounge at ten o'clock. Assuming none of us are in jail, it would mean great deal to me if you could all attend. This has been a memorable experience for me."

Everyone leaves except for Tommaso, Mickey, and Sarah.

"Can we talk, Tommaso?" she asks.

"Of course, Sarah. Mickey, do you mind?"

"Oh, ah, no problem. I'll just check out the venue one more time."

"Relax, Mickey. Take a stroll on deck. Don't overthink it."

He nods and leaves.

"They're closing up in here," says Sarah. "Can we go for a walk?"

"Of course."

As he stands, Fabrice comes by and hands him a note. He leaves as quickly as he came with no comment.

Tommaso looks at the note.

Vijay is missing. J.

Saturday, Nov 1st
~ Fiesta Mambo, Deck 13, Sports Deck ~

Elmo walks out into the sunshine and sees his friends on the court shooting around. Jerrell is running plays teaching the younger kids how to get open and to play defense.

"That's what I'm talking about," says Elmo. "When you guys try out, you'll find that everybody can shoot and dribble, but the fundamentals will get you on the team."

"Do white folks actually believe that?" asks Jerrell.

The other kids are laughing when Elmo pulls his medallion out of his pocket. He puts it around his neck.

"Who's laughing now, pipsqueak. Who's got the hardware?"

"Hardware?" says Duane. "That thing is straight up plastic. If you leave it out here, it'll melt in the sun."

"You got that for foul shooting," says Earl, "not for real ballin'."

"I'll have you know that foul shooting is the last bastion of the white man," says Elmo, "and I am proud to carry on the torch for my non-jumping people."

Desmond takes the ball from Jerrell and dribbles around Elmo for a layup.

"Shouldn't you punks be in school?" asks Elmo.

"It's Saturday," says Earl.

"What about the rest of the week?"

"We were at school," says Duane. "We're all home schooled."

"Really?" asks Elmo, "How do you play sports?"

"We can still go to the school for activities. Our Moms are trying to get a charter school started," says Jerrell.

"Interesting," says Elmo. "Listen guys, I need a favor."

He goes on to explain what he needs from each of them.

"Are you sure that you can do this? I don't want you to get in trouble with your parents."

"Yeah," says Jerrell, "we're on our own today."

"Alright, let's do a little practice," says Elmo.

The kids start toward the court.

"No, no, not that kind of practice. I'll be Mickey. Let's say I give Earl a note for my Grandpa."

"I'm so sorry about last night," says Sarah. "I don't know what came over me."

Tommaso leans on the rail and looks out to the sea.

"Do you think that's Cuba out there?" he asks.

"I'm not sure. I'm not from around here."

Tommaso smiles at her.

"That's better," he says. "You have nothing to apologize for. This has been a very strange experience for me as well. I'm not sure what to make of it. I've also been preoccupied with this other mess."

"I've never had a man be so…I don't know…respectful of me, maybe."

"Your father was abusive as well, wasn't he?"

"You see? That's another thing. We've never met but it's as though you can see right through me. It was this way with Meg. Sometimes, quite frankly, it freaks me out."

"Then you are really going to be freaked out by this."

"What?"

"The event tonight, in the lounge. It's for you."

"Me, what do you mean?"

"Elmo told me how well you sang, and how happy it made you. Apparently on many cruises, on the last night, the band and singers have kind of a cabaret show in the lounge. They do standards and show tunes."

"Alice mentioned something about it. How does this apply to me?"

"Remember when the Captain said that I could ask anyone on the ship for any favor?"

"Sure."

"I asked Mr. Blake, the bandleader to allow you to do a number during the show tonight."

"Oh my, Tommaso. That may be the nicest thing anyone has ever done for me. But why? Why would you do this?"

"For some reason, I feel compelled to do the nicest thing that anyone has ever done for you. I just don't know why either."

"Well, this is pretty weird, I must say. We both seem to be in the dark about this."

"You are under no obligation---"

"I want to do it."

"I would like to hear you sing, Sarah. You will need to go to the main theater at four o'clock to meet with Mr.

Blake to pick a song. I'd prefer to leave it as a surprise to the others."

"I won't say a word. Tommaso, this has all been the most incredible adventure."

Saturday, Nov 1st
~ Fiesta Mambo, Hernando's Hideaway ~

Tommaso stations himself on a fancy settee between the Photo Shop and Hernando's Hideaway. Elmo has already told the boys where to find Tommaso in the event that they have to pass notes. Alice arrives first to look at the preview. She is quickly followed by each of the others.

About ten minutes before the auction, the group meets by the photo studio to compare notes. They develop their bidding strategy and head back inside.

The biggest concern is the number of lots and the number of bidders. As expected, the Tamayo painting is not in the preview. Tommaso sees Shana enter the auction room.

The boys are all sitting with Mickey who has stationed himself off to the side to have the best view. They're all are wearing polo shirts as Elmo directed. Mickey is very impressed with their behavior.

Tommaso puts his magazine in front of his face as Melody and Ted enter the room. This is a wildcard that he failed to account for. There is always something unexpected in an operation.

Olivia is basically channeling Vanna White as she does little more than point to the items up for bid.

The first item is a Romero Britto limited edition lithograph 'valued' at $500.00. The bidding starts at $150.00 and immediately a Hispanic man bids on it.

Alice leaps into action and follows up with a bid. After two more bids, she wins it for $190.00.

Tommaso gets two notes from Mickey in rapid succession. The first, from Duane, tells him that there are about forty-five people attending including their people. A few minutes later, Earl brings a note saying that Vijay is not there, but Max Durkin is.

Tommaso asks Earl to wait a few minutes with him to make it look like he went to the bathroom. He hands him a note that says, 'keep an eye on this guy'. He tells Earl to go to Paul and ask him to discretely point out Ted. He is to give the note to Mickey and point out Ted to him.

After nine lots, there have been five not bid on and four going relatively quickly. Paul has won two while Sarah and Alice have one each. About a quarter of the bidders have already left.

On the tenth item, Ted bids first. Larry is up, but knows that he can't bid against Melody. He hopes that Mickey gets the hint. He waits figuring he has until Claude says, 'Going twice'.

Since Mickey already has his eye on Ted from the note, he bids at 'Going once'.

Ted continues to bid well past the value of the piece, and then considerably beyond that. Once Mickey is satisfied that this may be his man, he stops bidding.

Mickey is now wondering whether this lithograph could have some unseen value, or this is just a smokescreen for later. There may even be something valuable underneath, although this would make the provenance issue moot.

"Don't overthink it," he mutters to himself.

After the gavel goes down, Ted and Melody get up to leave. Mickey whispers to Jerrell and Jerrell follows them out.

Jerrell is giving them a fair amount of space, so Tommaso whistles in his direction. Jerrell turns toward him and discretely points toward his quarry. Tommaso shakes his head and motions him over.

"I know where he's going," says Tommaso.

He writes a note and gives it to Jerrell.

"Take this to Mickey, please."

The eleventh item goes without a bid and the twelfth item is the Tamayo.

"This one is not in your program," says Claude. "It is a last minute entry of a limited edition. The bidding will begin at $100.00."

"Clever," thinks Mickey. Original art is by definition limited, but he told no lies. It must be unnatural for an art huckster to downplay a piece rather than overvalue it.

A small man in the back who is sitting with a plain looking woman raises his hand. There is nothing at all noteworthy about them. They appear to be in their mid to late fifties.

Larry bids at $125.00 and continues to bid against the other man. The man shows no reaction and just keeps bidding. Max Durkin, on the other hand, looks clearly annoyed.

Mickey scribbles a quick note and gives it to Duane and nods toward Larry. Duane heads out of the room but drops the note in Larry's lap as he walks by. Larry looks at the note and reads, 'Stop at $650.00'.

Larry bids $625.00. There are now some 'oohs' and 'aahs' around the room. The other man immediately goes to $650.00. Larry shakes his head no to the auctioneer and the gavel falls.

The man and woman get up as though nothing has happened and head out. Max Durkin waits a minute and heads out as well. Mickey sends Jerrell and Desmond after the couple and Duane and Earl after the comedian. He stands and gives a cut signal to the others ending the operation.

They all walk out together and head over to Tommaso.

"It was surprisingly simple," says Mickey. "They were clearly after the one item, although I'm still not sure what was up with the guy you put me onto. That litho could not have been a target."

"The woman is Melody," says Tommaso. "She's the tablemate you missed at dinner last night. I'm still not sure about him."

"Well, Claude is the inside man for sure. His apprentice didn't do anything except move the paintings around. Olivia did more and I am convinced that she's not involved."

"It went so smoothly, I almost fell asleep," says Paul.

"Speak for yourself," says Larry. "I was at bat for both Ted and the painting. I'm looking forward to a nap before dinner."

"The best news is that now I can focus on Durkin as the next guy up the chain. It's a great scam. He probably manages this on several ships through his work. I'm guessing that he got word from Claude that Vijay screwed up and arranged to get on board."

"You don't suppose he hurt that juggler, do you?" asks Sarah.

"I'm certain of it," says Mickey. "A check into his travel should help us prove it."

"That sick bastard," says Paul.

At that moment Jerrell and Desmond run up.

"We got 'em," says Jerrell. "Room 4829."

"Yeah," says Desmond. "You were right Mr. Velez. They got on the elevator. I stayed to watch what floor they got off and Jerrell took the stairs. They never saw us."

"When you guys get finished with school, you should consider a career with the FBI," says Mickey.

"After the NBA," says Desmond.

The other two boys sprint around the corner. Both are panting.

"That dude went all the way to the big theater," says Duane.

"He went through Olvera Street so he was easy to follow," says Earl.

"You guys were a great help," says Mickey.

"Oh, man," says Earl. "Are you tellin' me it's over?"

Tommaso laughs and pats Earl on the back.

"So, it looks like we made it," says Tommaso. "Maybe now we can relax and enjoy this cruise. Oh, Sarah, don't you need to be somewhere soon?"

"Yikes," she says and heads toward the theater.

"There's just one problem," says Alice.

Everyone turns to look at her.

"I hate Britto," she says. "Anybody want to by some art work?"

Saturday, Nov 1st
~ Fiesta Mambo, Deck 3, The Ballroom ~

Mickey enters the dining room and heads to the table.

"Is there a spot for me?" he asks.

"Right here," says Shana. "My mother is dining with Ted at the Argentinian specialty restaurant."

"And I see that we are also missing Sarah," he says.

"I believe that she should be along any minute," says Tommaso.

As if on cue, she hurries to the table. She looks quite shaken.

"What's wrong, my dear," asks Alice.

"It's so horrible," says Sarah. "I just came from the theater. A man was killed."

"Oh my Lord," says Alice.

"It was the comedian from last night," says Sarah. "He was crushed by the part of the stage that goes up and down. I think I'm the only non-crewmember who knows."

"What were you doing in the theater?" asks Paul.

"I, um, I wanted to get a picture before we left the ship," says Sarah.

Tommaso looks at Mickey.

"That's not all the odd news," he says. "I was able to get a picture of our couple and send it to the office via my sat phone. They are Durkin's parents. Is it possible that he was the mastermind behind this whole thing?"

"I guarantee that the parents won't know," says Tommaso. "They probably won't even be able to lead you to the buyer."

"Damn it!" says Mickey.

"At least you recovered the painting," says Paul. "and I assume this will put an end to the ring."

"Maybe," says Tommaso. "In any case, as terrible as it might be, Durkin was a criminal. I hope that this does not spoil our last evening together."

While the mood remains somber, everyone agrees to do their packing after dinner and to meet at the Conquistador at nine-forty-five.

When they all get up to leave, Sarah tells Alice to go ahead to the room without her. Tommaso says the same to Mickey and Elmo, but before they leave, he hands the note from Jameson regarding Vijay's disappearance to Elmo.

"Share this with Mickey," says Tommaso.

"I don't know if I can do this tonight," says Sarah. "I feel guilty."

"Let's put that aside for a moment," says Tommaso. "How did the rehearsal go?"

"Oh, it was wonderful, Tommaso. Everyone was so kind, and it sounded amazing. Some of the other singers were there and they stopped to listen. They gave me pointers on phrasing. It was the best gift ever."

"The best part is about to come. You have nothing to feel bad about. Tragedies happen and this has nothing to do with us."

"Do you think it will be all right? I want so badly to do it."

"I won't insist as it is your call, but I will be very disappointed not to hear you sing."

"Thank you so much, Tommaso. I believe that the show must go on."

Saturday, Nov 1st
~ Fiesta Mambo, Conquistador Lounge ~

Alice, Paul, Shana, Mickey, and Tommaso settle into their seats in the lounge with a good view of the stage. There are two chairs and microphones off to the left, and Darcy Blake is talking with the piano player. There is a double bass player on the stage as well. In a few minutes a trumpet player and trombone player arrive.

Elmo walks in wearing his pinstripe suit from the first day and his grandfather's fedora. Sarah follows him in wearing her outfit from the first formal night.

"What are you two decked out for?" asks Paul.

"It was all I had left," says Sarah. "I guess I packed for a six day cruise by mistake."

"Where's Larry?" asks Elmo.

"I'm not sure he's gonna make it," says Paul. "He's missing Sylvia pretty bad. He said he needed some fresh air. I think he just needed some alone time."

The first set begins with two of the cruise ship singers doing a series of standards. They sound great in the small venue with the live band. The male singer, who introduced himself as Trevor, from Canada, started with 'Fly Me to the Moon' and 'Spanish Eyes'. Carly, from Carson City, Nevada, followed with 'At Last' and 'Besame Mucho'.

This pattern continues for several more songs before Darcy Blake announces a break, and a special treat in the next set. Tommaso orders another round of drinks. When the waiter hands Tommaso his drink he also hands him note.

Extremely urgent that we meet. Ten-thirty Deck 8 aft.

Tommaso looks at his watch and then he looks at Sarah.

"I need to take care of something," he says. "I'll be back as soon as I can."

Sarah looks surprised as he gets up and heads for the door.

~~~~~~~~~~

Tommaso walks through the door leading to the secluded deck at the rear of the ship. He is alone. He walks past a pair of deck chairs and moves to the rail. After a few moments he hears someone coming up behind him. He turns around.

"You," says Tommaso. "This, I did not expect."

"We all get old," says the Captain.

"And greedy, apparently."

"No, Tommaso. I don't even sell the works. I collect them in my villa in La Maddalena. I'll be retired soon. Can it be so bad to love beautiful things?"

"Watermelons? You like the conquest."

"I imagine that's a bonus. It doesn't really matter at this point. You've put an end to it."

"It was nothing personal."

"That hardly matters. Now it is a matter of honor."

"Honor? Did it take honor to kill Vijay?"

"I had nothing to do with it. That *pompinara* Durkin took care of that."

"Just like on your ship, you are responsible for the actions of your subordinates."

"And I honored that responsibility. I killed Durkin."

"Hmm, I suppose I cannot argue with that."

"I was serious about the debt I owe you regarding my father. It makes it that much more bittersweet that you must die as well. By now you must have realized that this is one of the few places on the ship devoid of surveillance cameras. It is a courtesy to our special suite guests."

"So I am to go over the side?"

"That would be easiest on you. It is in deference to my father's debt to you that I spare your grandson. Does this make it easier for you?"

"Might I ask a couple of questions first?"

~~~~~~~~~~

"Welcome to our second and final set," says Darcy Blake. "Before we bring out our next two singers, I have a special treat for you. One of our passengers, Sarah, from Iowa, is going to do a couple of numbers for you."

Paul, Alice, and Shana are genuinely surprised and applaud vigorously. Sarah takes a quick look for Tommaso as she walks up to the mike. She nods to Darcy and the band begins the intro.

Sarah begins with, "There's a saying old, says that love is blind."

The crowd applauds at the start of 'Someone to Watch over Me'. She had picked this song as a message to Tommaso. The fact that he is missing it does not affect her performance a bit. If anything, it adds just a touch of melancholy.

After the song is over, everyone in the place is either applauding, in tears, or both. Sarah takes a second bow, and acknowledges the band like a pro.

"I'd like to do one more, with my friend and partner, Elmo, from New Jersey!"

Elmo bounds up on stage wearing the fedora and grabs the other mike as the drummer starts a staccato tapping on the inner part of his cymbal. The pianist comes in a few seconds later followed by a trill from Darcy's tenor sax.

The band goes into a four-measure segue and Elmo begins to sing, "That old black magic has me in its spell…"

"oooh, that magic that you weave so well…," counters Sarah.

They go on to sing a spirited version of the Louie Prima/Keely Smith classic. Many of the patrons stand up and dance, including Paul and Alice. After it is over, everyone is hugging. Sarah is too excited to worry about Tommaso right now.

"It is rather unbecoming for you to stall," says the Captain.

"I would not want to disappoint you further," says Tommaso, "but I did not live this long voluntarily doing myself in. Even Durkin seems to have made you work for it."

"I actually am disappointed, but no matter."

The Captain takes an electronic device out of his pocket. Tommaso assumes it to be some sort of stun gun. Before the Captain can move toward him, Tommaso hears a loud clank. The Captain looks momentarily stunned, and then falls forward on his face.

Directly behind where the Captain was standing is Larry, holding a fire extinguisher.

"Larry, I'm so glad to see you."

"Is the fascist son-of-a-bitch dead?"

"I'm not sure. He's not bleeding, but based on this crease in his head, I can't say it looks good for him. As thankful as I am for your intervention, I'm curious as to what you are doing here. Were you following me the whole time?"

"This is going to sound strange, Tommaso. I wasn't following you at all. I just caught the end of your conversation, but enough to get the gist of it."

"So you just grabbed the extinguisher and bashed in his skull?"

"Again, this is an awkward situation for me."

"I'm a good listener."

"I was actually on my way here to…do myself in."

"Larry, no."

"I'm ninety-one. I just don't know if I can continue without her."

"I wish I could say something. I still grieve for my Marie, but I was such a young man."

"It's okay, Tommaso. I haven't had the chance to be a hero for quite some time. I suppose it might give me a sense of purpose."

"Where did you get the fire extinguisher?"

"Oh, on Deck 7, by my room."

"You brought it with you? Did you expect trouble?"

"No. It was for the weight in case I survived the fall. I had actually planned on putting it in my pants."

"So I can assume that this has not been a typical cruise. Otherwise I might be forced to complain."

"There's the Captain. Feel free to unload."

"What are we going to do with him? He's too heavy for us to lift him over the rail."

"Well then it's a good thing an engineer happened by. Let's see. If we can roll him onto this deck chair, we can roll him up to the rail using the back wheels. We can then tip the chair on the wheels until the front legs slip over the rail. We might just have enough strength to then lever up the back of the chair using the rail as a fulcrum. After that, this fat Mussolini lover becomes shark bait."

The two of them take their time and the sequence actually works. By lifting with their legs, they are able to slide the Captain off of the deck chair and into the roiling wake of his own ship.

"Pretty poetic," says Tommaso.

"How so?"

"You became a hero killing Germans. It took a while, but now you're working on their allies."

Tommaso throws the fire extinguisher overboard.

"Let's see. No blood, no cameras. We might be alright here. Also, there's no fire extinguisher for you to put down your pants. Are we done with this talk of suicide? After my loss, I completely focused on family. Can you do the same?"

"I was actually thinking of them. I'd want my ashes dumped off of a cruise ship. This way, they save a bundle by eliminating the middle man."

"Hmm, suicide. This gives me an idea. Can you help me out with one more favor, Larry?"

"Man, you kill for a guy and now it's one more favor. I'm pretty wired anyway. What do you need?"

They go all the way forward to the crew passage for the Captain's cabin. The officer at the door is the same one who let Tommaso and Sarah in earlier in the week. Tommaso tells him that the Captain wanted to meet his friend before the end of the cruise.

"He asked us to come here and wait for him," says Tommaso.

The officer lets them in asking that they remain in the living room. As soon as he steps out, Tommaso goes over to the desk and uses a pencil to open the Captain's laptop computer. After turning it on using the pencil eraser, there is a request for a password.

"What do you think, Larry?"

"B-E-N-I-T-O."

"Well I'll be damned. First try."

Tommaso opens Word.

They compose a suicide note implicating the Captain in the art thefts.

"Damn, that reminds me," says Larry. "I left a note for Paul. He's gonna be angry."

"That you lived or died?"

"Either, if he's already read it."

They leave and tell the officer that they can wait no longer and are disappointed that the Captain was too busy to see them.

Sunday, Nov 2nd
~ Fiesta Mambo, Deck 9 ~

Tommaso is awakened by the sounds of the ship docking in Port Everglades. He purposely left the balcony and drapes open when he went to bed at about three in the morning. Mickey is gone.

Tommaso gets dressed and puts his remaining belongings into a small carry-on bag. He takes the envelope for tips for the room steward and slips $500 cash into it to supplement the prepaid tips furnished by Milton.

Milton. Has it been barely a week?

Tommaso takes one more look around the room as he heads to the Embarcadero for breakfast. He sees Paul, Alice, Sarah, and Larry at a table and joins them. He's particularly glad to see Larry.

"I feel that by the looks of each of you," he says, "I must look pretty bad as well."

"They all know," says Larry. "Paul found my note and immediately went to Alice. They were all in my room crying when I returned from our adventure. They were not pleased."

"At least I know why you missed my show," says Sarah. "I had already been crying."

"I was just crying," says Alice, "because I was just so God damned confused by it all."

Elmo, Shana, Melody, and Ted walk in and squeeze around a neighboring table. They all shout 'coffee' as soon as a server comes near them.

"Did you all sleep well?" asks Tommaso.

"Out like a light," says Elmo. "Shana and Melody slept in the suite."

"I don't recall much sleeping," says Melody, as she squeezes Ted's arm.

"We're going to try it again," says Ted. "The last few days have really opened my eyes to what I've been missing."

"If you don't mind," asks Tommaso, "can you tell me what you were doing at the auction yesterday?"

"The auction? Oh, I just bought my lady here a piece that she liked. Unfortunately some other guy also wanted it and bid me up. I'd have stopped, but Melody really liked the piece. I don't get the other guy, though. He looked like he had four kids. I'm not sure where people get the money."

"Sorry, Tommaso," says Melody. "I didn't know what to do, so I just remained silent."

"No harm, no foul," says Elmo. "It all worked out."

"Well, thanks for stealing my thunder," says Paul. "I have asked Alice to marry me and she has graciously accepted. Now, we only need to bang out the pre-nup."

"Pre-nup?" asks Elmo.

"It's not for us," says Alice, "it's for our kids. We don't want them suing each other over our bones down the road."

"Assuming I am invited, it gives me something to live for," says Larry. "Please forgive an old fool."

"For me, it's back to New Mexico," says Shana. "I feel reenergized about my painting. I'm going to get back to my studio and get back to my first love."

"How about you, Elmo?" asks Sarah.

"Just work and nothing else…for a long, long, time."

There are hugs and handshakes as everyone heads to the debarkation station. Sarah hands Tommaso a card.

"Tommaso, this has been the most amazing week of my life. Here is my contact information. Whatever the future holds for you, you will have a special place in my heart."

"For me as well, dear."

After they all leave, Elmo slugs down the last of his coffee.

"Ready, Grandpa?"

"Yes, but I need to fill you in on a few things as we go."

Sunday, Nov 2nd
~ Port Everglades, Fort Lauderdale ~

Tommaso and Elmo are waiting by the curb next to a cart containing their luggage. Mickey walks up to join them.

"Our ride will be here any minute," he says. "Olivia is out. She's going home today. I also have some interesting news. The Captain appears to be missing. It's all very hush-hush, but I thought you'd be interested."

"Fascinating," says Tommaso.

A large SUV pulls up and a young agent hops out. He places the bags in the rear compartment and Mickey directs them into the back where he joins them. He makes a hand gesture to the driver, who immediately raises a privacy window.

"At least we have the artwork marked. We'll pick it up when Durkin's parents try to go through customs. That's federal weight and we can leverage them with their son's death."

"Don't waste your time or my tax dollars. They know nothing."

"Probably not, but at least I can recover the painting."

"About that," says Elmo.

He reaches into his bag and pulls out a rolled canvas. He opens it to reveal Shana's painting. Elmo pulls from behind it a picture of watermelons. He hands it to Mickey.

"What's this?"

"The Tamayo," says Tommaso.

"But how? I saw them pick it up."

"That's a fake."

"But, wait, I'm confused."

"Tell him, Elmo."

"My grandfather was always harping on the value of leverage. In Jamaica, we commissioned a very good fake of the painting. We were going to find a way to return it so you could track it after the auction and we could smoke out the other conspirators."

"Wow," says Mickey.

"That's not all," says Tommaso. "My grandson had a wonderful idea. We figured we could fool Vijay, but didn't know if the fake would pass muster with the inside man, or any others in the chain."

"I had Shana come with me to make a fake that wouldn't fool any expert," says Elmo. "I got that one to Vijay when I returned to the ship. As expected, he turned it in to his handler. Later, one of our operatives gave the good fake to the studio and implicated Vijay. The hope was that they wouldn't check the other as carefully."

"You guys are nuts. Vijay was most likely murdered over this. Also, how could I have arrested anyone for buying a fake painting?"

"They did not know it was fake, plus we left a trail."

"A trail?"

Tommaso holds up his finger with the bandage.

"My DNA was mixed with the paint. I told you my grandson was a genius. Oh, and I have another surprise for you."

"I'm not sure I can take this," says Mickey.

"Get a warrant and check the computer in the Captain's stateroom."

"What? You didn't kill him, too, did you?"

"I can honestly say that I did not. I have a feeling that it will close this case and lead you to a cache of additional stolen works of art."

"I never expected to make my career in this manner."

"That's why you weren't getting anywhere. It is pointless to try to catch rule breakers when you have to follow rules. Remember that. If you need any help down the road, I'm sure you can find me."

"The great Tommaso Pastor is admitting that the FBI can find him?"

"As a taxpayer, I would hope so. I'm in the phone book."

"You're a piece of work, Tommaso."

"Well this piece of work needs one more favor. Our travel credentials---"

"Say no more."

Mickey taps on the glass divider and it slides down.

"Eddie, tell them."

"Mickey had me check you both out. We found the video of you breaching TSA in Newark and scamming your way onto the ship. Very clever. As a result, we found out about your bogus tickets."

"We got you a flight back using your proper information direct to Newark leaving in ninety minutes," says Mickey. "First class. Oh, and your video will be used in training by TSA for many years to come."

They pull up to the terminal. Eddie gets the bags checked in and Mickey hands them two tickets and boarding passes.

They head to the gate and sit quietly. They both fall asleep immediately after boarding and stay that way for the duration of the flight. When they arrive at baggage claim, Marcus is there to meet them.

The ride home is quiet as well. Marcus drops off Elmo and heads to Tommaso's condo.

"You guys were awfully quiet," says Marcus. "Did it go well?"

"Interesting question. I'll fill you in during therapy on Thursday and then at lunch. It's quite a tale."

"It doesn't surprise me. Are you done with travel for a while?"

"Actually, I don't think so. I'd like to see Iowa."

"Iowa? What's in Iowa?"

"I have a friend there. I promised her that I would hear her sing."